Praise for *Skin*

"[A] beautifully written first
eloquent, and occasionally gruesome ... but there are many flashes of joy and humour, and hope."

—*Quill & Quire*

"Ibi Kaslik's debut novel is a luminescent read ... Kaslik's harsh realities are well-painted, her characters' emotions and mistakes vivid.... The book's emotional grip is fierce, and the hunger of its characters for love and understanding is compelling."

—*eye weekly*

"Kaslik is a talented storyteller. This book captured something visceral and alive in every family: the power of its secrets and how we can choose to be either haunted or healed by them."

—*The Georgia Straight*

"[A] profound portrait of girlhood.... The psychic inner worlds of both girls ring painfully true ... Brutally beautiful."

—*NOW magazine*

"One of the most elegant, beautifully written novels about female self-immolation to come out in a long time.... Comparisons between Plath and Kaslik are inevitable, but should be taken as a compliment."

—*Montreal Mirror*

"Ibi Kaslik has written a first novel that is vivid, compelling, at times even darkly funny."

—*Montreal Review of Books*

"It's tender, empathetic, and heartbreaking."

—*Saturday Herald Sun* (Australia)

"Kaslik is a gifted storyteller.... Kaslik's writing is so vivid that the reader feels rather like a peeping tom who is watching something intensely private yet cannot bear to turn away."

—*CM Magazine*

"*Skinny* is a painful book to read, but this is an accomplishment on the part of Ibi Kaslik. It's a painful, haunting, and depressing story, and it's a sign of Ibi Kaslik's brilliance that the reader is able to feel that."

—*Curled up kids*

"Ibi Kaslik's ambitious debut novel looks at eating disorders in a way that both avoids chick-lit and self-help clichés ... her prose cuts like a scalpel."

—*The Gazette* (Montreal)

"Unflinching and raw, this story ... is powered by a frenetic energy that can't be ignored. Brave and unique."

—*Kirkus Reviews*, starred review

"Intricate and heartbreaking.... Kaslik's unblinking eye shows a psyche fatally incapable of digesting life's hurts, turning every blow into another round of self-abuse ... Kaslik's last chapters bring a bitter end as engrossing as it is uncompromising."

—*The Globe and Mail*

PENGUIN CANADA

THE ANGEL RIOTS

IBI KASLIK is a novelist and freelance writer who writes for North American magazines and newspapers. Her debut novel, *Skinny*, has been translated into many languages and nominated for several awards, including the Borders Original Voice Award (U.S., 2006) and the Books in Canada Best First Novel award (2004). Ibi currently lives in Toronto.

the angel riots

Ibi Kaslik

PENGUIN
CANADA

PENGUIN CANADA

Published by the Penguin Group

Penguin Group (Canada), 90 Eglinton Avenue East, Suite 700, Toronto, Ontario, Canada M4P 2Y3 (a division of Pearson Canada Inc.)
Penguin Group (USA) Inc., 375 Hudson Street, New York, New York 10014, U.S.A.
Penguin Books Ltd, 80 Strand, London WC2R 0RL, England
Penguin Ireland, 25 St Stephen's Green, Dublin 2, Ireland (a division of Penguin Books Ltd)
Penguin Group (Australia), 250 Camberwell Road, Camberwell, Victoria 3124, Australia (a division of Pearson Australia Group Pty Ltd)
Penguin Books India Pvt Ltd, 11 Community Centre, Panchsheel Park, New Delhi – 110 017, India
Penguin Group (NZ), 67 Apollo Drive, Rosedale, North Shore 0745, Auckland, New Zealand (a division of Pearson New Zealand Ltd)
Penguin Books (South Africa) (Pty) Ltd, 24 Sturdee Avenue, Rosebank, Johannesburg 2196, South Africa

Penguin Books Ltd, Registered Offices: 80 Strand, London WC2R 0RL, England

First published 2008

1 2 3 4 5 6 7 8 9 10 (WEB)

Publisher's note: This book is a work of fiction. Names, characters, places and incidents either are the product of the author's imagination or are used fictitiously, and any resemblance to actual persons living or dead, events, or locales is entirely coincidental.

Canada Council for the Arts Conseil des Arts du Canada

We acknowledge the support of the Canada Council for the Arts which last year invested $40.3 million in the arts in Ontario.

Manufactured in Canada.

ISBN-13: 978-0-14-305512-9
ISBN-10: 0-14-305512-7

Library and Archives Canada Cataloguing in Publication data available upon request.

Visit the Penguin Group (Canada) website at **www.penguin.ca**

Special and corporate bulk purchase rates available; please see **www.penguin.ca/corporatesales** or call 1-800-810-3104, ext. 477 or 474

And it was that terrible sense that things would never change that changed everything, terribly.

—Sherwin Tija, *The World Is a Heartbreaker*

part1autumn

1
jim

I remember driving.

Slashes of blue appear above the horizon, the air sucking wasps and leaves into the car as I open the window and dip my hand over the highway.

I remember how, on long summer nights like these, Yawnie and I would run to the fields, our extended shadows sprawled under the sun's hold out against night. We would bring objects: an old rusted lock, a hockey stick blade, our father's amateurish watercolours of sailboats. We'd rolled his paintings into a thick scroll, and Yawnie would bonk me on the head with it before he blindfolded me, before he spun me around the levelled circumference of wheat—which we both knew wasn't crafted by aliens, only by a tractor dragging its shovel low.

Arms out, he spun me like a propeller, and the nausea rose up inside me like the first seconds of ingesting some terrible news. But I was twelve at the time and so far the only bad news I'd heard was that the cat had been maimed by coyotes, Mom's hair had caught on fire, and there wouldn't be rain for another three weeks.

I can see Yawnie, at twelve, perched above the lake, ashen hair falling over his face.

You can't dive there, Yawnie! It's too shallow!

But Yawnie knows only to dive, is familiar only with the dangerous instincts that force his pale body into the water like a jacked knife.

Later, for me, danger will be seeking out the guy with the most tattoos at a party. Fear is a purple feather earring I pierce into my lobe with my mother's biggest sewing needle. Stupid is letting Jessica Tribeca clamp my throat in the girls' changing room while I hold my breath and splotches of green appear before my eyes. Pure insouciance is smoking twelve cigarettes and two joints in a row in the rafters of the barn.

But, in this still-kid moment of blindfolded twirling, Yawnie runs, buries our father's rolled-up paintings, the key. The lock he tosses into the field while the hockey blade he boomerangs into a prairie-dog hole with his pitcher's aim. In my mind I see where each object goes and, when we finish that game, we play another. For this one, I lie on the dusty ground, place my body carefully between wheat stalks, and time Yawnie to see how long it will take him to stumble over me.

What, in god's name, were we preparing for? The ESP Olympics?

We never failed to locate the object or the other within minutes, and sometimes—if we were feeling particularly telepathic—while still blindfolded. We trained ourselves, became Team Kov from Saskatchewan. And we became good.

Yawnie explained to me that we couldn't permit bits of our brains to focus too long on quotidian subjects like homework and television. Baseball, soccer, and musical instruments were acceptable topics. And sex. We could think about sex alone. In these respites from the other's invasion, we could fit in other secrets, as, I learned later, my brother often did.

Yet we couldn't permit our minds to focus too long on matters of our changing bodies, the astronomical library fines we'd accumulated, our mother's frustration with the wringer-washer, our older brother Simon's curious chin hairs growing in like paramecium squirming under a microscope—though these matters indeed distracted us.

Too many people, activities, TNFB—Thoughts Not From Books—could not go untethered without our shared approval. Information was a physical transaction between us. In quick lid movements, his eyes silverfish, I could tell Yawnie was tired, that his back ached. Watching him bounce a bloody knuckle on his knee, I knew he was thinking of a Loretta Lynn song and of the Native girl named Stella I worked with at the DQ Grill & Chill. Stella was tall and wore her white sneakers unlaced, their thick white tongues lapping over her feet. Yawnie was in love with her: he longed for the folds of her heavy black hair to rest on his neck *like a pelt of hope*—Yawnie's phrasing, not mine.

At thirteen, my twin brother hadn't yet learned to filter out his teenage lust, so I'd demur and tune him out, ordering a hot dog from the stand while he sat in his blue and white baseball uniform and thought about Stella. When ideas like these came into his head I'd turn away, and hoped he'd learned to do the same (he had). But mostly I could read him in as many ways as there are days in a lifetime.

Yawnie.

What?

Where did Victor's monster go—quick, it's a test—at the end of the book, where did he go?

Do you think if people could choose between going blind and never telling a lie again, which one? Which one would they choose?

Yawnie. I need you to focus here.

The Arctic, Frankenstein goes to the Arctic. Where else? Idiot.

Each day we would check the psychic knots we'd moored to each other. We were waiting, perhaps, for a time when the knots between us might slip loose, or at least Yawnie was.

The time came.

* * *

I AM HEADING EAST, my car is stolen. I can feel each kilometre clicking away in my gnashing teeth. The Transcona gravel, the thick August air is trapped in my sweaty fingers and hair as I grip the wheel and press the gas.

And yes, it's filmic: a blazing cigarette in hand, the bottle clinking against the steering wheel. I'm drinking Jim Beam—my accidental namesake—straight from the bottle, with the windows rolled all the way down.

An eighteen-year-old blond girl named Jim, me, driving by myself across the country. And drinking, never losing my coordination, my clarity. Drinking myself east, I wonder: *Is this what pain is—never feeling drunk again?*

East is colder, the oxygen is rich with the swell of green forests. Unable to gulp down the changing air quickly enough to stop my sobs, I pull over to the shoulder, my voice screeching into the still night. I reach out the window and throw the bottle at the sky. He won't find it, he's beyond these baby games.

And so am I.

I rev the engine to swerve back onto the road, but the shift's in reverse and I end up slamming into a pine tree. My head ricochets off the top of the wheel. There are too many trees here. I hold my bloody nose in my hands. And then he's behind me, urging me to keep driving, that I'm not that hurt, that I need to ditch the car before they realize it's missing.

Just before I black out on the side of the Trans-Canada—somewhere near the Manitoba–Ontario border—before I'm woken up by a trolling, snitchy squirrel that has mistaken my splayed arms for branches and crawled into the car, I remember Yawnie's warning.

He said the words aloud because I never could have found them, or guessed them, buried so deep in the whorl of one of those knots we'd tied to each other. I'd missed it. An explanation for our games, the strange rituals that, at thirteen, I suddenly deemed "immature."

Okay. But one day, Jim, you might need it.
Why?
You might lose the map to me.

* * *

WHEN I WOULD RIDE to Isaac's house on my bike, I never felt as happy, or as free. I loved the ride to the west end, with my shoulders straight against the wind, my violin strapped across my back. I liked the way the houses got larger and more impressive. I liked the shops: there were nice yuppie stores that sold baby clothes and smelly French cheese. There were bistros and cafés, not art bars and gas stations like where I lived, the Plateau. I imagined I was some slim young crook making my escape, and if someone looked at me I fixed my face into a snarl, though I felt like smiling.

The days Isaac insisted on seeing me, I'd pedal harder, my calf muscles bursting like propane tanks. I'd lock my bike up and look at the barren trees that lined the sides of his opulent street. I especially loved the silence of Isaac's rich neighbourhood, and breathed it in gratefully. There was always too much noise where I lived, traffic, sirens, trucks.

From the very start Isaac and I lived in suspended moments, and, when his body shuddered against mine, I'd imagine he was an acrobat. If he slipped, I caught him inside me. My mind would open up when he entered me and there was a kind of relief in this, a chasm of quiet nothingness; it was like sand pouring into the folds of a cave. At first we spoke little, needing only to relearn the rhythms of each other's bodies since our last meeting. Despite our long silences, he filled my mind, my flesh, what was missing from me, at least for those stilled moments. The only other thing that filled me that way, that made me forget and froze time for a while, was playing.

Those days in his cool dark house nothing, or few things, indeed reached us. We never talked about what we were doing or where our relationship was going, and this made it impossible to imagine endings. In the beginning it was just sex, and mutual understanding, I suppose.

We often began stories and then ended them abruptly. We would smile when we felt like weeping, roll over into the heat of the other when we felt like talking. Though we never acknowledged our future we were always tethered by it and this always made our lovemaking a little fiercer.

This was the beginning and, at the beginning, each time I stepped back out into Isaac's quiet street to unlock my bike I remembered the real reason I loved the west end so much: every time I made the trip there, some small, outraged voice inside me said it would be my last.

* * *

AT TIMES, it strikes me that other children had choices. Limited as those opportunities were, they had them. Me? I couldn't remember a time when I didn't play violin. It seems absurd to me now that my mother drove an hour, twice a week, to deliver me to the downtown steps of the Conservatory of Music. Case in tow, with three dollars for a vanilla milkshake, I waited for my mom while she parked the car and university students asked me if I was lost.

My mother would knit during my violin lessons, so the constant clack of needles was my metronome. Pauses to wind wool on her finger signalled breaths and cued me to relax my grip. She, and Mrs. Henderson, my tall, thin, chain-smoking violin teacher, were always there to correct, listen, and guide my shaky hands over my quarter-sized violin.

Mrs. Henderson inspired and terrified me.

"You didn't practise this week, did you?" she'd say, tossing a half-lit cigarette out the conservatory window. I imagined her smoke landing on some poor sucker's head, or joining the mountain of yellowed butts in the park below.

To this day I can picture her kneeling in front of me before a performance, as she did before my first recital. "Play, gypsy, play!" she'd cry, flinging her arms into the air before sitting down at the piano to accompany me on whatever pathetic little allegro I was butchering that day.

When I was six my mother enrolled me in Suzuki, the happy-group Japanese program where you listen to tapes and learn the music from memory. Suzuki attracted my mother, who thought it was important for children to learn an instrument, "for their little brains."

During those long afternoons in the overheated rooms, while the floors creaked in the conservatory and my mom knit one of her bulky sweaters, my blood-brown, quarter-sized violin promised me something, though it never did reveal to me what that was, beyond escape. I discovered pretty early on in my career that it was my mother, not me, who had a passion for music. But if you can inherit taste, gesture, looks, and brains from your parents, then you can at least learn passion the way you would a favourite recipe. So I did. For whatever reason, my mother needed a musician in the family, and with Simon interested only in metal and Yawnie being Yawnie, well, let's just say I was my mother's only hope.

The thing about Suzuki is there's no music theory. You can come away from the program able to play loads of music, but you can't actually *read* any of it. Mrs. Henderson herself never succeeded in teaching me theory. Whenever she tried it was at the end of the lesson, and I'd be too groggy from the heat to absorb anything.

When I started to play in orchestras as a teenager I'd figured out the basics, but I was still so far behind, theory-wise, that I'd have to buy recordings of whatever we were playing so I could keep up. By the time I turned sixteen I'd learned the bass from one of Simon's friends and I'd left the afternoons of Mrs. Henderson's cigarettes and my mother's sweaters far behind. My Walkman, a constant sore point between my teachers and me, was my life support: it enabled me to get through high school. I mixed tapes of hard-core punk and Tchaikovsky symphonies and fell asleep with my finger lodged on Play. I dressed like a punk for school but at night wore long flowing dresses for chamber concerts.

When I wasn't listening, I was memorizing the music I'd heard on my earphones. Find notes, rewind, rewind again to master timing. My mother liked to cook or knit while I practised and she never commented on the Walkman. The only thing she ever criticized was my speed.

"Too fast," she'd say, when a bass line or a scale slipped out of my reach.

Because of my ear, I could pick up any riff quickly. My mom and Mrs. Henderson, now older, not so tall, and with a bad case of emphysema, came to my first rock show.

They sat at the front sipping wine. It was just like dozens of other chamber and orchestra nights they'd attended together, only with booze and smokes. They sat through the feedback, scooched their table over to make room for the growing mosh pit, and endured the baying of Lyle, our lead singer, who sounded like an off-key Iggy Pop.

Afterward the three of us went out for cake and coffee at an all-night café, and Mrs. Henderson, a little drunk and wheezing badly, laid her hand on mine.

"Rock-punk stinks, my darling."

"I know, Mrs. Henderson." I looked to my mom, who shrugged and smiled.

"You might lose your beautiful ears from all that cranky garbage, no?" Mrs. Henderson added.

I played with the icing on my cake. "Maybe."

* * *

"YOU WANT A PIECE OF ME?" were the first words I heard when I walked into my inaugural Divine Light Orchestra rehearsal, fifteen minutes late. Seems the violins hadn't tuned themselves to Kellogg's perfect-pitch satisfaction and he could no longer endure their flatness.

"Because if you guys want to piss me off, all you have to do is play one more note, one more, and I'll come over there and rip your arms off."

I stood still for a minute, watching Kellogg flip his long black hair as the violins bent over and adjusted their pegs. I studied the way this tall, intimidating man-child tapped the baton and hummed to himself. Then he focused his crazy blue eyes on me.

"Whaddaya want?"

"I'm replacing Charles, I talked with you on the phone, ah, Mr. —"

"Kellogg. Call me Kellogg."

He pointed to a chair next to a girl with spiked bleached-blond hair named Lhisa. "The 'h' is, like, silent," she explained, "so it's not, like, La Heesa, it's just Lisa."

Charles was a guy I'd been playing with in a chamber group at school. He'd said he had a flu that "might last the rest of the year." So this was my informal audition, I suppose, because Charles had no intention of returning.

Even then there was a buzz around The Divine Light Orchestra, and spots in the band were like Plateau apartments: you didn't give them up, you passed them on to your friends. It was tough to get in and Kellogg trusted his musicians to understand the calibre of player he wanted. If you begged out you had to offer a replacement; otherwise you'd be blacklisted by Kellogg, who knew everyone in both the classical and indie music scene. It wasn't just me on the line; Charles's reputation was at stake too.

Luckily, Charles had prepped me with recordings of all the pieces we were doing that night. And Lhisa—not La Heesa—played right into my ear so that I could fake the nuances I hadn't learned. "Kellogg's all bark," Lhisa said, as if I couldn't tell he was a hammy showman.

During rehearsal, Kellogg had intermittent tantrums that would crack up half the orchestra and mortify the other half. His mad-conductor act was part show and part authentic, for Kellogg, whose real name was Kalvin Krajensky, got his sobriquet, Special K, from his former proclivity for designer drugs. When he wasn't terrorizing Divine Light or doing drugs—now only seldomly and recreationally—he worked as a studio drummer, managed a local group called The Angel Riots—a group he occasionally moonlighted with as lead guitarist—and studied Buddhism. Rumour had it he was about to launch a new indie label on major-label money, which would propel The Riots, and The Divine Light, out of their provincial status and into the American music scene. But bands were always being talked up only to end up staying in the same little incestuous circle. The whole getting popular thing was a crapshoot and I'd learn that whether you got panned or exalted on Pitchfork determined your status. For me, it was best to avoid website ratings and chatroom diatribes and just focus on playing.

Finally, after two hours of blaring cacophony, Kellogg let us go.

"Go play to your lovers, your parents, anyone who'll listen. And hey, Trisha, are these your running shoes over here? Did you step in dog shit or what? They're right next to the radiator, and man, they're really stinking up the place."

A cello player smiled and waved goodnight to me on my way out the door. I went outside and lit a cigarette, thinking about the music, about my bike ride home. I rolled my pants up and blew smoke high into the dusky shadows, inhaling the smoky fall smell. I did a two-step in my sneakers. For the first time since I'd left home it felt as though something positive might happen; I had a good feeling about Kellogg, despite his abuse. I felt like I was joining something important, something big. Everyone in the orchestra was excellent. So what was *I* doing there? Good question.

"Dancing? What don't you do?" Kellogg appeared before me, lighting a smoke himself. "So, you wanna stay?"

"Sure," I said, like it didn't matter.

"Play me something, then."

My eyes widened at him.

"Why not? I could see you were doing a good job keeping up tonight, but you were hiding behind La Heesa."

"Lisa," I giggled.

"Right. So, play."

"Now?"

He nodded.

I hoped my violin was in tune. I played him one of my mother's favourite Mozart allegros, and as the music slipped into the fray of Montreal traffic I thought of how her hands had held the notes in her clacking needles.

"I like how you delivered that," Kellogg said before the last note got swallowed into the rush of night.

"Thanks."

"Now, come inside, try out this new thing we have coming up."

I went numb. "I can't, ah, I have to go home."

Kellogg smiled and we both laughed nervously. I felt as if I were at a job interview, which, I guess, I was.

"It'll take two minutes, come on." He butted out his smoke and opened the door. I followed him in, frozen inside. I'd have to read music. How was I going to avoid this?

Kellogg and I went back into the gymnasium. I sat down as he put a music sheet in front of me that had been scored by hand. I perched, with my instrument on my knee, my posture perfect, and swallowed repeatedly. The first notes made sense, but the jumble afterward was a complete mystery. I loosened my bow and got up to pack my violin away.

"What're you doing?" He crossed his arms over his skinny chest.

"I can't," I whispered.

"Please, play it."

I walked right up to him and stood directly under his nose—Kellogg was almost a foot taller than me and was staring into my hair. And, in one of those moments in life when you are unquestionably going to make a huge mistake but decide to go with it anyway, I said:

"Look, don't you get it? I can't read that. I don't know what it means." I snapped my case shut, but making a graceful exit was hard because my eyes were blurry.

"Wait!" he yelled. Then he ran up and offered me a card.

"What is it?"

"It's this guy, buddy of mine, a theory teacher. He'll give you a discount. And, well, I'll pitch in, if it's still too expensive for you."

Ridiculously, I still felt pride. "I can't accept."

"Is it true you play four instruments?"

"Yeah."

"Do you play them all that well?" he asked, nudging my case with his knee.

I shrugged.

"But you can't read music?"

"That's right."

He paused for only a moment. "Aren't you at the university? How did you pass the theory test?"

"I'm an excellent faker. There's a huge gap in my knowledge. I know, it's weird."

"It's the most retarded thing I've ever heard is what it is," he barked.

"I said, I know."

"Is it true that you're only eighteen?"

"Yes." I studied the card, not wanting to meet his eyes.

Then I looked up at him, hurt, as he laughed at me. "Wow. You really thought you'd blow through an accelerated university music program, join a rock orchestra, and all without a stitch of theory?"

I shrugged again and then smiled. "I guess it's kind of crazy."

"I'll say one thing, you have balls." Kellogg winked at me. "What's your name again?"

"It's Jim."

"Jim? You're a girl named Jim."

"Yes, Kellogg."

"Well," he said, oddly formal, "you can join us on the condition that you take theory classes. I'd like to have you in The Divine Light, Jim, so, if you're up for it, start taking the classes, come to rehearsal. I have a good feeling about you and my old guts never lie." Kellogg opened the gym door for me and gestured that I keep moving.

"Now, would you care to join me and some more of my fake musician friends for a beer?" He winked at me again with those insane sparkling eyes and swung my violin case from one long arm to the other as if he were plucking up my baggage from an airport carousel. As if I had been on a long trip and was finally home.

Tonight the downtown marquee reads:

The Angel Riots

All Your Dead Lovers tour

$10

With Special Guests: The Divine Light Orchestra

2
rize

He'd been asking to meet Margo's best friend, Kit. Margo kept saying no. *Kit's not at all right for you, Rize.* Then, one day before a show, Margo turns up backstage with her arched eyebrow, Kit trailing behind.

It's The Divine Light's first show opening for The Angel Riots. Before tonight the orchestra has played their dirge-like jams in half-empty community halls and at after-after-hours parties. But the cops always break up the party before they're through their second ten-minute-long song—if the music Divine Light make can be called songlike.

Kit's smoking Benson & Hedges and wearing a long peacoat. Rize tries to be gentlemanly, asks her if she'd like him to put her coat in a safe place, and Kit rolls her eyes as if to say *Nowhere around here is safe, buddy.* She is full of nervous energy and Rize likes this about her because it makes him feel as though something important and different might happen.

It's chaos backstage. Margo is yelling at Kellogg, who's telling her not to smoke because it makes her voice sound like shit. Kellogg subs as lead guitarist for Riots' shows when they can't get anyone else, even though his specialty is management and his preferred instrument percussion; like Rize, Kellogg is a preternatural instrumentalist and could juice a song out of a rock if he had to. Margo is the only girl in The Riots, and is also Jules's wife of four years. Jules sings, and plays the shaker, while Margo backs him and plays rhythm. Rize can't remember a time when he didn't know Jules. He tries to, but he can't. They got Guy, the drummer, two years ago, when Margo finally joined the band.

Ten minutes in and Rize is already exhausted by everybody's yelling, so he lies on his coat in the windowless green room and falls into a fitful, noise-filled sleep. When he wakes, he finds himself holding his lips together tightly; he's dreamt that his teeth have fallen out, as if someone had smashed his head with a two-by-four.

"Your father used to have those dreams too," his mother told him when he was fifteen and first started to have them. "They're about death."

With one eye open, he can see Guy smoking a blunt the size of a carrot, which means Guy's drumming will be off all night. Jules croons "Blue Moon," then sits on Rize's chest.

Rize wants to remind Jules about that twenty he owes him for the cab, wants to tell Jules he is his best friend but that sometimes he dreams he murders him in the desert. And to pleasepleaseplease get the fuck off him.

He pushes Jules off and Jules rolls next to him on the floor, as if they're camping and staying close for warmth. The smoky room is suddenly very crowded. Kellogg, The Riots' manager, is in the middle of it all, puffing on another joint. Kellogg is holding court for the benefit of an entourage of young musicians covered in tattoos. There's also a gap-toothed girl, who looks about twelve, with blond hair down to her ass, hanging off Kellogg's every word. When Rize asks about the girl, Jules shrugs. "Some kid from the sticks. Supposed to be an amazing string player. Kellogg's trying her out tonight. In the orchestra, I mean."

"What's her name?"

"Dude, or something."

"Her name is Dude?"

"I don't know. She's got a dude's name."

"Oh."

Rize flicks his eyes at the child-woman and she sneers at him under her bangs. He sticks his tongue out as she tightens her violin bow. Then she cracks a slow, careful smile. *Good girl,* he thinks.

The Divine Lights are all there tuning, banging things around, yipping at each other in French and English. It's all too much sometimes: the noise, the permanent stench of hash and stale beer on his clothes, Jules going on about socialism and revolution. Rize turns away from his friend and curls over his coat, minding the beer and broken glass.

He thinks about the question Kit asked him before he told her he had to lie down for ten minutes: "What do a trombone player's fingers smell like?"

He'd felt ambushed by her weirdness, had clutched his drink, pretending he hadn't heard her over the sound of duelling flutes. He thinks about her long arms and questions, her nervous smoking and her lips that look bee-swollen, fat as a model's. He thinks about her until his balls begin to ache with something like sorrow. Someone spills beer on him and Margo knocks over all four guitars Rize has spent the last hour tuning.

Then Jules karate-chops his ears and tries to insert a pepperoni stick down his pants: "Wake up, you bastard, we're on."

Now he wishes Margo had never brought Kit backstage.

He hates pepperoni.

* * *

"WHAT DOES a trombone player taste like?" she asks him as they ascend the emergency stairs to the top of the club. Stunned, he shoulders her, she climbs over him. His eyes flick open and he can see her ribs beneath her sweater.

Elegant on the roof, they are show dogs, prancing on the thin autumn ice with their boots. The ice cracks. It's so cold that they screech and tie their scarves over their heads, like cartoons of people with toothaches, before they fall over laughing. In the first pink light of morning, he tucks inside her warmth and lets out the breath he's been holding all night.

"Like this," he says finally. "I taste like this."

Later, naked in Kit's bed, he puts his head in her lap and forms a gun with his hand, points it to his skull, and pulls his trigger finger. Drool catches at the corner of his mouth. Kit puts her thumb in the invisible point of entry and a half-remembered guitar riff flies through him like a shocked roach. She's saying something to him as she pulls at tufts of his hair, but he can't hear her voice, there's only the wailing sound of feedback in his head. Then she plugs his mouth with two fingers and makes an exploding sound, which he catches. Then he remembers: Kit owns a gun.

* * *

EACH TIME AFTER SHE LEAVES in the morning, Rize goes to the corner of his room and kneels naked on the cold floor. It is habitual. Feet overlapped, sphincter stretched, he splays his hands and tries to think about his breathing.

But his thoughts creep, inevitably, to money. How to obtain it. How to save it, how not to squander it. Maybe he can sleep all day, all night, not eat or drink or smoke or buy Kit drinks. Maybe he can steal. No, not stealing. In this prayer pose he must at least try to think good thoughts. He should stay in bed reading books. Books are free; she brings them to him but they stay there, where she leaves them by his bed, covers fading a little more every day from the sun that glares into his large room.

He wants to tell her to bring food, cigarettes, but his pride won't let him, so he accepts the books without comment until Kit grins and notices their unopened covers.

"Illiterate, are you?"

Each time she leaves, he doesn't know where or when he'll see her next. The thought of today's leaving causes him to cough out a breath. The way she crashes out into the world in her black cop boots makes him nervous.

"What do you do all day, Kit? Where do you go?"

"I spy," she had told him, a piece of melted cheese hanging off the corner of her mouth.

"I spy, with my teeny eye."

He puts his head on the floor, his small nose unable to take in enough air. The gasps quicken. He can never get a straight answer out of her.

All he knows, so far, is that she seeks him out when she is tired, when the clutter of other people's crimes becomes unbearable. She pulls on those leather boots, dusts her eyes with blue powder, and steps into his night. Into whatever club he's playing. She usually turns up when he's tired of unhooking cords, exhausted by the squawks of the sound system, of sighing into the horn. Just when Jules's sweet voice becomes a tedious drip of lament, she turns up at the back, by the bar, sipping vodka with a beer chaser.

I am not illiterate, he wants to say, every time he comes out after a show. *I have text, reams of words, and ideas and feelings and all sorts of things to say and write and do and tell to you.*

Then, just as he wants to say this, she grabs the scruff of his collar and bites down on his jowl.

And then it doesn't matter that he thinks he is a fucking epic, that he's been collecting interesting things to say to her because, of course, he can't remember anything when she does that kind of stuff. It doesn't matter that Jules, in his concerned but condescending way, asks him what they talk about. *You know, Kit has two degrees in criminal psychology (one in French and one in English) and is going for her master's, Rize. You know that, right?*

It doesn't matter that he can't explain it to his band and, when he tries to, he says something stupid like *There is a lot of energy between us.* And it doesn't matter that he dropped out of secondary at fifteen, that there are bouts of paranoid frenzy that seize up his veins and his mind and confuse him. Cause him to erupt and break women's things with his puffy fingers. To make errors in judgment.

It doesn't matter what anyone else thinks of him. Because Kit knows.

Because, when he lies in her bed, Rize makes Kit laugh so hard snot bubbles come out of her nose. Because this is his intelligence: that he makes a girl as smart as Kit pee her pants giggling.

Kit isn't specific about her job, but Margo says she works for the RCMP. Kit talks about firebombs and bikers, dirty politicians and businesses he has never heard of. He knows she wiretaps people and follows them around sometimes. Wiretap, like her body, wound tight and ready. He welcomes her talk, too, when he collapses into her bed. It's a relief not to have to entertain anyone.

He wants to tell her that he hears her arrogance in her vague spy stories. He understands that they are not stories about her job, that they're designed to make her look better, bigger than a bony girl in well-heeled boots. He wants to tell her he likes this arrogance; her big ego impresses him more than her job. Instead, he leans into her face and calls her beautiful.

He welcomes her silence, too, when she pulls her hands through his hair and sighs in her sleep. Because when she's quiet and asleep he's able to take his retribution on her, with the cruelty that only a lover can execute. This is when he pulls the sheet from her body, inspects her long legs, and dips his fingers between them to pull out his own smell. This is when he pushes his mouth under her nose and draws on her sleeping breath. Using a circular breathing technique, he sucks all her air into his lungs then breathes it back into her shallow breath until, annoyed, she pulls away from him.

Why do we want to do such nasty things to those we adore? he wonders.

When she settles back into sleep, he curls up at the base of her hip. In this levy of flesh between her belly and hipbone, he traces his name with his tongue. *Mine.*

He doesn't think of money then, of the hours spent arched and silent in the corner of his room. There are no songs in his head, not the new Angel Riots tunes, not even the stupid pop songs that constantly stream through his radio mind.

Swathed in the smell of sex, of smoke, he tries to stay awake, to relish this unworried span of time and flesh. He breathes in the singed taste of her skin; it burns the back of his throat just like the fourth rail of blow. So that every time you swallow you feel higher, more alive.

* * *

IT'S LIKE WHEN YOU LEARN a new word and then hear it everywhere. *Impunity. The American soldiers went about their business with impunity.* Rize sees this word on one of Kit's files and looks it up later, learns its meaning, and then sees it in a newspaper article, then again in a fax from the band's lawyer.

It's like that now, ubiquitous reminders of things he doesn't understand, systems of language outside and within himself he cannot decipher. He feels a camera's eye is trained on him everywhere he goes. He walks into the grocery store, examines the ceiling cameras, nods, grabs what he needs, and then goes to the cash. Paranoid, he checks his clothes for bugs, hangs up the phone if he hears clicking.

Now when he kneels in his room it's different; he wears clothes, his head twitches backward. He feels as though someone is watching him. Onstage, he dresses better, makes sure he's shaved, pulls the slide precisely, careful not to slur a single note. He takes care, scans the dark crowd for eyes that trace his movements. He trawls the streets, head down, and doesn't make eye contact with anyone.

One day it becomes too much, so he decides to turn it on its head. He shuffles through his wallet for the card with her work address on it. He goes. He waits on the corner, blowing smoke into the hair of schoolgirls. Then he ducks through the doorway of a fancy Westmount brownstone when it gets too cold.

Through his sunglasses he sees her come out. She's dressed conservatively, in a black blazer with a white shirt, like a waiter or something. Two large men in black suits flank her. They laugh at something she says as one of them flicks on a lighter for her cigarette. They continue to talk, till one of them grabs her arm and kisses her cheeks, twice—Montreal style—before he leaves. *Kissing colleagues, fucking cops.* The other cop stays and lights his own cigarette. Her arms are wrapped around her waist, she nods at her colleague's words, biting her bottom lip.

Rize gulps and looks away, at the two lanes of traffic that pass between them, then he opens the door for a woman with grocery bags. When he looks back to the window he realizes he's been so close to it that he's fogged it up with his breath. Alone now, Kit looks up and down the street, shivering. She aims her eyes directly at Rize as she pulls a hand up, wiggles her fingers at him.

His throat tightens. Startled, he takes a step back; a truck drives by slowly, blocking her out. When it passes he looks back and blinks, seeing only the ghost of her eyes that follow him everywhere now.

* * *

ONCE, when he was a kid, he won a colouring contest during a family vacation to Ontario. The prize was any free ride he wanted at the lakeside fair. He chose the pedal boats. When his mom got in the small yellow boat with him they went around in circles. June started to laugh and screamed "Oh my god!" while the boat churned up dead water in the middle of the pond and his father, Clay, fed their baloney sandwiches to the ducks. They finally managed to get out of the "Bermuda Triangle," as his mom called it, and were back on the dock when she said, "I guess there are no free lunches, eh kiddo?"

He feels like that now, like he's peddling around in the muck, trying to move in a straight line, a woman's roaring, nervous laughter always in his ears.

* * *

SOON, a longing for the road pulls at his lungs like his tired, sobbing, unborn child. Lately, it wakes him up in the mornings.

He misses American cities, metal hubcaps reflected in the highway sun, the hum of an L.A. air conditioner at two in the morning. Dust. Wearing sunglasses all day and night, two sets of clothes and no underwear. He misses the shiny teeth of young girls smiling at him while he bounces on stage.

"How can you miss a place you've never seen?" Kit asks him when she brings him coffee in bed and he tells her about it. He doesn't tell Kit that he's been everywhere in North America, twice, that he's been touring some way or another since he was fifteen. Kit likes to ask questions like these. She also likes to make portentous statements. Rize, in turn, likes to leave her metaphysical phrases and questions hanging in the air like smoke rings.

It's not just the going he misses, it's the money. Real, dirty, American money. Money to spend on crap. On Twinkies, cigarettes, beer, guitar strings, cheesy clothes, sunglasses, and now, postcards and presents for Kit. He misses the cabal understanding of travelling bodies in a van, the rush of seeing darkness descend on a different city every night.

No eyes on you, eyes that trace you like a suspect, a thief.

I gotta get outta here. I gotta get ...

He bolts up from her bed, slips on his jeans.

"Where are you going?" she asks, as if there is nowhere else to be except in this cold, high-ceilinged room, with the threat of winter screeching to be let in.

He pulls the sleep from his eyes, undoes the three locks on her door after lighting one of her cigarettes. Suddenly awake, she leaps at him, the lighter ricocheting off the wood floor.

He doesn't move as she holds him.

"I'm not like you. I can't stay here," he practically spits. He can't describe to her the need to move.

"What are you talking about? You've just spent the last three days eating, watching movies, and having sex with me."

"I know but, Jesus, Kit, you're a cop." He pulls at the door, it doesn't open.

She focuses on the floor, at the protective circle he's started tracing around himself with his boot; her chest caves in as she unhooks the latch at the very bottom, the one he's failed to undo. Then she kicks the door open with her too-big foot.

"Go."

"Kit!"

"You're right, we're not the same. And if you showed up one day like you did last week, stoned, dressed like a—"

"But I wasn't—"

"You act like I'm clingy and you were the one fucking stalking me? Talk about mixed messages, Rize." She pounds a bare foot on the floor, her calves flexing from the pressure.

"I wasn't stoned. I wasn't stalking, I just—I just wanted to see where you worked. I'm telling you, they're watching me."

"You're paranoid. Just go, already."

He walks out, face burning. She slams the door behind him. He hears the snap of locks. He shivers. Freedom.

And then he hears the chord of A minor, played low on a piano, the sound of penitence.

3
jim

My first week in Montreal I found an apartment in a damp brownstone at the western tip of the Plateau. It was a cheap one-bedroom at the end of a long hallway, far enough away from the other tenants so that my practising wouldn't reach them. The other tenants had the same wide, stretched-out look in their eyes as I did, so it seemed like the right place to survive the coming winter.

I sent a note to my mother telling her that I'd started school and to contact the police about the car, which I'd left in a ditch in a small town outside Montreal. For money, there was still a couple grand in savings from my four summers at the Dairy Queen.

Isaac I met during my fourth week in Montreal, after stumbling out of a stuffy orchestra rehearsal. I was outside debating whether to go to a music department party that promised to be a screamingly boring affair with lots of Cheezies and little booze. I felt restless, lonely, as usual.

I had played badly at the rehearsal, my chinrest sloping off my neck at an awkward angle so that now my arms were throbbing with pain. All I wanted to do was go home, take a hot bath, down some Nytol, and forget the day.

But Isaac was walking toward me. He was with two other men and they were all dressed in suits. Massive shoulders, with wild hair, Isaac resembled a medieval warrior dressed in Hugo Boss. His brown eyes snagged on mine, would not let go. He stopped. His friends, two good-looking young Québécois guys, shifted behind him, smiling, a little drunk.

"We're going to a tapas bar. Come with?" He reached for my hand and shook it. I could feel his wedding band against my palm.

"Wow. Aren't you forward?"

I had a ridiculous bow in my hair which I pulled off as Isaac turned to his friends and quipped something in his quick Anglo-French. They laughed, but not unkindly. I wiped rosin on my black dress and was about to say no. How random, not to mention unsafe, would it be to put myself at the mercy of three strange men? But they didn't scare me: I hadn't learned to fear people yet.

Trees, ghosts, rain, hail, wind, what I had left behind somewhere on the Trans-Canada, and Montreal itself, with its infinite permutations of suffering and garbage—these things terrified me. But, I decided, this man and his gang I could handle. Isaac stared at me while his friends fidgeted: *"Allez, Isaac. Vite."*

I scrunched my face up and looked at the tall downtown buildings, wondering what kept them up. Isaac pulled my violin case from my hand and I caught a glimpse of myself in a car window. My face was swollen; I looked like a child who hadn't gotten enough sleep and my hair flew upward in perfect vertical spikes. I looked young. Younger than eighteen. Then I thought about my options again—the dismal string-player party ahead or a drugged night in a bathtub—and let myself be escorted into the front seat of a cab by this stranger. Isaac's meaty hand felt like velvet. *Trust me,* his push said as it dipped into the small of my back for a golden instant.

* * *

AT THE BAR, Isaac and his friends, François and Fred, ordered plates of spicy sausage, garlic-smelling dips, and unrecognizable vegetables swimming in olive oil. Sangria flowed, digestifs were ordered, plus imported beer to clean the palate between courses. French and English: Franglais, swirled around me, and the more the men drank, the louder they got. Only Isaac's voice stayed at the same decibel. I learned that he was an importer, forty-four, Jewish, and a great lover of classical music. Or so he claimed.

"What grade are you in?" he queried.

"I'm at the university, actually. In music."

"I see." His eyes were focusing on my hair. "I don't even know your name," he whispered, his hand making its way to the back of my chair.

"Jim."

"Really?"

"Yup. James Neil Kov. Jim."

"Why—"

"It's a long story."

"Okay. Later then, tell me later," Isaac said, turning back to his friends. *Fat chance, mister,* I thought, sneering to myself. I sneered a lot in those days. *Later?* Who the hell was this guy? Did he think I'd be impressed by his money? By his cheesy, playboy attitude? Did he think his wide arms could contain me and my past?

Oh you and your fucking past.

It occurred to me then that I was becoming callous, detached. Part of me—the busy, forward-thinking farm girl—had been carved out. I'd left her in Yawnie's room a month ago. Like so many depressives, I existed day to day, waiting for the next disastrous blow. Sometimes I caught myself striding down a sidewalk like some impatient French officer in my unfashionable, flapping coat. The absurdity of my restless gait, my dwindling funds, my empty life in a city where I didn't know a single soul, save for humourless string players—these facts had not escaped me.

I was lonely, so ridiculously lonely; I had become a train wreck of a girl to manage. To the outside observer, it may have seemed that Isaac was getting the better end of the deal: a precocious eighteen-year-old vixen. But, in fact, *I* was the lucky one.

After the last round of drinks had been ordered, Isaac offered me his card and asked for my number.

"Are you nuts? I hardly know you. Plus, you're married."

I held up his paw of a hand and dropped it in his lap. Isaac made a face as if his wedding ring were a petty detail he didn't have time for. He waved for the bill. I saw the flash of a single gold tooth when he opened up his mouth to smile at the waitress. It reminded me that Isaac was from another generation, that he was closer to death than I was.

Maybe it was simply that I was wedged between isolation and the forced, drunken hilarity of strangers, and that made me desperate for contact. Whatever the reason, my hand crept back into Isaac's lap and, when it did, he plucked it up toward his heart. Then crushed it like a blossom.

* * *

WE WENT TO HIS MANSION in Westmount that night. He took me from room to room, pulling off cover sheets to explain how he'd just finished renovating, how he'd decorated all the rooms himself, his wife having no taste in such things. The living room clashed: severe Bauhaus metal shelves stood against bright orange walls. In the kitchen, bronze pots hung at the exact height of halogen lamps and tiny pretentious lights were pinned to the ceiling with what appeared to be hairclips. I was a country girl, it's true, but I still knew it was gaudy, so I told him this. He laughed, pulled a hand over his brow, and shook off his jacket. Then he lifted me up to the cold marble counter and spread my legs open with a slow twitch of his right hand, all the while keeping his brown eyes on my face.

Later, in his big room, with nothing in it but a king-size bed, we did it again and he fell asleep almost immediately afterward. I pulled the cover from his body and he shifted uncomfortably, cold. He'd looked so large at the bistro, so strong, and now he was lying on his stomach, arms and legs splayed, his breathing collapsed as if every bone in his body were broken.

* * *

IN THE SLOW MOTION of discovery's silence, as Isaac peels off the layer of gauze from my arm, he says:

"Jesus Christ, Jim, what're you doing to yourself?" He holds my left breast in one hand, my right wrist in the other.

As he examines the lattice of cuts on my wrist, I hold out my angry arm, daring him to judge me. Cowed and naked, I trace my steps behind this moment: How did I get here? Offering my scars out to this gentle millionaire?

You sought me out, remember? I was standing still when you met me, going nowhere and just fine. So heal me, save me, goddamnit, it was you who found me.

Screw being a modern woman: I needed saving. And I'd found just the right man for the job.

"Tu me manques déjà," Isaac said that first night, after he had rewrapped my bandages and made me promise I would stop cutting my arms.

Tu me manques déjà. I miss you already. *Manquer.*

In French, the word sways toward the sentimental only to double back on itself, true onomatopoeia. The mouth opened like a kiss, tongue shuddering against the teeth, it spits out the disgust of need in two exact syllables: *Mon key.*

I wanted to tell him that I hadn't been born alone, was only just learning to cauterize my own wounds. I wanted to tell Isaac that the lacerations would eventually heal. Before I met Isaac, I thought I would try to follow my brother. But Isaac's smile had rearranged things for me, and I needed him now.

But I didn't say a word. My body felt paralyzed, my mind glazed with sex and hope.

Besides, Isaac was asleep, and the blue morning light had already started to creep into his room. Plus, you cannot say such things to a stranger so early on in the day.

4
rize

He remembers the very first time he saw Jules: an underdeveloped nine-year-old, trembling slightly at the front of the room as he was introduced to the rest of the grade-six class. Jules was wearing a too-big pair of purple ladies' glasses, which no amount of playground mockery would force him to part with.

Later, Rize would learn that the glasses belonged to Jules's dead mother and that he is pathological about not losing or destroying them, though he seems to have no other earthly attachments. Something about the boy's confidence captures Rize's attention. That, and the fact that Jules is small enough to be folded into the air vent, alerts Rize that the new boy may need some sort of support in the weeks to come. Rize watches Jules's shaky walk to his desk, and while the other kids break crayons and roll their bowl-cut heads on their desks, Rize stabs the meat of his palm with his sharpened pencil just to feel something.

At recess he finds Jules alone, digging a hole in the snow. Rize taps a mittened hand on his shoulder and the blond boy turns around with a gruff, adult "What is it?"

"What are you looking for?" Rize asks as snowballs hammer around them. Jacques, Alessandro, and Harold, the popular boys, the boys on hockey teams, the boys with dads, are watching this new alliance with amused interest. Rize's inquiry has earned both Retard-Rize and the New Kid a hearty snowball pounding. Just as Jules is about to squeak out a reply, a glob of ice plummets straight into his mouth, thankfully missing the eyewear.

In the nurse's room, Rize piles Jules's drenched winter clothes on top of the heater and arranges tongue depressors in a neat row on the green counter. Then he produces a half-eaten pack of Rolos, presses the sticky chunks of caramel and chocolate onto the ends of the sticks, and feeds them to his small yet captive audience.

"They're energy bolts, go on."

Jules groans and makes a gagging noise, but chews the caramels gratefully, sucking on the tip of a wooden tongue depressor like a pacifier. Rize pats Jules's staticky hair down only once and watches the snow fall on top of the teachers' cars as he sings the Big Mac song, over and over.

Most of his childhood memories of Jules are like this: the two boys squatting in unseen corners, away from the gloomy, shadowy presence of adults. One or both of them sick, injured, depressed, drunk, or asleep, with the other one awake, on watch, as if they are the only two people in the world. Where are the grownups? The people? The others? They are nowhere.

When Jules dates an aspiring theatre actress, the last girl he sleeps with before he marries Margo, Rize will go, with Jules and the girlfriend, to a terrible play. The play is about two old guys sitting on a bench waiting for a third guy, who never comes. Rize will fail to recognize the great pronouncements about life and death and "Beckett's allegorical perspicacity" (as Jules says to impress the girl), but something about the rapport of those two losers reminds him of all those grey days in cold rooms listening to Jules talk.

After the snowball incident, Rize and Jules form a planet of two. It doesn't matter that Jules finds grade six useless and is pushed up another year, skipping two grades in total. They aren't deterred by their collective nickname "Runt 'n' Retard" (RR for short) all through junior school. It doesn't seem to register that beyond insults, the loss of a mother and father between them, and the odd and endless discourse from sneakers to punk rock to Salinger, led mostly by Jules, they have little in common except their alienation. It's enough, somehow, to be in these quiet rooms, waiting for autumn to end, the bullies to leave the school, the looming grownups to go to bed.

When he thinks about his late childhood, Rize can recall only two players: Jules, and his own mother, June. Sometimes he wonders if that's normal, if a boy shouldn't have more social experiences.

But whenever he tells Jules that he thinks he might spend some time with Larry, his Ping-Pong champion buddy, or his cousin Anthony from Boston, who owns his own Casio synthesizer, Jules recedes from him, leaves him alone for days at a time to catch up with his own cousins, studying, and music listening. The possibility of a contracted, solitary universe—without Jules—is overwhelming to Rize. Jules's absence frightens Rize more than the idea of June's intense and ferocious sex life and enforces an even greater sense of loneliness than his mother's swift, orgasmic abandonment. He didn't think it was possible.

* * *

HE DOESN'T HEAR from Kit for nearly two weeks after fleeing her apartment. Finally, after two shots of tequila and half a pack of cigarettes, he gets up the courage to call, but gets her machine.

"So, yeah, hi," he begins, making his voice breezy and casual. "So, I'm just hangin' out and I guess you're not home so, I'll, you know. Hey! Listen! I wanted to tell you, my head hurts, not like a headache or anything but, like, my head, the skin on my head around my temples, and maybe the bone, too, haha, like, I guess you'd call it, my skull. Anyway, my head feels kind of soft, in around there, my jaw hurts, too. I can hardly eat anything. I've been drinking milkshakes for three days. Vegetables, fuggedabowdit. Anyway, I'll call you back another time. Bye!"

He stares at the phone as if it were a large tarantula he has to ingest.

He's still sitting by the phone when his roommate comes home an hour later and tries to use it.

"No."

"Why not?"

"There's lightning. On the radio, they said there might be a thunderstorm and I don't want you to get a shock."

His roommate smiles and picks up the phone. "I think I'll be okay."

"I meant to call this girl, because the last time we were together I acted like a total ass. So, I meant to apologize, but instead I told her my head was soft."

"Your head *is* soft."

He nods.

"It'll be okay."

"I launched into a monologue about milkshakes. I said, 'fuggedabowdit.'"

"Dude, what happened?"

* * *

HE'S ALWAYS GETTING HIMSELF into situations like this with girls. It reminds him of the time with his ex, Sally, when he came home after a salsa gig and told her he and the guys were moving to Mexico to start a mariachi band.

Sally was half asleep and half Spanish. She was also an aerobics instructor at the Y and had a short temper.

She pushed him away and said something sexy to him in Spanish.

When he found out the next night from the guys that she had *not* told him he had a nice ass but had called him an asshole, he got drunk with Sergio, the singer, and, when he came back to their apartment, he cut the toe part off all her good dancing tights. Then he started to defrost the fridge to make up for it but passed out midway. He woke up with all the condiments on the table, two large bloody steaks in the sink, and Sally screaming at him in Spanish. She threw all his eighties records off their third-storey balcony and called him an asshole again.

When he and the guys came to her window and serenaded her, mariachi style, it was late February and he noticed that she had put plastic on her windows to conserve heat. Someone from another apartment threw an apple juice can at him and Rize knew then that he had overestimated Sally's capacity for forgiveness.

* * *

"RIZE?"

"Yes."

"It's Kit, calling you back."

"I know. Listen—"

"They told me about you."

"Who?"

A pause, her throat clearing. "Margo and Jules, they said you were a bit emotionally disturbed. Look, Rize, I think you're great but if it's going to be like this all the time—"

"Be like what? Look, I'm not a fucking psycho, Kit, I have some problems but—" His chest, full of pride and shame, feels as if it might tear and fly away like a flimsy shopping bag. But then he gains control of his fury. He clips it in and says, "I'm sorry, Kit, my brain gets scrambled sometimes. I get restless. But I want to see you again." He wants to know the meaning of the black ink scrawled in her steno notebooks. He wants to crack her anger open, push his fingers into her skull.

He could, perhaps, learn something from her anger; they could construct something magnificent from it, like a song, or the promise of not being left behind. It might be impossible. But at least he could try. He could stand to learn something new, he figures. Kit is smart, she could teach him things. In return, he could try to peel back the layers of her hard words, understand what connects their angry, mismatched souls.

"I need to see you, Kit."

A sigh; she is curious, too. "All right."

* * *

HE THINKS MAYBE he needs a vacation from Jules. Thinks maybe he doesn't need him calling at eight-thirty a.m. to tell him he just saw a squirrel on his windowsill that looked like Nixon, and that, for a gas, the band should cover Rush.

"Why do you pick up the phone? Just let the machine get it," Kit says.

"Jules is the only person who calls me every day."

"That's weird, Rize," she says, pulling his favourite pillow down between her legs.

"Why is it weird? You and Margo talk every day."

"That's different. We're girls."

He imagines going up to Jules and telling him, *Buddy, you know I love you to death, but I need a little space.*

Space?

Yeah, like it's too much sometimes, I feel like we're married or some shit.

These days Jules would probably laugh, try to put him in a headlock and then wash his trombone out with Tide, leave a note that said: *I AM the boss of you.*

He thinks maybe he needs a vacation from his life. He could become an optometrist like his cousin Anthony from Boston, who says "caw pawk" and pronounces his name "Antanny." Anthony is his favourite cousin and has a two-car garage, a garden, a wife with coloured contacts. He could forget this music thing for a while, open his own practice and make some money like other people. Real people. He could get Anthony to help him.

"First of all," she tells him, unrolling a fresh Tootsie Pop and throwing the wrapper on his floor, "you don't have to go to med school to become an optometrist, and second, you gag when I put my contacts in."

"Do not."

She hits him. "You do so! Besides, you couldn't cut it, you'd get nauseous, up and close and personal with some old lady's rheumy eyeball." He wishes she wouldn't say words like *rheumy.*

"Third, there's nothing else in this world that you could do except play music."

"Not true."

She twitches her eyebrows at him and then closes her eyes.

"What colour are my eyes, Rize?"

"I forget."

She opens them.

"Grey."

"Very good."

"So, you don't think I'm wasting my life?"

She pulls the sucker out of her mouth, shrugs.

"I think the world needs more trombone players and fewer optometrists. I think you are very talented, if poor, and I think you are lucky to be so talented because some people aren't good at anything true."

By way of changing the topic, he tells her how Anthony once ate three sloppy Joe sandwiches at a roadside diner then puked his guts out the window doing eighty miles an hour. Then he tries to lick her eyeball.

"Jesus, Rize," she gags.

The next day, the morning of the day he wants to tell her he loves her, two things happen: he unintentionally rips off the cover of her first-edition copy of *By Grand Central Station I Sat Down and Wept* with his foot, and crushes her reading glasses under his stomach.

Both of these things happen between turning off the alarm and answering the phone, in the first moments of waking.

Merciless, Jules starts right in, but Rize interrupts him. "I gotta go, Jules, I just made Kit cry."

"Oh god, you didn't show her your—" dial tone.

Kit is still sleeping, she still has no idea of the love or destruction he has wrought upon her life.

Duct tape. Duct tape is essential to this situation. He grabs a spool of it and starts to tear. It doesn't rip easily. Scissors. Naked, he bolts to the kitchen where his roommate is enjoying a delicious English muffin and reading the paper. He grabs the scissors from the drawer.

"Can't talk now! Emergency!"

He tapes the book up and then breaks the arm off her glasses trying to bend them back into shape. "Oh, Jesus," he whispers, winding the sticky mess around the arm clumsily. When he looks up she's awake, her head propped up high on several pillows. Her small breasts perch like alien anchor people, inquisitive. They watch the horror, tactfully silent. His belly shrinks.

"What is it? What's wrong?"

He hands her the glasses, then the book.

"I—I broke your stuff." He crawls beneath the cover and pulls a pillow over his head. She sighs and begins to unwind the tape.

"It's okay."

"I'll get you another book."

She gives him a sad smile, which he can't see.

"Today was supposed to be special," he says, trying to open his eyes which are pressed to the sheets. "Like, not retarded special, but nice special."

"It's okay, Rize, really, it's just stuff."

He imagines her shrug. A bunch of minus signs trail through the lids of his eyes. She puts her one-armed glasses on, covers her breasts, and turns on the radio.

He decides to put it off to another, more auspicious day, without phone calls or alarms, weak spines or arms.

He decides it's a sign: bad things come in threes. He'll break one more of her things, by accident, of course. Then, when that's over, he'll say it; like Jules, he'll croon, he'll sing sweetly into her ear and then she'll know he can talk about love and duct-tape what's broken.

* * *

THE FOLLOWING WEEK, as he sits waiting for her in a Saint-Henri diner where the liver and onion special is only $4.99, he thinks about how he still hasn't said it.

He's eating french fries and reading his horoscope: *Those around you will introduce you to the fine art of argument. Show them that you are not superficial, only flexible.* I am flexible, he thinks, smearing ketchup on the paper.

Then he reads hers: *The world seems to be making unreasonable demands on you at this moment. Dismiss those with outdated claims on your good nature and slip out the back door while you still have the chance.*

She is half an hour late.

He smokes one of the four Gitanes he stole from Guy.

When she arrives, her face is wet with sweat.

"I ran into my friend Hal. Hal used to be a real asshole. All he wanted to do was be a writer, and now he's published, so he's stopped being an asshole. He's relaxed now, nice to everybody. It's so simple: when people get what they want, they stop being assholes. Eh, Rize?"

"Some aren't, some are more asshole-y when they get what they want."

Kit crooks an eyebrow at him. Then helps herself to his fries.

* * *

SHE COMES OUT of the rain into the studio. She smokes and talks to Jules, her naked shoulder blades rubbing against the band stickers on the wall. While she chats, he thinks about what Jules said to Kit, that he was emotionally disturbed. Jules makes Margo and Kit laugh in a way they never do with him, unless he is doing something stupid like sticking chopsticks up his nose or mooning cars at red lights. Kit appears at just such moments, with his hands down his pants and Jules screaming, or his face covered with ice cream, and once, right after the worst haircut of the year.

Why are you the only one who gets someone? I want someone, too. I want her, he thinks, jabbing his thoughts into Jules's smug little face. As if reading his mind, Jules cocks his head at Rize and smiles, a real nice, toothy Jules grin—a rarely seen wonder of the universe, lately, what with Jules wound up on three different strains of paranoia-inducing weed and his recent root canal. Following Jules's stare, Kit walks toward Rize, almost hypnotized. She hardly says anything to him, just pecks him on the brow and folds her hand over the bell of his trombone as if her fingers want to crawl inside the hole and rest inside the moisture of his breath.

In the studio she runs her hands over speakers as if she is securing the site. She touches beer bottles, cables, adaptor cords, the drum kit, and the amps before the band begins to play. Then she sits on the floor and looks at her hands throughout rehearsal. Rize clutches his fists between songs, thinking about how he has to touch all those things again to undo the spell she's cast on the equipment.

Sensing Rize's discomfort, Kit gets up in the middle of a number, stretches her long body out, and waves goodbye. He hears her boots knocking down all three flights of the studio's stairs. He loosens his grip on his horn and decides that, in about two hours, he will begin drinking in earnest.

Don't leave me alone with this song. With the memory of your warm hair. In this cold room with one low light bulb and two thin walls. Today, I am afraid.

Please don't leave me after hauling my body over yours, after you've taken the last drop I had. Not after I've brushed the cigarette ash off your fingers and caught you sprawled over my place in bed. Not after you've told me about the magicians who throw knives at you in your sleep. Don't leave me to chase myself in circles, around your words and secrets and favours, on this corner, with the scalpers and hookers. I am not brave like them. Like you.

* * *

IT BUILDS until it breaks in him.

It builds until he is at her door, knocking. He's wearing two toques and a scarf on his head, despite the fact that it's a balmy Indian summer day. He has black bags under his eyes, his cheeks are flushed. When she opens the door he stumbles over the step.

"Jesus, Rize, I'm fifteen minutes late for a meeting I organized."

"But you smell so clean!" he shouts, before doubling over. She catches him.

"You look like hell." She pulls her hand beneath his toques to feel the fever emanate from his skin, then pushes him toward the bedroom, wraps him in a blanket, and pulls out her cell to explain to someone that she'll be late.

She prepares tea, a handful of vitamins, along with a sliced orange and a piece of toast. Then she returns to the bedroom to go through the two plastic bags he brought. They contain: six mismatched shoes, a tricycle wheel, two broken umbrellas, a dog leash, several eyeglass cases, dirty vacuum cleaner parts, and half a smashed pumpkin. Kit puts her hand on his forehead again and pulls out a dirty red sneaker from one of the bags. "What is all this, this junk?"

He wants to tell her about the two days he's been collecting it. On her streets. Where and how he found each item, hugged it to his body. "They're lonely. They make me feel so goddamn lonely, all these lost little guys. They're clues, for you." Lately, he's been talking a lot to inanimate objects. He's been high-fiving bicycles and discussing stardom with garbage bags. He takes the sneaker from her and sniffs it, almost weeping.

"Hi, buddy," he whispers.

She sighs. The phone rings again as she lies down beside him and takes his hand. But she doesn't answer it. They lie there like that for a while until Kit makes him swallow the vitamins, eat half the orange, and blow his nose. Then he puts the sneaker over his eyes, like he's embarrassed.

It's night when he wakes up, alone, in her bed, fever abating. He can hear Kit and Margo talking about him in the living room. He lies back on the pillows, wondering how Margo is explaining it to her, how he gets like this sometimes. Unlike Jules, he trusts Margo not to be too mean, or hysterical, or to scare Kit off. He hopes she mentions that he could be taking mild drugs for these episodes but that he chooses not to because they affect his playing and dull his sense of humour. He hopes, too, that Margo's not making a big deal out of it.

Because it isn't. He just gets like this, especially when he's got a fever and hasn't gotten much sleep.

As the girls talk, he watches the orange streetlights bounce off the high ceilings of the room. He stares at the ceiling without blinking until he sinks, face first, into the brown shag carpet of his childhood and dreams about the day he woke up and Clay was gone.

His mom is crying, smoking cigarette after cigarette in the living room, while he tries to open his eyes in the carpet. The threads kind of scratch his eyeballs; the smell of dog, basement, and popcorn fills his nose while his mom sips at her vodka tonic and stares at the television. It isn't even on.

* * *

AT REHEARSAL, the sound of Jules taking a bong hit reminds him of blowing bubbles in his milk glass as a kid.

Kit, Margo, and Jim are huddled around the hallway heater, wrapped together in a fleece blanket, drinking gin. Jim is asleep, and the girls have braided and pinned up her long hair so that she looks like a Mennonite or an angel, lying there on the hardwood, swaddled up in a plaid blanket. Rize is on his stomach, listening to Jules talk.

"Art isn't sanctioned any more, and we have to make a living eventually. Where are our patrons? I'm sick of this poverty shit."

"Sanctioned," Rize repeats, placing his arms in a triangle and preparing himself for the yoga handstand Kellogg taught him. Just as he is about to push his legs up, the girls let out a shriek.

"Also, we need to run through the set again," Jules says,

ignoring the hysteria in the hallway. "We need to practise more, tour's less than two weeks away."

"I don't have it in me tonight, man," Rize whispers, pointing his socked feet at the ceiling.

He can hear Jim wake up and say something that makes the other two girls giggle. A cocktail is knocked over.

"My ears hurt, too," Jules says, inhaling another hit. The girls start to sing "Rocky Raccoon" and Jules joins in.

Rize drops his knees to the floor and lets out a long groan. Everyone sings louder.

"I need you here, baby," Jules tells him. He's so stoned it looks like his green eyes are dripping blood.

Later, Margo wraps herself in a blanket tightly for warmth, tucks the microphone to her chest. In her best warble, she sings a simple piano tune Jules wrote for her that morning. Kit sits by the high window, looking down into the street. Jim and the boys come in and watch, hands tucked into their jean pockets. When Margo peeks her head out of the mass of covers, she blows Kit a kiss then stares up at the sudden darkness of the room. She counts the white-corded Christmas lights that line the crumbling walls of the studio. Counts the stars.

That same night Kit dreams she is cleaning out her father's refrigerator, which is the size of a small bungalow.

Margo dreams she does heroin and finds a human toe in a can of Campbell's soup.

Jules dreams the band's lawyer disowns them for showing up late for his son's bar mitzvah.

Jim dreams she is effusive and gorgeous at a social gathering, though she is unsure whether they are celebrating a wedding or mourning a death.

And Rize dreams he is making love to Kit, that he comes into the new morning tide. In the dream, when the cops handcuff him and show him pictures of her battered body, he remembers that she is his only alibi.

5
jim

Margo was drinking a glass of red wine while the band set up on stage when I first saw her. She was talking to a long-legged woman in high boots who, it turned out, was Kit, Rize's the trombone player's, girlfriend. I approached the bar and ordered a soda water while Margo sipped her drink and went on with her conversation:

"So, anyway, this guy's talking to me, and I can just feel it coming, so, I go to him, 'If you say my voice sounds like Tori Amos, I'm going to throw this drink in your face.'"

I leaned against the bar, feeling almost normal. Both women looked at me.

"Hi," I said finally, turning toward them, offering my hand, which they looked at curiously.

"That's what you're drinking? You know, I'd love to buy you a real drink," Margo said, calling the bartender over.

"It's okay, I have this," I said, indicating my beer glass full of soda.

"That's not a drink," Margo hissed, before she ordered a bottle of wine and three glasses.

"I'm Jim. I know Kellogg," I said, apropos of nothing, as Margo passed me a glass.

"I know who you are, Jim," she said, lowering her lashes as the bartender uncorked the bottle. Kit left her glass and went backstage, leaving Margo and me to make conversation. "To being plucked from the prairies," Margo said loudly, raising her glass. "To the city!" She looked glamorous; her bits of silver jewellery complemented her red dress and her clothes clung to her as if they were wet. It seemed that Kellogg had already told her all about me, or at least the basics.

"So, you're like, what? Some musical prodigy or something?"

I shrugged and sipped my wine. It tasted off, but, then again, I had never tasted anything stronger than Pilsner.

"Kellogg says you're an academic musician," Margo said in a more careful tone, "that you're borderline genius, or something."

This caught me off guard. It was true, my old super-twin mental absorbency had kicked in the minute I started studying theory, and somehow I was acing both my private course and the university classes.

I wasn't used to people knowing things about me, private things, but soon, under Margo's tutelage, I'd be initiated into the band's collective brain. I'd learn that gossip was currency and everybody knew everything about everyone. As my role became more established, I also discovered that if you saw something, anything, amiss, it was best to suspend judgment and pretend you hadn't seen anything odd, in order for the common good to prevail: for the band to survive. Later, of course, this tactic would serve to devastate us, but at that moment I was flattered by Margo's attention.

"So, where's the famous Jules?" I asked, wanting to divert the conversation away from the subject of my negligible genius and over to Jules's controversial persona. I could already feel the wine warming my insides and tongue.

"See that adorable man with the jeans hanging off his ass? The one in the homemade underwear shirt? That's him."

Margo looked at the stage and yelled out a couple of orders to the guys, as if to prove she was intimately connected to them, but they ignored her and continued with their tasks.

At this point I started babbling about her dress, how great it looked, about how people in Montreal dressed so stylishly. Babbling was a trick I had learned from Simon. He used it when he found himself in awkward situations, such as trying to explain why he had poured his own beer from the tap while the bartender wasn't looking, or where Mom's emergency cash stash had disappeared. Margo, Jules, and the band intimidated me; they were minor celebrities around town. Rock stars. And I was, well, I was the underaged hick who wanted in.

"Wow, everyone sure drinks a lot here," I said, almost yelling, as I took another sip of the wine, which tasted like clover and wood.

Margo laughed in a throaty, actressy way. "You'll see that you need a healthy amount of alcoholism or some kind of addictive behaviour to get through these shows."

I cracked my fingers and took off my windbreaker, well, Yawnie's windbreaker, actually.

"So, what's your secret?" I asked, pulling up a stool next to her in what I thought was a cozy way as we watched the boys arguing about where to put what on stage. Margo pulled a calloused finger over the zipper of my windbreaker, half in admiration, half in disgust. It was a small, unconscious, almost sexy gesture, even though I noticed that her red nail polish was chipped and her nails were filthy.

"What's the secret to what?" she asked in a rougher tone.

"To surviving The Riots."

She looked up and I could tell she was assessing me. My "genius" versus my naïveté, my youthful looks versus my awful, unfeminine, un-rock 'n' roll style. Was I friend or threat? Was I even worth befriending?

Then I noticed something else: Margo was already drunk. Despite her glowing white skin, her vampy dress, something in the weakest point of blue in her eyes was grasping, trying not to drown.

Margo blinked at me, as if willing me to disperse into non-human matter. She was pacing herself socially; I suppose she couldn't waste all her charm on me. I was just a stupid child, I was useless to her: I had nothing to trade, offer, or sell. Margo, I would discover, was nothing if not a shrewd manipulator and self-promoter. Instead of answering me she ordered herself another glass of wine and turned her attention back to the stage, to the boys. Their tired voices echoed through the microphones like satellite transmissions from another time.

* * *

AFTER THE SHOW we all went up to the roof. While Rize and Kit made out by the fire escape, Margo and I shared cigarettes and another bottle of wine. By now she was well greased and talking to me was easier for her, I guess, as no one else was paying her any attention.

I learned that she and Jules had been married for four years—dating for eight—and that Rize was a little psychologically unstable, and that Margo was worried, frankly, about his involvement with her best friend, Kit. She also hinted that she was seriously concerned about my fashion sense and that she wanted to take me shopping.

Even though I didn't trust her, I liked Margo: she amused me. She was one of those people I had imagined meeting in Montreal. Meeting her was déjà vu, in a way. I would later learn that her confidence was as fake as her auburn hair, but I believed in her, then. I loved how she was completely aware of her own ridiculousness, her own ridiculous charm. She said things that people back home didn't, things like "Maturity is overrated" and "Who has sex without lube?" She was kind of like Isaac in the way that she didn't really edit what came out of her mouth. Despite her obnoxiousness, she had a way of making you feel significant.

That's why I almost slipped up and told her about Yawnie, because she had a way of getting things out of me.

"So, I'm sorry, let me get this straight, you took off, on your whole family, on your own birthday?"

"It was my brother's birthday too. I'm a twin," I said, staring into the spaces between the fire-escape steps to the cement below, imagining how it might feel to be so small you could slip through those metal gaps. I looked up at Margo, and as she held me in her dark blue eyes I felt I was being pulled in by the force of some large magnetized creature.

I suddenly became quite terrified about where my little emancipation story was going. I was one of those people who spilled their beans too early in relationships and told strangers inappropriate stories in an effort to ingratiate myself. During a high school science class, I'd told my lab partner that my parents did it the first time they met, in a silo, in the middle of a 4-H Club auction. Luckily, my inclination to spill was aborted by Jules, whose feet cracked the thin ice before he leaned down and offered us a drag of his ever-present joint.

"How are you, my love?" he asked Margo, smiling.

"Jules, this is Jim."

"I know." As he laughed at the legendary combination of our names, his eyes twinkled. They seemed gigantic through his big, eighties dewdrop glasses. I wondered, vaguely, how those glasses could have been fashionable in any decade.

"Yes, they are his mother's glasses," Margo said, reading my mind. "He can't go a month without breaking a pair, and we can't afford new ones any more, so we figured he'd just have to wear the old standbys till some record company dumps a load of cash on us."

"You should get those neat geometric frames when you have some money. You know, architect glasses," I suggested, wanting Jules to like me.

"Like, those faggy ones?" he quipped. A plume of smoke slithered under the glass of one of his exaggerated eyes.

I laughed as Jules coughed.

"So, Jim was just telling me a heavy story, babe."

"No, I mean, I was done, done talking."

Margo flashed her teeth at her husband and he retreated. He stood there throwing rocks at Rize and Kit on the fire escape, but I could feel him still listening to us.

"So what happened, on your birthday?" Margo prompted in a whisper. "You know, that made you leave the farm?"

I shrugged. My guts were busy churning up bile as Margo slipped one of the folds of her long coat over my shivering knees.

"I stole a priest's car," I said, in an effort to distract her from the meatier bits of my narrative.

She laughed. "Really?"

"Uhuh," I slurred. "A '74 Impala, to boot." Margo wrapped an arm around me and held me close as the alcohol continued to slosh around inside like lighter fluid in an arsonist's canteen.

"I have a boyfriend," I stated. "He is twenty-six years older than me."

"Sure, honey," Margo said, in a voice that betrayed the fact that she didn't believe a single thing I'd said. I remember laughing inwardly, realizing how bizarre it was that the contents of my life were too strange to digest even for someone as wild as her. I congratulated myself on having fooled the savvy, urbane Margo by distracting her from the truth with the truth. But somewhere I also knew that I couldn't tell her everything, and that if I was going to tell anyone it would be Isaac, whom I implicitly trusted. Margo, I suspected, collected information about people for the wrong reasons.

But maybe I was too cynical: perhaps Margo, like Isaac, was just waiting for the end of my story. And with Isaac maybe it was some kind of thousand and one Arabian nights thing, where the life of our relationship was extended each new night I filled his head with talk. But I couldn't get to the end with him either, not because I mistrusted him, but because I feared he would hate me if he knew what I really was: a renegade, a coward.

Margo had stopped talking now, and this sudden lapse in the feverish pace of our exchange, along with my wonky guts, made me throw up.

She sat there, calm as a stone, rubbing my back and watching Jules's profile against the clear night as I bowed off to the side. I tried getting to my feet, feeling humiliated about all the undigested fragments of my life I'd so unceremoniously dumped upon this friendly, glamorous, slightly terrifying stranger, whom I'd only wanted to impress. I remember feeling proud of myself, though, for not telling her my whole story, for holding back. Something told me not too many people could resist Margo's wilfulness.

I'd had enough of people, music, my great big new life. I needed to find a quiet place where I didn't need to be so on guard. I needed to get going. I said as much to Margo, begging her to call me a cab. Instead she pulled me toward her with surprising strength.

I fell on top of her, my body jerking as I cried. Luckily, it was so cold both my puke and tears froze quickly. Jules stood by us, oddly still, as if he'd witnessed this kind of exorcism before.

When I finally relaxed, Margo tried to bury me in her body, in the warmest place, between her breasts and her belly.

"Sorry, must have been all that wine," I mumbled.

She laughed. "You had three glasses, Jim, a good country girl like you—I know you can hold your liquor." Then my body relaxed and my physical resistance to Margo evaporated. Maybe it was because she was could be so warm and kind when she wanted to be, or maybe it was because I was tired and sick. Maybe it was simply the fact that, at that moment, Margo saw what I had been waiting for someone to identify in me. "Look at you," she said, holding onto my hair as if I were a little girl who needed to be told I was pretty and good. "Look at you with all this filthy guilt inside."

* * *

TWO WEEKS LATER, after a short hiatus from booze, I was working my way through a mickey of bourbon in order to drown out the voices in my head that said I was a charlatan. Isaac's wife was out of town and we, or rather Isaac, were renting a room for a week at the Ritz-Carlton. We were watching a documentary on natural disasters.

A tornado blew a dog into the air as I contemplated the fact that I couldn't go on tour with The Riots and The Divine Light for at least the next couple of weeks because of class. I was nervous about telling Kellogg that I couldn't go. Plus, there was the new quartet I'd been asked to join. They were desperate after one of the original violinists had wrecked her arm in a bike accident. The other violinist, Henry, a bland-faced Czech, had gotten my number from Kellogg. Stressed, and brain-dead from having attacked reams of new music in front of three great players, I was also feeling guilty for being with Isaac in the first place, and not going home immediately to memorize the new music.

"Maybe you'll go back there. Go back to the farm one day," Isaac said whimsically, hypnotized by the glow of the muted television. He was fascinated by the idea of me as the farmer's daughter; he could hardly believe his luck.

I gaped at Isaac's stupidity. "Me? A farmer? Are you kidding, are you watching this thing, or what?"

"I know it was hard, but there must have been some kind of satisfaction in, you know, living off the land and all that."

I looked at Isaac. He was shirtless, wearing only blue silk pyjama bottoms and smoking a cigarette even though we were in a non-smoking room. I realized that, though I liked to think of him as different from the rest of the city people I'd met, he had the same romantic notions about farm life as everybody else.

How to tell him? About my father, who was always recovering from one injury or another, whose face was sun-beaten and crumpled as a browned apple by the age of forty-four,

Isaac's age. How could I describe my mother's hands? Welted and cracked like pieces of baked shale.

My parents would cry when it rained too much and rage when the sun stayed out too long. The weather was never right. Waiting for the elements to align themselves was a constant experiment in how to beat the gods. While other children whooped and swung their towels as they walked to the lake, my brothers and I would look at the huge sun in the sky and drag ourselves along like sad sacks. We dreaded the last words our mother would impart to us before sleep: "Pray for rain."

I often thought of my parents as gamblers. The way they tracked the weather reports was like watching cigar-chomping, high-stakes bettors at horse races who compared odds on newcomers and jumpy thoroughbreds.

What do you think of that cloud?

Looks like something, then again, it's windy today.

I wasn't responding to Isaac's glib "living off the land" comment. I was going to "that place," as he put it. That same place where Yawnie would go when he withdrew from our family.

On the TV screen, a hurricane gulped up a green and white clapboard house in the middle of an airless field, all in a matter of seconds.

"That's why I didn't stay."

"That's Kansas. There aren't hurricanes in the Prairies."

"No, but there are potato bugs that you can spend your whole life squishing and it makes no difference. They come back threefold. Don't even get me started on grasshoppers. Why do you even care about this stuff?"

He shrugged, took the mickey from my hands. He smiled his "businessman who gets what he wants with his charm" smile. I had seen him use it on waitresses and concierges and it worked every time.

"You think it's cute."

"What?"

"You think it's cute that I'm this little girl with hayseeds in her hair."

"Maybe. But I like your stories, too." He grinned, rolled over onto his belly, and stretched my sore fingers out with his big hands. "Besides, I want to know everything about you," he said with mock lasciviousness.

I pulled away. "No, you don't."

Isaac had many bad points. He was a cheat, a shady businessman, a pseudo-intellectual, but he managed to make up for it, with me anyway, through his genuine curiosity about the world. He was an open person, and most people are like shut boxes with their agendas and opinions already arranged. They ask few questions and sit there nodding, not really listening when you talk. You can see they're already thinking about what they're going to say next, or figuring out their shopping list, or what kinds of adjectives they'll use. I know this because I am one of these people: reactionary, opinionated.

But some people are open, ready to engage. And while I loved Isaac for this, for his curiosity, for his ability to listen and absorb, the fact that he lacked a frontal lobe also meant that I never knew what the hell would fly out of his mouth next.

"How big are potato bugs? How is it you can play every kind of crazy arpeggio with those magical fingers but not screw off a beer cap? What kind of backward town could've named a girl as pretty as you Jim? You said once your grandmother was half-Russian—do you think she was a Jew?"

"You really want to know about potato bugs?"

"Yes!" he trilled, clasping my hands to his chest.

"Okay, if I tell you about that, you have to divulge a secret."

Though an expert at pumping information out of others, Isaac kept his own secrets well. His refusal to tell me anything about his wife, even her name, for example, was typical of his subterfuge tactics. Early on, I'd learned that one of the things that kept Isaac coming back to me was that I understood he was easily bored, that he liked to be challenged, and a little abused, by his women. Each time we met I'd answer one, maybe two of his questions, never more. But he'd never answer mine.

Still, it was easier to fill his head with facts and images about the landscape I'd left behind. I thought that maybe one day I'd be able to tell Isaac about Yawnie, about the real reason I had come east, but not yet. So, I sighed and told him about the striped black and orange potato bugs that were the size of tacks, that ate up every living thing in their paths. I told him about strains of canola, and made up differences between quarter horses and shag ponies—though I knew as much about horses as he did—and his eyelids drooped as we waited for room service to bring his egg-white omelette.

That night Isaac fell asleep right after we made love. His body felt heavier than usual, and I made a mental note to tease him about going to the executive gym a little more often. I worried that I'd taken on too much by joining the quartet when I remembered the twisted expressions that Henry, the unimpressed Czech, had made while I sawed my way through that night's Haydn piece. I worried about seeming too young to fit in with The Riots on the road, whether I could even get the time off class. I worried until, finally, I coasted off to sleep.

That night I dreamt of the mud storm. How our mother had shuttered the windows and secured the lock on the flimsy screen door of our house. How she'd banged two pots together as if the wailing mass of dirt and sand were a bear she could spook away with our false childish thunder. She'd marched us around the Formica table as if she were leading us, two small twins and a gangly ten-year-old boy, into the greatest battle of our lives.

In the centre of the kitchen sat our father, in his jeans and plaid shirt, with his untouched breakfast of oatmeal and tea in front of him. He looked across the table, out through the kitchen window, not moving, as the heaving mass of rock and sand headed straight toward us.

I separated myself from our resistance parade and watched as the curtain of rock and sludge battered down the road leading to our house. Ten feet before our door, it swerved toward the fields.

I remember feeling like we were the only humans left in the world.

"Holy shit," our father said, over and over, until it became a new kind of prayer. Because that's what it was, those fractal spires of swept earth. Biblical, crushing. A wall of holy shit.

I can't go back there. Don't you understand?
You can't go back somewhere you never really left.

6
rize

Sometime after Kit leaves for work, Rize goes to the kitchen, peels a grapefruit with his teeth. He watches the wind whip white plastic bags into trees as the bitter juice rolls into his mouth. He throws an old yogurt container of mouldy pasta in the garbage and licks the crumbs off the counter from her morning toast. He finds her note there, tucked between a tea bag and a can of sardines. He purses his lips; despite so much practice his mouth feels oddly out of shape. Too warm, too soft.

Rize,
and shine my love. There's some granola in cupboards. Voilà du lait. Want to have dinner at eight? How about Eduardo's? My treat. Pick me up after 6, at work.

XXXXXX
Kit

* * *

PERCHED ON A CEMENT COLUMN, he waits for her outside headquarters, where she works. Today is the day. He's clutching a fistful of white roses while a bunch of jockish guys in RCMP training jackets eye him. He looks at the yellow maple leaves mulched to the ground, the cars swishing down the ugly boulevard-cum-highway.

He averts his eyes from the phalanx of young recruits, some of whom work under Kit, as he wonders why tourists always say

Montreal is so pretty. It's not pretty at all, it's devastating. The people who like it don't have to live here because if they did they would see the weird, disgusting combination of garbage found on every second corner in March. Like, for example, spaghetti mixed with children's hair and Tinkertoys. These people would not think that's romantic, or cool, or that twenty-four-hour bagel bakeries make up for it. Rize never likes the places other people like. Like New York, or L.A. He likes Montreal, maybe even loves it in the way you love an annoying relative, or a smart but ornery friend who's always stealing change from your pockets, but to call this freezing island-city pretty is too much. He doesn't get it.

While he waits, he thinks about the story Kit told him a week ago, in the stillness of her high-ceilinged room. How she hadn't been able to pass one of the physical tests during her cadet training. She'd had to drag a hundred-pound wobbly weight out of the water for the lifeguard part of it. He agreed that her being part female and part feline made the task difficult.

"So, what'd you do?"

"I swam, woke up at five every morning to do weights. Gained six pounds of muscle in four weeks and finally dragged that goddamn duffel-bag corpse to the edge of the pool." She pounded her pillow to emphasize her point.

"Wow."

"The officer in charge felt sorry for me. So, finally, after the millionth try, he just passed me. Told me to stay away from beaches," she laughed.

"You were the only woman in your troop?"

Kit nodded as he traced a hand over her nose.

"Six months, thirty-two cop-wannabes, one me."

When she finally comes out of the mirrored doors, distracted, loosely checking her pocket for a cigarette, Rize springs off the column and runs to her. He wants to thank her for showing him her weakness, her cracked pride. To say he is sorry about all the men, all the time, in her world and his. Men are tiresome; even though he is one he knows this. He wants to tell her that she is the strongest, out of all of them, and he knows this because she has felt the weight of dead things floundering in her empty hands.

Instead, with the wall of recruits watching, he stumbles over to her, acutely aware of how fey and dishevelled he appears. He pulls her jacket like a child, and pushes the white rose petals into her black hair.

"Love is this," he says. Their bodies lace into an inept, unpractised dance. And just as a thorn pierces his playing finger, she says, "Okay, Rize, I get it. I love you, too."

* * *

HE'S NOT SURE what love is but he knows what it isn't. Love isn't his father, who leaves him and June when he is eight. Love isn't a cheque for thirty-three dollars every month from Clay signed in his father's tremulous handwriting. It isn't in his mother's vodka tonics, or her string of boyfriends who can't even speak English and think it's okay to sit on the couch and smoke Export A's and leave their socks for her to wash.

Love isn't a clean white T-shirt that smells like Clay's brand of smokes and his wonderful, tinny musk. Though it takes Rize a long time to figure that one out. Whenever he plays onstage, Rize mentally piles a bunch of sticks over Clay's white V-neck

T-shirt. He sees the shirt when he plays. He sees it now, before he falls asleep.

In his child's eye, the shirt hangs over the edge of a dining room chair. He imagines the T-shirt being pulled on by an invisible man, his father, and walking out the door. He sees it flapping in the wind, like a kite. He sees it flattened out next to his mother in bed, smothering one of her stupid boyfriends.

One night, when there aren't enough sticks to pile over it, he tells Kit about the shirt. He explains how he came into the living room one afternoon and saw it dancing on the stucco ceiling. He explains the shirt, its perfect smell, how he'd move it but then find it days later in another spot, living a secret life, doing crossword puzzles, doing godknowswhat all over the apartment.

Kit takes a piece of his black hair and plays with it while he talks. "Is he dead? Your father? 'Cause I can find him if he's not, I can try. That's what I do. I find people. Rize, don't you want to know? Don't you want to know if Clay's dead yet?"

Yet.

Rize ignores her and explains how the shirt disappeared for two years and how, one Christmas, when he was looking for his presents, he found it wrapped up around a trumpet underneath June's bed. He unwrapped the trumpet then beat it against the walls of their apartment. He placed the shirt collar in his mouth, ripped it seam to seam, wiped his shoes on it, then took his mother's sewing shears to it.

"To stop the dancing," he explains, his voice floating above the bed.

When he was finished with it he hid it at the bottom of the garbage can, under the banana peels, coffee grinds, and cigarette butts. Then he picked up the trumpet and put it to his mouth. When his mother came home from work, she stood in the doorway of the living room watching Rize trying to play. Her empty face twitched as the boy farted out a couple of notes.

"What happened then?" Kit asks, staring into the dark ceiling.

"I was ten years old. I thought it was magic, that if I played it he'd come back. Pathetic, eh?"

The next week, his mother pawned Clay's trumpet for an inferior trombone and saved the rest of the money for his classes at the conservatory.

"I am a natural musician," he says, in someone else's voice.

"I know, baby."

Then he falls into his familiar dream where Jules's father is his father and so he and Jules are brothers. Only, for once, he is the good brother, he is Abel.

In this dream, he is walking toward a stray piece of white cotton flapping at the edge of a fence in the middle of a hot field. He knows that if he keeps walking Jules will shoot him in the back. Jules, his best friend, doesn't want him to have this reminder. Still, he moves toward the tiny white flag, understanding it's his only proof that he, too, owns something precious. It is a dream of childish stealth, anguish, and confusion. His heart feels turbid and freshly wounded as he picks the fabric off the fence and tucks it into his pocket. It's not love, this little piece of shirt, he knows this, but it's something like hope, something he can't yet part with.

* * *

THE NIGHT HE LEAVES for the fall tour, Kit comes out to the hallway of her building where the EXIT sign glares down on them like a nuclear star. He can already taste the Midwestern highway grit in his teeth. Kit's wearing a long brown sweater over a slip and a pair of wool socks on her big old feet. She slides out the door, as if they are joking around, as if it were simply another Sunday when they hang out, half-naked, and drink pots of coffee. Those Sundays when Kit reads the paper and unplugs the phone.

"See you in a month, babe."

Kit looks at the ceiling, points her foot out like a ballerina, and then looks back down at him, as if he is just some random piece of dust caught in her line of vision.

"What?"

"What are we, Rize? What are we doing?" She pulls her hand back as if she is aiming a bow and arrow.

For an instant, he closes his eyes and thinks about how much Kit likes to define things, how much she likes structure, good guys, bad guys. Even her face, pale against the mane of her dark hair, resembles some artful Eurasian mask done up in violent contrasts. He wants to tell her that, for all the strange edges and opposites in her features, she is easily the most beautiful woman he's ever been with. He means to tell her to wait, to be patient, to let the restlessness get beaten out of him. He's not quite ready to surrender to the structure of her days. If only she could wait a little more. If only he could tell her that she needs to wait a little more.

"Don't you get tired of it?"

"Of what?" he snaps defensively.

She shrugs. "Of drinking, of driving around, having strange little teenagers think you're a rock star."

He lets her words fall between them without comment, side-steps her invisible arrow. Then he grasps the edges of her slip tightly and, pressing his mouth into her ear, whispers, "Sometimes, when you wake up and ask me what I want for breakfast, with your hair undone, with your Chinese eyes, I forget there's a world outside."

"Wait," she says. "Let me get dressed. I'll walk out with you."

* * *

HE CALLS HER from a phone booth by a roadside diner where semis keep rolling by.

But she's not home, and when the machine beeps he feels like his guts are going to expel the Mr. Noodle soup he ate all over the gravel road. He holds the receiver away from his ear; the grinding sound of a semi shifting gears becomes his only missive.

Because he can't, he can't squeeze anything out of his mouth into the black phone because his gun-shy body, his guts, are in his head and his head is buzzing a Stevie Wonder harmonica solo. He drops the receiver and curses Mr. Noodle.

The semi runs over a plastic bag in the middle of the road and it sounds like a bullet exploding into a body.

Nobody plays the harp like Stevie.

* * *

IN A DANK MINNESOTA ROOM he lies in bed, sandwiched between Margo and the wall, as he watches Margo cry. It is the band's first day off in a week and Margo has become delirious with fever. Plus, she's been drinking all morning and babbling about Jesus, how she'd like to be more like him. "Because Jesus,

Rize, Jesus turned the other cheek. Everyone forgets that part, everyone's so down on Jesus. Everyone just wants to get back at everyone else. It's hard to be good. So hard."

He doesn't know what she's talking about so he sticks a thermometer in her mouth, pats her wet hair down, and kisses her forehead. It's been a sucky week of playing backwater Midwest towns with no more than twenty-five people at any given show. The audience is barely present, most of them just out to drink or get away from their spouses and children and mortgages. In one bar, a guy with a hearing aid throws a piece of stringy cheese at Jules and declares him a homo in an embarrassing nasally whine. Plus, there's a flu going around—the reason for Margo's fever. When they're all in the van, each member becomes completely immersed in his own anxiety; there's no yelling, or stupid knock-knock jokes from Guy, or "I spy a polar bear in a snowstorm," or arguments about the radio, or Crosby, Stills & Nash (and Young) singalongs created for the sole purpose of driving Jules up the wall. No, there are no random grabs for the steering wheel to set them off course and keep them on guard (Margo's specialty), there's none of the fun that keeps them tolerant of the extended journeys and time wasted on the road.

Money's tight due to the fact that no one's buying T-shirts or CDs. Since they aren't selling much merchandise, Margo and Jules have been arguing about money, how they don't have any. Rize wants to tell her that she shouldn't feel bad, shouldn't make herself sick over this because Jules is a hard person to argue with. Whenever you make a good point he starts yelling over you. Rize wants to remind her that she has not slept in three days and that soon they'll be in warm California, playing bigger clubs. California loves The Riots, loves Kellogg and his bullshit, and soon Kellogg's going to sweep in and get them off these small-town circuits. Rize takes out the thermometer. "You have a fever, Mar, you should stop drinking."

Jules sits on the edge of the bed, turns on the TV, mutes it, and smokes a joint. He yells at the screen every once in a while.

"Abersizer? What the fuck is an abersizer? Go to hell you steroid monkeys."

Rize doubts that Jules would even recognize a medicine ball. Margo rises from the bed and perches on Jules's lap, her big eyes wan and apologetic. Jules buries his head in her chest and wraps his arms around her waist. Rize watches them wading in the other's forgiveness and then leaves the room.

What are we?

In the washroom, he puts on one of Jules's old sweatsuits: it's blue with grey stripes and comes up only to his elbows and knees. On the way to the elevator he grabs Jules's trumpet from the closet and goes down to the pool, which is covered with leaves and an orange plastic tarp. It's a halcyon autumn afternoon, despite the cold.

He plays jazz by the pool on a weathered plastic patio chair. It's a habit Rize got from his father; Clay used to play like this when his mind got stuck on something, aimlessly, the notes punctuating the night with an insistent curiosity, a sorrow too vague for words. Rize plays till it gets dark, till the security guard comes by with Jules at his heels. Jules is wearing a trench coat Rize has never seen, like he's Columbo or something, looking just as crumpled up as Peter Falk too. Somehow, Rize knows Jules is naked underneath.

"You got a call," Jules says.

"What?" His ears are full of echoes.

"Kit. Message for you." Jules takes the trumpet from Rize's hand and replaces it with the band's cell.

The very last time he saw her she was wearing a long flowing skirt and kicking rocks across St. Urbain. He can't believe that the last thing he said to her, before she stepped out to cross the busy street, was, "Hey man, how many of these here chestnuts do you think I can fit into my mouth?"

He feels them in his mouth now, even though he's in Minnesota, and so far away from St. Urbain chestnuts. The stones are shiny and smooth, like ocean-swept glass rubbing the inside of his cheeks. He sees her long fingers wiggle at him as the cars swish by. *Bye, bye!*

He dials the number to retrieve messages.

"Um, hi, Margo, hi, Jules. Message for Rize. I'm going away for a while. I don't know when I'll be back. I'll call you, or something, soon. Bye, bye."

7
jim

After I left my family there was a great airless space inside of me, always waiting. Like a fallowed field, I imagined this place lay under frost while I washed dishes, practised violin, made plans with Isaac, slept. These weren't real moments, I told myself, while I went about my business. I believed my real life to be quietly resting inside me.

But one morning when I looked in the mirror I noted a new crease in my face, a single strand of white hair amid the blond ones. I caught myself there, slowly aging, changing. I examined my new face briefly. Time was actually passing. This was it, my life. But this carpe diem moment slipped out of my grasp and then I had to pretend, as we do in our more private moments of denial, that it had never happened. I straightened my collar, brushed my teeth, proceeded as usual, in a gauzy web of unreality.

Even though she didn't know what I'd been through or done, Margo said I was depressed. This was a new concept for me and at first I didn't buy it. Idle, lazy, weird, city people, fifties housewives, and mentally unbalanced artists got depressed, but I was none of these.

"Jim, you sleep fifteen hours a day," Margo would say matter-of-factly when I told her I wasn't depressed. "I've seen you. You're goddamned narcoleptic: you fell asleep in the middle of band practice right next to the amps the other day."

"I was still meditating," I argued.

Kellogg was always encouraging the band to meditate to increase our focus while playing, but so far I was the only one—besides Rize, sometimes—who had taken him up on his offer to instruct us.

Shush, now. Sit on the pillow. Feel the pain in your leg. Count your breaths. Acknowledge your perpetual discomfort. Prepare for your dying.

Margo was right, I slept too much. Most days I could barely gather the strength to get to rehearsal and then go out with Isaac. I used Kellogg's meditation classes, and my endless need for sleep, as a means to escape back into those torn, moonlike landscapes of my unconscious where, I thought, I might reconnect with my twin or, conversely, at least be free of him for a few hours.

When I first met Isaac, I was half a person, half-asleep, and fearful of being completely awake. A May–December romance. Is that what they call it? A farm girl matched to a quasi-Renaissance man, whose life of culture and money gave me access to almost any means of instant fulfilment. Isaac laughed at my jokes, bought me drinks, clothes, and groceries, and for this, for this safety and security, I felt grateful.

When Isaac and I were together I was more lucid than usual: I didn't feel as though I was waiting for anything terrible to happen. Yet part of me remained absent. Maybe that's why he wanted me, because he was absent physically, emotionally, too. The fact that he went away almost every week—to the States, to Hong Kong, to England—didn't exactly help with our bonding. Because if Isaac was in love with me, he was also in love with the distance between us. And even though Isaac's body moved like a smooth dark boat under my hands, and our sex levelled the edges of my rocky panic into a wave of relief, I knew it wouldn't be long before he left for work and I would, once again, be sucked into my inner vacuum.

But I had something to offer Isaac too, besides an absent-minded love that didn't require too much of his attention. A fantastic speaker but an inveterate non-reader, Isaac bought me books—classics, political science, and bestsellers—and then asked me to recount them to him so that he could be *au courant* at business socials. Isaac was smart—lazy, but smart; he could speak four languages and explain the Big Bang theory to you by arranging pieces of penne on his plate, but ask him to read a five-page article about anything except finance or current events—forget it.

I can still see him, in my mind's eye, on our first proper date together. Isaac felt embarrassed about that first night, about picking me up off the street and taking me to his dusty house, so, in order to prove to me that he was a gentleman and not some middle-aged near-pedophile, he'd insisted on taking me to what he claimed was the best Italian restaurant in the city.

In my memory, he stands there, under the halogen street lamps outside the restaurant, as the smell of expensive perfume wafts out and women in plush black coats and red-stained lips leave, glancing at him and glazing their eyes over me.

"You like pasta?" he asks me, almost bowing.

"Like, spaghetti?"

Isaac laughs. "Yeah, spaghetti. Expensive spaghetti."

I shrug as he opens the door for me. At the table, he orders two plates of linguine and a bottle of wine that costs as much as my rent.

"Excuse me." I go to the washroom, find the stubby end of a lipstick pencil, and pull wet hands through my hair.

He's drinking the wine and talking to the owner in Italian when I get back to the table.

"You look nice."

I grin at him and refold the napkin in my lap. It's the first time I've been to a place that charges over twenty dollars for a heap of noodles. I tell him this and he laughs. It's also the first time Isaac and I have been out in the world together—just the two of us—and I wonder what the world thinks.

The waiter brings our food. I sit with my hands in my lap, watch Isaac twirl his fork and sip wine. I imitate him, enjoying the creamy flavour of the sauce. We don't talk. When we finish, he leans in.

"So, what were you doing today?"

"Practising," I lied. That day I had, in fact, managed to get through only half an hour of scales before I crawled back into the womb of my bed.

"You're always practising. There's a world out here, Jim."

"I know, there's a world in here, too." I point to my chest and smile.

But he was right, I was avoiding the outside. My world had winnowed down to narrow experiences. I didn't go out to bars and clubs like Kellogg and his friends—except to play music. Instead, I could be found practising in my box-sized apartment or wrapped up in Isaac's arms. Every part of my life, from music to my soporific tendencies, was designed for escape.

I didn't want to think about how I would survive and pay rent in Montreal with hardly a word of French, how my savings I'd come east with were dwindling fast. I couldn't think about the fact that I seemed to be setting myself up for a world of pain by getting involved with a married man who was old enough to be my father. I didn't consider how I might adjust to a choking skyline that spewed cold hard pellets when the only horizon I had ever known absorbed three-quarters of my vision. When I thought about it all in the silence of my apartment, with the radiators clicking out waves of stuffy heat, I ended up having to lie down in my bed, sheets pulled up to the whites of my eyes.

After dinner, upstairs in the hotel room, Isaac loosens his tie.

"You like the view?"

"Yes."

"What's your real name?" Isaac asks, nursing a martini in one hand and patting my legs with the other.

"Jim. I told you."

He smiles, like his head hurts, and walks to the window.

I'm lying on the bed. I prop my arm up and watch him poised there, lacerating the moon with his profile as he kneels before the bed to kiss me. I hear the small furious sound of his desire, the tune of more than being; it's being without pain. *This is alive, is all the world I need,* I tell myself. And when Isaac bites my lip I feel something sharp there amid the kinesis of his desire, and I almost forget who I am, why I've come here. But then I recall what, exactly, I am, and, for the first time ever, I want to call my mother and say:

I kissed a man. My first. My first big-city man. Yes, I'm fine—

Except. Except for one thing. I had come here to run away from Yawnie but he had followed me. The thought of him always leaked into my brain like a slowly bleeding hemorrhage.

Mama, I'd say, ignoring the blood flushing my brain.

My man's got diamonds in his mouth.

* * *

"WHAT DO YOU MEAN you'll be gone for two weeks? What about the quintetlets?" Presently, Isaac was finding it hard not to raise his voice with me and, because of this, the waitress was giving us looks. "Or is it quintuplets?"

"It's a *quartet*. Four people, not five, you know? Plus, I'm pretty sure they've already found someone else to replace me." This was a lie. I hadn't even considered the quartet or the ramifications. Henry, and the group of stiffly Mcstifferson musicians, could rot in those hot practice rooms for all I cared. My grand plan, of playing with a rock 'n' roll band, was finally being realized. But, ever the planner, ever the controller, Isaac was already anticipating complications.

To be honest, I was too excited to worry about what he thought. I was psyched to be the one to leave, for once. I thought about how excited Margo had sounded when she called me from the road. She'd shrieked and cried and begged me to bring some special soap and moisturizer she wanted that was available only at Holt Renfrew.

"How are the shows going?" I asked her.

"Smelly boys in a van, you know how it is. Lots of fighting with Jules this week for some reason. But the shows are getting bigger: there were over a thousand people at the gig last night!"

"Wow."

"What about school?" Isaac asked, bringing me back to the moment.

"I did my mid-term recital and all my other work. And they're not going to spring any more new material on us this late in the term."

"How do you know that for sure?"

Isaac and I slid our eyes away from each other. We both realized how fatherly his last comment sounded. What I'd said, about finishing all my mid-term work, was true. However, I didn't mention how many classes and important rehearsals I'd be missing (a lot) by going away on a two-week tour. Between my private theory classes, Divine Light rehearsals, and all my other activities, like sleeping and going to chic new restaurants and vernissages with Isaac, school seemed, well, distinctly secondary. Besides, university no longer mattered to me; I was a real musician now, playing in a successful group. Music school was for chumps, or at least academic musicians who planned to spend their whole lives teaching or doing regular orchestra gigs.

I sighed. "Look, Isaac, it's all going to work out. I won't flunk out of school, this won't change us, I promise. But you need to be happy for me. Please don't get pissed off," I begged. "Besides, you're going to Hong Kong next week."

"I know, I know. I'm not pissed off, I'm just curious, why is Kellogg expanding the band? What's the point in having a huge collective?" Isaac asked, slowly, as if he were discussing a financial investment rather than a ragtag rock band.

"I'm sure there's no financial point but, otherwise, it's probably because Kellogg thinks there's power in numbers," I said defensively. Isaac was getting on my nerves. I felt as though he were an old person judging me.

"And I'm not being an asshole when I pose that question, really. I'm genuinely curious. I just can't understand how—" Isaac looked down at the tablecloth as he spoke, swishing his cognac around so that the burnt-coloured alcohol dripped down the side of the snifter. We both watched it, hypnotized, as his voice faded into the background sounds of the kitchen.

"So, when are you leaving?"

I pasted a weak smile on my face. "Tomorrow night?"

He looked at me as if I'd just told him I owned a cockroach circus and we were setting up rehearsals in his house. It was a funny look to give your eighteen-year-old mistress and I felt sorry for him, suddenly, because I realized that my decision to go had shifted the power dynamic between us. It occurred to me then that he was in love with me, perhaps very much so. It also occurred to me that I might be doomed in my relationships with men because I lived like one, freely. It wasn't fair: what I had waited for my whole life, to find a band like Kellogg's, had finally happened, and now my married, itinerant lover was angry with me. Angry.

Just as I was about to blurt out what a disgusting hypocrite he was, Isaac waved over the waitress and ordered a bottle of the most expensive champagne. He sighed, fiddled with his diamond signet ring, and looked into the street where the Friday night parade of gorgeous, suburbanite twenty-something-year-olds had begun.

We were dining on the ostentatious stretch of St. Laurent—between Sherbrooke and Prince Arthur—where the beautiful people liked to strut on weekends. I thought of my own friends, shaggy-haired and bohemian. I imagined them slumped over mugs of beer at Flora, a dark, cavelike, third-storey bar on the Main. They would be there or at the Rio, a somehow sadly themed tropical bar that was red inside. Being at the Rio was like being in the thrombotic centre of a heart. I thought of Margo, her mouth painted in a red slash, and how Isaac would rather suck on a raw egg than spend five minutes in the types of dives my friends liked.

Though Isaac and I connected in a fundamental, emotional and sexual way, his money, and the designer quality of every aspect of his life, often made me uncomfortable. As did his habit of shoving hundred dollar bills in my jean pockets.

"No, baby—" I'd say, crushing the bills back into his hand.

"Why? It's just money, Jim."

"Because, I have to learn. I'm a grownup and can barely pay rent."

"Those things don't matter," he'd whisper, stuffing the money back into my underwear. "I'll pay for everything, always. You're an artist, so be one."

Isaac always seemed both inspired and deflated by my bands, my voracious reading, my ability to pick out a tune on four different instruments. Some say couples always fight about the same thing, and for Isaac and me it was always the difference in our lifestyles and how it pulled us in different directions. Yet it also brought us together; Isaac liked to take care of me, and I needed taking care of.

But right now I felt smothered by this giant man who sat across from me sulking, despite his big champagne gesture of support.

"Isaac."

He positioned his face away, like a scolded dog.

"Isaac, please, quit being so dramatic. I can't stand it."

"Does this mean you'll stop dressing like that?"

I looked down at my grey pants and rosin-covered T-shirt, which I wore sometimes just to rankle him. My closets were now filled with all kinds of designer clothes, heels, and bags—courtesy of Isaac—but sometimes I just schlepped around in rags.

"Dressing like what?"

"Well, can we at least go shopping tomorrow to get you some decent rock star clothes?"

I laughed. Acquiescence: a shopping trip to celebrate. I knew I'd won.

8
rize

At the Roxy in Los Angeles the crowd is eerily quiet all through three long sets. Apparently, this silence means they love the band. *They want more,* Rize thinks, *but they don't know how to untangle their eyes from the* People *magazine gloss of celebrity.* Celebrity. The word makes him giggle into the cuff of his shirt. The slick, silent crowd is mesmerized by the scruffy Canadians. In the crowd he sees two pretty but emaciated girls—must be actresses. All the girls he meets in L.A. are actresses. They sip energy-boosting cocktails. They balance on the balls of their feet in their high heels to see the band better, to watch this collective mass of Canuck dysfunction, which is now, to use his mother's phrase, "a sensation." Ridiculous, somehow, that at the end of the night music journalists with dictaphones and the two painfully skinny girls clamour around Kellogg and Jules.

Ridiculous, but logical, too, that those two have become the voice of The Riots while Margo slams JELL-O shooters (another American phenomenon); Jim—who's just been flown in from Montreal with a host of other Divine Light musicians to complete their new sound—chainsmokes Winstons in the only bathroom backstage, seized by an uncharacteristic bout of performance anxiety; Guy hauls on a joint; the brass section light each other's cigarettes, while the sensible guitar players sip cola, dog-ear their DeLillo books, and to try to call their girlfriends with their calling cards. It's logical that only Jules and Kellogg have some talk in them when everyone else feels as if all their dirty wants, words, and underwear have been blared out in an endless musical narrative all night long.

At the end of the show, when Rize finds out that they've sold more merchandise in L.A. than in all the towns they've toured collectively, he figures his thesis—that next to New York, L.A. is hell's main outpost on earth—has been confirmed.

Something's happened to catapult them here, to this shaky terrain of success. Rize doesn't know what it is, exactly, except that it has something to do with Kellogg's infectiously optimistic presence and the way The Divine Light and The Riots bleed into each other now. There is hardly any distinction between the two bands, what with the new orchestra arrangements embedded into almost every Riots song. The Divine Light just plays along with the core group and the crowded stage gets more and more chaotic as everyone from random bongo players to Kellogg yelps into microphones and messes up his carefully duct-taped cables. All this, coupled with a favourable review in an online music magazine, has created a kind of excitement Rize can barely wrap his mind around. He has ceased clipping articles from newspapers to send to his mother. He has lost track of Jules's and Kellogg's interviews, somewhere near Topeka, at the same time losing his favourite fleece sweater and a pack of naked-lady cards he lifted from a gas station.

As they load out, he thinks of June's seventies Farrah Fawcett hair, how she'd wake up at six-thirty to make coffee, pat his bum lightly when he walked to the bathroom for a pee.

Kellogg, seated at the wheel of the van, is talking to some journalists about The Riots. In the past couple of weeks, Kellogg talking to even larger entourages than the ones at home has become a familiar sight. Rize hauls amps in through the rear door of the van. He pauses for a second to look at his hands, which are bloated and slightly too small. They look as if they should belong to someone else.

Sometimes I think you're right. That this is no kind of life, where all we know how to do is drive, play, and party.

Kellogg kills three flies in one easy strike against the windshield while one of the writers looks on in horror at his swift appendage of death.

Rize goes back to the empty theatre, noting how efficiently the crowd has packed itself out into its next SUV adventure. Two Japanese girls rush him and push their pens into his hands.

"You're our favourite!" one of the young girls yells, wrinkling her nose and offering him a purple sucker from her purse.

"Thanks. I play the horn, and the guitar," he says, talking extra slow just in case they don't understand English.

"And the triangle," says the prettier girl, in a perfect Californian accent.

Rize hugs the pair and takes a picture of himself with them, using their digital camera, then he goes back to the van and finds a small space that smells like beer. He wedges himself between the sampler and the amps.

At the front of the van, the guys are playing hip-hop and drinking the beers they took from the rider. Margo, surprisingly sober, sits in the driver's seat, working on some knitting. Rize leans out to slam the back doors of the van, the signal to the rest that load-out's done.

Kellogg winds up the interview and offers a tentative date to the L.A. company. Then, with a wave and an "All right, is this goddamn circus ready to go yet?" from Kellogg, The Riots are off and running into the requisite midnight Los Angeles traffic.

Someone puts on a T-Rex CD and Rize mouths the words about cloaks full of eagles and his dirty sweet girl. He thinks about Kit's body, how, if there is music playing while they make love, she can come only in the silence between songs. He thinks about Kit in bed, the way she is all legs and arms. The way she climbs his body like a sun-starved child angling to get closer to the sky. He's been thinking about her body a lot, about all the tiny, sacred secrets they have culled from each other's skin cells and what all of it amounts to now, with her body so far away.

At the Roosevelt his night opens up to the smell of chlorine, a short massage from Margo. People run back and forth from the hot tub to the room and get water all over his sleeping bag. Kellogg slaps people's asses with a wet towel, spills champagne on the dresser littered with half-empty bottles of Cuervo and beer cans, and piles the merch money all over the beds. Sachets of coke are opened, and Jules sits in the centre of the floor, trying to roll a joint, looking a little stunned.

Suddenly, everyone feels too close to Rize. Everywhere he turns there's a body doing something messy, stupid, or illegal. Everyone's talking at once and he realizes that they are all high. He can't get into the spirit of it. The cocaine talk. About how great the show was. How much the crowd loved them and how the band is going to do an unplugged performance on national radio tomorrow, thanks to Kellogg.

What are we, Rize?

You are cogent and I am this. I am Margo's dirty nails and sorrow. I am Jules's chronic cough and Kellogg's contagious powder smile. I am Guy's cheesy shredded jeans.

Filled with the ghost of Kit's sex, he watches Kellogg do a bump off the van key. Rize sits back on the bed to take in the chaos, feels a terrible hollow pain ascending from somewhere between his pelvis and his heart. K offers him a flap of blow but Rize refuses. "Nah, man. I'm exhausted."

"Exactly," Kellogg says, seated like a Buddha on the adjacent single bed. "But what else can you do to kill the soul of this empty city? Buddy, I'm asking you."

* * *

IN KANSAS HE'D BOUGHT HER a postcard of a cowboy and a cowgirl lying in bales of straw. The caption reads, "Makin' Hay in Kansas." He doesn't send it till they are halfway through the desert, smudging the words with his sweat.

Kit,
Pray for me, I am beginning to lose my shit a little these days. Pray for me and please don't leave me. Because nobody prays for me, and everybody always leaves.

xxxxxxxxxxxxxxxxxxxx
-r.

* * *

"LOVE IS FRAGILE," Margo says, as if in the middle of a dialogue. She seems to be talking to herself when the four of them pile into a hotel room. She tries to balance a champagne bottle on her head and dance in time to Rize's strumming fingers tapping the bedside lamp like a high-hat. Margo's on one of her quick-drunk monologues, which begins in the form of French carbonation and ends in a fizzled heap of shoes and clothes, with Jim piling blankets on her and Margo under the covers, mumbling to a can of Coca-Cola.

The girls are trying to cope with their lack of privacy, their fatigue, and the indignation of the last club owner's stiffing the band out of three hundred American. For her part, Jim just pulls up the hood on her windbreaker and smokes unfiltered Winstons out on the balcony, refusing to communicate even with Rize, who's become her preferred confidant and arcade buddy. In order to work through these upsets, Margo, apparently, needs to stand on the bed and announce that she and Jules haven't had sex in exactly two and a half weeks, three days, and six hours.

"Here we go taking our love out for a night on the town in every city in the States, when I should be wooing it with white wine in Montreal summers," Margo begins. "Here I go, crashing it into cars and getting it so drunk it can't even find a taxi home."

Jules, who has been oddly unvocal for the last stretch of days, suddenly finds his voice. "If you are so unhappy with our sex life and our lifestyle, why don't you ease up on the fucking champers at one o'clock in the afternoon, eh Margo? Try to get a little personal clarity?" He plucks the champagne bottle out of her hand and squares off in front of her.

Margo's eyes become engorged. "You, of all people, are talking to me about personal clarity, you chronic?" she says in an acid voice, staring at Jules until he can no longer take it and flicks on the television. He cautiously lights up some Mexican dope a fan brought him and watches an infomercial on Rogaine. He says nothing more about Margo's drinking, knowing that if he did she'd throw him, and his stash, into the bathtub.

"Here we go again," Margo mumbles, grabbing the bottle back and shooting Jules a dark look while she adjusts a lily in her hair, bought by Jules earlier in the day when she got mad at him for eating the sprout-and-brie wraps she'd packed for them all. "Here we go, ruining it all for rock 'n' roll."

Jules shaves, kisses Margo on top of her messy head of hair, then grabs her neck to whisper something in her ear that could be a warning. He's going to see another show, The Stay-At-Home Dads. The singer once accused Jules of being an insufferable phony during an interview and he's going to see whether the lead is worthy of his public opposition.

Margo kisses Jules quickly. She chooses to avoid the night out in favour of *CSI* reruns and takeout Chinese with Rize. She tries to teach him how to angle the chopsticks into his mouth, but he fails, ultimately, and drops a piece of spicy moo-shoo pork on a pillow. Gagging and laughing at the televised inner journey of a bullet through a human brain cavity, Margo flings the pork at the screen; it slides down slowly.

"I think this is the best program ever made," she says, suddenly transformed into someone happily drunk. She kisses Jules's blond head one last time and tucks in his shirt while Rize, who was only feigning ineptitude, expertly piles a wad of spicy pork into his mouth and waves vaguely at Jules, who plucks Jim off the balcony, dragging her along for moral support. Jim is the best person to go to gigs with as she can determine whether a band is sincere or having an off night within two songs and Jules is planning to get her into the club by pretending she is a deaf-mute musical prodigy with six months to live.

After four egg rolls, two gelatinous noodle dishes, and enough pork and bok choy to feed a sumo wrestler, Rize and Margo polish off a second bottle of champagne and play gin rummy on the floor in front of the television in their pyjamas, half watching a biography on Janis Joplin.

"I could sleep in the other room, with the other guys, you know, in 427, if you want, Mar. Sounds like you and Jules need some private time."

Margo shrugs. "It's okay, I was just being a shit. I don't really feel very sexy right now anyway. Plus, Jules is all stressed out about our 'success.'" Margo shrugs. "You know how he is. He's becoming paranoid about Kellogg, for some stupid reason. He's not sure about all these new people on board, all these big plans. I don't know. It's hard to be with someone who doesn't trust anything new." She pauses. "No, it's better that you're here."

Rize knows Jules is also stressed because he has a criminal record and has been driving the van without a licence and is afraid of getting caught. But he doesn't say anything about these facts as Margo smiles at him and lets out a fruity champagne burp.

"Jesus."

Sometime later, Rize passes out during a particularly lively rendition of "Summertime." Margo pulls a smelly duvet over his body and collects the cards into a pile, smokes two of Jules's leftover roaches, and then, deciding that the bed smells like a food court, lies next to Rize, wrapping herself in a sheet.

Their van-weary bodies are mired in grave-dark stillness. The room smells like Margo: fermented French grapes, dead summer bees. Landlocked, their bodies stew and hover over the surface of this black town. They lie, with noses turned toward each other, singing a silent song of grace and distance. In this hotel room on the main drag they try to find a deep sleep until finally the bass beats, the screeching cars on Hollywood Boulevard fade, and their soundscape goes slack.

Rize drifts into a dream about June. His mother is making him choose between a dog and a dolphin for a pet. "Only one, sweetheart," she says, smiling at him as a blast of Florida-blue water spurts out of the dolphin's blowhole. Deciding firmly on the golden retriever, as opposed to the cost of a large aquarium, he wakes up. He has been deprived of dreams for so long that the quick unconscious activity of his brain induces panic; an alarm sounds off in him.

He reels up, throwing off the duvet. Sweat coats his body. He thrashes into something soft. He's drenched in the odour of fear.

A dolphin?

A woman.

There's a woman next to him: Kit. He reaches for her, feeling the warm pressure of her hips closing in on his. Feeling her, fearing her sudden dissipation—*because every time, every time with you feels like the last*. He grips her hips, kisses her for some unpronounceable length, and holds her mouth in his. It's like unpeeling a warm grape in slow motion. Oh, hi, Kit.

She doesn't move for a stretch, tethered to the silence of his breath. Then, compelled by the energy of her tongue, which is fast and testing and new, he looks at her, really looks at her. And wakes up to a tapped longing.

Her eyes aren't dolphins. Aren't Kit's.

Suddenly a new image fills his head as he remembers the fox they killed on the road that day, its body completely unscathed but for the orange and white decapitated head flung up like a small furry lid. He remembers how Margo pulled her hat over her eyes even though she was going seventy. How she screamed, "Just don't tell me it was someone's cat!"

Now he knows why Jules comes to kill him in his dreams and what he must do to avoid his own murder. He closes his eyes and sees Jules turn into a wolf with long, pearl-white incisors. As the Jules/wolf sweeps a piece of hair from his scalp, there's the smell of blood and fur mixed with the sugary smell of trapped alcohol, and another smell, too terrible to name, the same one before a heavy rain.

Another suspended moment and it's over. Rize leaps to his feet and curls himself into the bathtub.

In the morning, Jules nudges him awake with his sneakered foot and pours a Bud Light on his head.

Margo doesn't open her mouth except to sing until Mendocino.

* * *

RIZE TAKES TO SITTING in the parked van for long periods of time as a sort of atonement. When the doors are locked and the vehicle is empty of human smells, save for the gasoline and salt 'n' vinegar potato chip remnants of the long journey, he gets to meditate on why he is such an infernal fuck-up. It is also the only time he gets to be alone. For some reason, he can't say why, he keeps returning to this memory. He picks at it like a tired scab during his solitary hours in the van. It's his default, this sadness, this past day:

Three days after his dad leaves them, his mom's friend Marcia, a Newfoundlander from St. John's who lives in the apartment next door, stands in the doorway talking about all the good for nothingness of men. Marcia tosses pillows onto the sofa, removes bedsheets, collects glasses swimming with the citrusy dregs of June's vodka sodas and throws them in the sink.

Then Marcia grabs Rize by the hand to take him to the supermarket. The lines in Marcia's face remind him of a map he once saw of crashed ships shored up on Sable Island. He remembers Clay telling him about the stumpy lost horses that lived there. One day June brings home a photography book about Sable Island and he rips out a photo of the horses all curled up together, their round little bums lined up like potatoes. The lines in Marcia's eyes are like crevassed routes, while the ones around her mouth fortify her great stories about all her brothers lost at sea.

"Now, don't you do anything foolish, mind," Marcia quips to June before yanking Rize out into the dingy hallway that smells of overcooked cabbage.

On the way to the store, Marcia tells Rize about a woman in her town who stuck her head in the oven after her husband left her for a college teacher in Toronto, but, not to worry, because she knows his mother has more sense than that.

Marcia buys him a KitKat and a Spider-Man comic book. The pretty cashier smiles at him when she leans over the conveyor belt to give him a lollipop and her hands smell like dill and Ajax. He fears that if he opens his mouth globs of blood might come out, so he tightens his grasp on the comic and jams the sucker into his pocket.

When they get back to the apartment, his mom is on the phone.

"Clay's left us. Three more days, Ted, and I'll be back."

June works at the library with a tall man named Ted who

calls him "Sonny" and blushes when his mom laughs. While Rize sits on the couch and tries to read his comic book, his mom and Marcia mop the kitchen floor, pull boxes from the bedroom closet, sing Carly Simon loudly, and smoke. Marcia leaves, finally, with the promise of returning later with a tuna-fish casserole and cherry Jell-O for Rize. He scrunches up his body under the threat of her hug.

Afterward, his mom sits next to Rize on the couch and combs out her long auburn mane. He crawls into her lap while strands of her hair descend on him like soft webs. He falls asleep thinking about woolly horse legs and sandstorms.

During the next three days, June buys new orange curtains for the front room and empties ashtrays. She reads a book about herb gardens and does all the crossword puzzles from all the *Gazettes* piled up by the telephone. She throws out his dad's old razors and sews a patch of a monkey on Rize's favourite pair of Levi's. She gets a prescription filled for Rize's eye infection and, at the end of the three days, the night before she has to go back to the library, to Ted, they order Chinese food from Kim-Sun: the place Clay claimed made the best sweet-pork ribs in the whole world. Only his mother doesn't order the ribs, she orders mushroom fried rice, egg rolls for Rize, and sweet and sour chicken balls steeped in bright pink sauce. They are breaded, heavy, and sink in his stomach like lures.

As a child, he'd never considered the Herculean task ahead of her, but now he thinks about what it must have been like to run through the dailiness, the unwarranted vacation from marriage. What was it like for June to have her shared life abandoned as unceremoniously as dumping wet clothes from a washer into the dryer? Plus, there's Rize and his eye and nose infections, his problem with reading, his teachers complaining that he throws sand at other kids in the playground despite his trenchant refusal to join in the weekly dodge-ball poundings disguised as gym class.

But she'd turned it around when, maybe, all she wanted to do was sink into their dirty couch and abandon herself to a vodka-soaked quiet. She could have drowned Rize in her unlove but she didn't.

Because buried inside June was a livid, impassive rage that could have mangled his childhood. He'd had a glimpse of it when, at eighteen, after a couple of beers with Jules, he'd come home, flicked on a cigarette lighter, and flashed his teeth at her flirtatiously.

She'd clocked him hard, in the face.

"What was that for?" he shouted, reeling, angry, but also impressed by his mother's strength.

He knew what the smack was for. It was really terrible, how much he knew about his mother, how he sometimes played her with Clay's own face. He knew he looked exactly like Clay, even though she threw out all the photos of his father. And he knew it was wrong to weaken her with certain expressions and ignite her fury with others.

But June had locked down her anger and stuck to the glue, the mundane fabric of life, when the bottom of hers had crumpled like a wet cardboard box. Maybe it's her fault, maybe he's inherited her obdurate wrath. Maybe June's the reason he's disassembling the simple anatomy of his life. Why couldn't she just knock him around a bit, get it over with, instead of being a single-mother martyr?

It's not his fault, he thinks, banging his head against the dashboard of the empty van, experiencing that deep inward shudder of hot-cold lashes one gets when caught in the act of lying, of unreasonable bitchiness. It's not his problem that he always happens to be in the wrong place at the even wronger time, reminding women of an ache they'd rather forget.

* * *

IN A SAN DIEGO HOTEL ROOM Kellogg's yoga teacher treats the band to a choice slew of drugs for discount prices. Laughing at the exorbitant narcotic display laid out on a glass table strewn with crushed begonias, Kellogg and Rize sift through the tiny white bags and pills. Jules and Margo are out getting a large order of fish tacos and the others—save Jim, who is in her room reading a book about suicide—have piled all the available mattresses by the hotel pool in order to vault themselves into the deep end. Guy's curled up on the edge of a stray mattress, trying to sleep off a combination of booze and coke. He twitches like the dying cicada bugs around him.

The boys take turns diving off the edge of the Princess-and-the-Pea construction and end up soaking all the beds. It's only eleven-thirty a.m. and everyone's shitfaced. Rize wishes he had the strength to get up and help Guy inside, or at least into a poolside chair. Wishes he could pull apart the mattresses and put an end to all this nonsense. The pounding in his head has become as continuous as his boredom.

He remembers days ago—or was it weeks?—when he felt the surge of his first un-hungover morning. He'd woken early, before everyone else, swum eighty lengths in the pool, drunk a beet juice, and sent his mother a large book about mummies he'd found in a discount store in San Fran. That morning he swore he would be good, would ease up on the booze, would flush out the memory of Margo's mouth on him like a damaged whisper.

Now, one hungover morning bleeds into the next. The unbroken highway is punctured only by night when his swollen wrists get loaded with bullets of energy while, for two hours, they get to play. Besides the odd moments of van isolation, it's only onstage that Rize feels good, as though there's a rhythm and a meaning to his life. Secretly, he agrees with Kellogg, who says being on stage is like communing with your maker, only he wouldn't say it in that flaky Waco way. Plus, on the scale of bands God chooses to commune with, The Riots are probably pretty near the bottom. But there's something to it. For Rize, it's enough to imagine that God tunes in for a riff or two before heading off to Joan of Arc's potluck.

Since the Chinese takeout night, Margo has said only two things to him as they've zipped around the West Coast: *Give me five dollars for lattes* and *Do you have an extra set of batteries? The ones in Jules's electric razor are shot.*

He is trying to put it to her, organize the ideas in his head, when Kellogg throws a dimebag of coke at him.

1. You are my best friend's wife.

"What do you say, Rize, you going to take a little edge off with me?"

Rize throws the bag back at Kellogg.

"What's this blue one with the Mercedes thingy on it?" Kellogg asks, looking to his yogic pal.

2. You are my best friend. (And I miss you Margo. Hate you not looking at me, making a concerted fucking effort to keep your eyes and legs and everything away from me. Miss you waking up and laughing at all my stupid jokes at Jules's expense.)

"That, my friend," the smiling sage intones, "is a beautiful E that makes you look at bag ladies and see fucking unicorns. It comes on the house, with a purchase of two bags of H, which, I might add, contains none of that quinine bullshit."

"H, eh?"

Yoga-boy pulls a half dozen sealed needles out of his fanny-pack and lays them on the glass-top table.

"You're cool with this, right?"

Kellogg nods. He's shot up with executives and their high-class hookers in Toronto penthouses, as well as with street junkies. The ultimate recreational imbiber, Kellogg upholds his spin on an adage: everything and everywhere in moderation.

3. The sort of on-and-off girl in my life is your best friend. (You see, I understand why this is complicated for you, why you'd rather not talk and are still sulking and afraid of me even after a week and two days.)

"Rize!" The rest of the band, in various states of sopping undress, are standing around, staring at him. Rize feels himself caught unprepared, as he often does, by the dubious honour of being one of Kellogg's favourites.

"No way, man. I don't even smoke pot. Are you crazy?"

"I've noticed you've been a bit, ah, depressed lately. This will cure what ails you."

"Me, depressed?"

"Yeah, you lock yourself in the van like a dog and Margo has been so unbelievably bitchy lately. Like, I don't know, you two are no fun any more."

At the sound of her name, Rize's knee jerks reflexively. He looks around to see if anyone can tell his heart has sped up.

"All right, man, suit yourself. We don't play till tomorrow

night and it's not like, I don't know, you have a schedule or anything to adhere to." Kellogg laughs as the yogi produces all the necessary accoutrements. Kellogg sticks his arm out and lights a cigarette.

"Look, dude, it's me, am I a junkie?"

"No," he says, watching the yogi tie Kellogg up.

"Would I let you, one of the sweetest and most talented musicians I know, become a junkie?"

4. I blurred you. (I'm sorry. I blurred you. I kissed her and I saw you. I saw you and kissed her. I don't know. It was a blip, a blip, Margo. I had no idea what I was doing. I knew exactly what I was doing. It was like that time in the van when we were both so hungry and started eating that meatball sub at the same time and raced to see who could get to the middle first and then you started cracking up and spitting up on the van floor. Jules got mad, remember? He yelled at me, said I made you choke, but really he didn't understand that it was the first time you'd laughed, or eaten, in three days. We'll laugh about this, years from now, I swear we will, after I've put your kids to bed. We'll laugh. Except, if we don't talk about this now, at this juncture, it may become insurmountable. Even I know this. It could get bigger than the band, bigger than you and me.)

"Well?"

Inside himself, he imagines he is shirtless and on his knees, prone before the trinity of women he loves: June, Kit, and Margo. He puts his hand over his eyes and sticks out his arm. He watches the injection through the gaps in his fingers.

He's trying to explain it to them as the warm glow invades his blood.

He tries to cope with the fact that he has violated the only two rules he has ever made for himself: first, to never, ever, meddle with Jules and Margo, and, second, to never try to keep up with Kellogg's consumption habits. He feels his breathing slow. His muscles slacken. It feels as if he is peeing himself inside, no one can see, but he's getting wetter and more and more uncomfortable.

5. (This is the last one and it's the hardest to say.) There was nothing inside me except for a rusted can and an old pair of Kit's underwear that had long ago lost its scent. There was nothing inside me for weeks on end, except at night when the stage lit up and we took those kids inside and walled them up with our noise. There was nothing there, except for these scraggly remnants; the memory of emotion. So when you opened your needful mouth and let me in, I knew I still felt something.

* * *

WHEN HE WAKES UP he's in the washroom. A yarn of bile connects him to the toilet bowl. He's naked, his arm is bleeding a little, and everything's foggy. Sounds return only after he's bashed his head against the ceramic bowl a couple of times. A constant banging that is his head, must be, but no, it's the door: the sounds that remind him that he is always among people. He looks at it, sees the doorknob turn fecklessly. More banging. Jules's angry voice. Jules knows. Is coming to kill him. Best stay here, in this pool of his own vomit. Best not give Jules any more concrete evidence to despise him.

But then he hears something that forces him to drag himself across the trail of puke and push the doorknob in. The door opens and reveals all of them, dressed up, so nice, all his nice, almost-famous, rock-star friends. Then they all take a collective step back. Oh. Skin must be green, hands shaking, and naked, too.

Right, it's not normal to be lying passed out in a hotel bathroom floor in the middle of a sunny California day.

Everyone backs up against the wall, all of them looking—what? Guilty? Is that it? Of what? He's the guilty one.

Words try to arrange themselves in his mouth, but all he can think of is how people in America say "raspberry" all the time and he has no idea what that means. *Then he makes a raspberry at me, and I freak, right?* So he says "raspberry" out loud, which makes everyone look even more scared. Then he hears what made him unlock the door in the first place: Margo. She tears through them.

"You pieces of shit. Rize can't even take an antihistamine without hallucinating little blue men! You bastards. Do you even realize what you've done? He's not a clown for your fucking amusement."

And then it seems he's solved all his mistakes by making another, because not only is she relating to him in a way that suggests he has not ruined their working relationship, she is pulling him up off the floor, holding his swollen face in her hands.

"These L.A. kids don't mess around, do they?" he slurs, as she slams the door and they are alone for the second time in three weeks.

9
jim

The day Yawnie and I were born marked the end of a month-long heat wave. Our mother had planted her enormous self in Simon's inflatable pool for a week and a half prior to our birth and so she had almost missed the whooshing of her watery insides that preceded our arrival. But she certainly knew when I entered the world because I tore her up like a machete-happy farm boy. I was long, screaming, and I struggled with the doctor who was desperately wiping at my genitals to find a penis.

My brother, on the other hand, slipped out soundlessly, when our mother's initial wails had abated and all eyes in the delivery room were on me. It would be Yawnie's first gesture of quietly supplying what was lost or missing amid my bluster and audacity, but definitely not his last. The doctor and nurse switched their attention to my twin, who was half my size and strategically wrapped in placenta and the umbilical cord I had fought so hard to gain freedom from.

Soon after, he was moved to a bubble-shaped incubator where a gurney had to be wheeled in so that I could lie beside him. Apparently, I wouldn't be held or calmed by anyone in those first few days of cold August rain and nothing, except the constant sight of this hand-sized boy, could soothe me.

A sleepy prairie town, where the world is mostly sky, names my brother and me. No one knows exactly how it happens. Mrs. Martha Jr., an honest if gossipy spinster, has been working for the city for years and has made few, if any, mistakes. In fact, her own mother was the first woman to have a municipal job—the first sign of feminism in our town—and the legacy is passed down to Mrs. Martha Jr., who is in charge of birth and death certificates.

Only Mrs. Martha Jr. makes a mistake on our birth certificates and types that Janice Stella Kov's sex is *male* and that James Neil Kov is a *female*. In town, there's speculation that Mrs. Martha Jr. snuck one too many Pilsners at bingo the night before. On any given day, if you walk by her office at city hall, you can hear her on the phone, openly criticizing the hygiene of other people's children and complaining about the heat or cold. So, what would compel the woman to make such an egregious error? And to spread it around town till it stuck?

No matter, there's something to Martha's accidental logic: at age two our mother's friends at the farmers' market lean over my pale twin, pinch Yawnie's cheeks, and exclaim "What a pretty little girl!" as he opens his mouth and yawns at their clucking. While Yawnie swims in his baby clothes I burst the snap-ons of my pink jumpers and the market women use words like "husky" and "handsome" to delicately describe my sausage limbs and oversized potato head.

At four, our identities are cemented and Yawnie and I are irrevocably named: I am Jamie to my friends in kindergarten, and Jim to Yawnie, who's called me that since we were two. Our church-going mother is oddly indifferent to the matter that my intended name, Jan, has become perverted into Yawnie. Perhaps it was easier for her to put up with weird nicknames than to actually cope with two babies and a six year old. Maybe a lost name or two was a small price to pay for the fact that Yawnie spent more than half of his early childhood in a languid sleep. Years later, when I examine the baby book where our mother tucked away our first locks of hair, I will learn that my name, my original name, Jan, means "God is gracious." When I ask our mother whether she regrets the loss of this subtle nod to the Lord, she shrugs and says that God's grace is everywhere and, besides, God obviously has a sense of humour.

But not everyone is into the joke, the noncommittal way our somewhat conservative parents have allowed time and disposition to toy with gender. "You've got to get it changed, Mom. A girl called *James*? A boy called *Jan*? It's stupid," a ten-year-old Simon says as he bites into a hamburger and flashes his eyes at us. In unison, Yawnie and I stick our tongues out at him across the dinner table. We hate our ten-year-old brother and have no time for his shame because we know, secretly, that our names chose us just as we chose each other.

Ten years later, at fourteen, there is a shift when Yawnie has an enormous growth spurt that evens out our family's lopsided dynamic. Years of bony awkwardness, coupled with his bent for academics, music, and poetry, have earned him a second nickname from Simon: "faggot." Yawnie only shrugs at this. Even before gay culture was cool, Yawnie didn't mind having his masculinity challenged; god knows he was used to it. He found, in fact, that it worked in his favour; he attracted more girls as a dreamy non-threatening boy. But one day this dreamy skinny boy disappears when Yawnie surpasses me, and Simon, in height and weight. Baseball, farm work, swimming, and soccer have sculpted his body to near-perfect proportions and he has inherited the high, angular cheekbones of our Ukrainian ancestors. Though Yawnie's colouring—his green eyes and near-white hair—is identical to mine, at fifteen he begins to look more like Simon's twin, despite the fact that Simon is black-haired and brown-eyed.

So, Simon stops calling Yawnie a fag and turns his attention to me, whom he merely calls "Freak Job," or "Freak" for short. Why? I suppose because I'm a farm girl named Jim who wears her brother's ripped jeans and cuts her own hair into jagged punk-rock styles. Who fiddles along in the dark garage to classical records that skip, who sleeps in the tree house on summer nights and tries to keep up with Yawnie, who kicks up dust with his red sneakers while he runs on country roads. I may have been born bigger but he's faster. He does everything quicker, he does everything first now, and this has begun to make both Simon and me uneasy for different reasons.

Another fact that has me feeling uncomfortable, at this age, is my encroaching femininity. I am proud of my almost-boyness, my two hulking, handsome brothers, and like a child raised by wolves who believes herself to be vulpine, I believe myself to be an honorary male as there has been no evidence, so far, to suggest the opposite, except. Except the monthly blood that seeps through my midsection and stains my pants. Except that sometimes I catch myself crying unreasonably during Guns N' Roses videos and long-distance phone commercials. Except that I am more secretive and take long walks in the fields, collecting flowers and things too sacred to mention here.

When I get back from my walks, I tell no one but Yawnie my stories. Only he has the patience to nurture my emerging female side, only Yawnie understands the art of listening: he deposits questions into the lacunae of our conversations. And it's here, in these spaces, where I sometimes catch him appraising the changes of my own growth spurt: the ill-fitting cut of his jeans on my hips, the new layer of fat on my face and limbs.

But I ignore his looks and keep talking because no one else listens to me. No one else understands the significance of the hushed, nearly missed moans of field owls, how their small garbled sobs can remind a person of death and pride.

* * *

AT SIXTEEN, Yawnie still understands everything I say, despite the fragments of light breaking his eyes apart and his distant, medicated smile. Since the accident, he doesn't talk much, but welcomes my descriptions of music lessons and softball practice.

He sits in the corner of the kitchen, at dinner, twitching his hands and mumbling. Since the accident, he has stopped eating beef, chicken, and "anything with vertebrae." This has the rest of the family confused, but he's explained it to me. "Animals are implanted with sensors. When we eat them, we swallow those tags and become tracked. There's already enough electricity in me to light up New York City, Jim, so why the hell would I want the government to confuse me with a cow signal?"

Across the dinner table, I look at Simon's tanned arms. His complexion is golden after helping Dad with the hay baling. As I talk to Yawnie about what I saw on my walk, Simon eyes us between the pages of his car magazine, like he's irritated. He's twenty-one now and always irritated. I consider my older brother's character: his unsmiling, angry presence and his ability to shot-gun ten cans of Pilsner and still drive everyone home after the bush party. Reliable, but humourless, Simon wears the stigma of Yawnie's damage like it's his.

"You're a stigmata," Simon says, out of nowhere.

"What?" I ask, getting more vexed by the second.

"What you said. I'm not a stigmata, you are."

"It's *stigma*, idiot, and I didn't even say it." Pause. "Out loud."

The wires crossed for a second, Yawnie turns his head to me, a faint smile on his face.

"Whatever. Just get your shit out of there. I'm going to sleep in the tree house tonight, not you."

"Ma—"

"Why can't you both sleep there?"

"You're twenty-one years old, why do you want to—"

Suddenly I know Simon wants to take a girl up there. I see the image he sees, a girl smiling at him, her golden hair spread over his shoulders. Her name is Jen and she doesn't think Simon is that serious and grumpy; in fact, she thinks he's charming. Butt-face Simon, charming.

Simon then gives me a look I've recorded as The Silencer. There's nothing but trouble for me in this look, hours of endless physical and emotional torment.

I pull Yawnie over to the living room couch so he can watch *Cops*.

Simon peeks over Mom, who's bent over the sink doing dishes and setting a plate aside for Dad, who comes in late on dry nights like this. Simon gives me the stink eye. Confused, I glance at Yawnie, who is smirking at something on TV. Or is Yawnie laughing at me?

This is just great, I think, making sure Yawnie doesn't burn a hole in the couch with his cigarette. Lucky me, never to own a thought or moment—even with Yawnie gone mad he's still exerting his power. Only the fields are void of boys now.

* * *

BUT THERE I GO AGAIN. Mixing up time. Mixing up before-accident life with after-accident life. Because there was a before-life at the farm when I didn't have to fight Simon on my own, let alone have the two of them gang up on me. All that changed early one July morning when Yawnie drove Dad's tractor into a ditch, through an electric wire fence, and broke his arm and collarbone. Though a relatively minor accident, as far as farm accidents go, it was monumental to Yawnie, forcing his mind into a vacuum he never managed to escape.

Before that July morning, it was the two of us against Simon. Yawnie would grab my hand and run into the centre of the field, spitting sunflower seeds out of his mouth, singing Leonard Cohen's "Hallelujah" with exaggerated vibratos to make me laugh.

"But you don't really care for music, do youuuuuuu?"

Yawnie had conceded to going to Montreal someday to help me find Cohen.

"No gushing, though," Yawnie had insisted. He personally thought old LC was a secondary poet, an absolute phony, and that the world loved him only because women did.

In the before-life, there were lots of plans like these. And it was these plans—our limitless possibilities that Yawnie had convinced me of—it was these goddamn hopes that drove me to pace the floor and sucker-punch the thin walls of our house until my father and Simon had to tackle me so I wouldn't tear the place down.

Yawnie is alive, my parents had told me, right afterward, at the hospital. They tried to convince me that all that mattered was that his heart was still beating. I blinked at them stupidly, knowing otherwise. Because I knew the future, our future, was dead.

I could try to explain it better, in my way, in more complicated language. About the anger, with images of guts exploding and all that. I could try to explain how heartache isn't just absence, and how in the end it wasn't ever enough for me simply to survive it. But I'll come back to this later. Besides, Isaac, of all people, had captured it perfectly, without all that gory stuff I'd add to it.

Because one morning, after I'd arrived at Isaac's house while he was out, I came across some hotel stationery on which he'd scrawled *The end of a couple is like the end of the world.* Beneath it was a bunch of financial figures and client phone numbers.

Turning the page over, I wondered briefly who Isaac was thinking of when he'd written this down—me? His wife?

Whose end could he see?

* * *

THREE NIGHTS AFTER Yawnie comes home from the hospital, I hover over his bed, my fingers encircling his frail wrist. Everything about him seems brittle, so small.

"What are you? Some kind of crazy person, now? Why won't you talk?"

Eyes open. Blank. Not a twitch of fear, of pain, of anything. I grab his good arm, try to crush the bones in his wrist, hoping to elicit something.

"Come on, or I'll break your other arm."

His face turns up, a small, automatic spark, of what?

Look at me. Your face remembers, show me it remembers us.

Using all the strength I have, I drill my thought-words into his thick, fuzzy skull as I straddle his body and pin his free arm to the headboard.

It remembers when you somersaulted on the last of fall's yellowed leaves and promised me you'd never die.

He doesn't even feel the physical threat, care that he's stronger than me and that I'm preparing to kick the shit out of him.

I don't remember. This. You. At. All.

I drop his arm and give him a shove, good and hard, before I slam the door to our room and run outside.

I don't believe you. You're a fucking liar. You lie.

Later, the psychiatrist explained that sometimes it takes a catharsis to dislodge the latent mental illness inside a person's mind. For all my reading, I had no idea what the word "catharsis" meant, imagining it to be either a place in Greece or a catheter needle. By the time Dad found Yawnie, with his left arm crushed under the wheel of the tractor like a stray branch, my brother had gone completely catatonic. It took a month before he started talking again, and then, the things he said, the lines connecting his thoughts to the words, were short-circuited. Crossed.

"Best not walk too close to those electrical fences, Jim," he'd whisper when I tried to hug him, cajole him out of a long stare.

"I know, Yawnie."

He'd turn to me with sudden clarity in his expression.

"They are conductors of light. On our own land, imagine. Now I have a chip in my brain. They can hear everything."

"Who?"

He pointed to his plaster cast covered with the big floppy daisies I'd drawn in pencil crayon.

"This is only the beginning. Next time they'll break my hip, or worse," he whispered.

"It was an accident. You were going too fast."

"Okay, we can't talk about it any more."

He slapped at imaginary flies and tapped his fingers on the edge of his cast, looking beyond me, outside.

In those early post-accident days we were pretty convinced that Yawnie had brain damage, so our parents kept taking him to the city for tests. It took almost a year before I heard my parents saying things like "psychotic episode" and "schizophrenia."

In the before-life, Yawnie's emotions and thoughts would seep into my head in strains of colour and musical fugues. Sometimes he took up so much space in me I'd have to block him out. His emotions would rise up and dance upon the white screen of my mind, like splats of Pollock's reds and blues. Sometimes, depending on what mood he was in, they'd be accompanied by Beethoven's loud, defiant chords.

His fear, slashes of black, would tear into my skull and wake me from dreams, or they would make me miss a perfectly good pitch during a baseball game. His joy swarmed into my consciousness in hot swabs of orange-juice light.

But after the accident, when I closed my eyes and waited for him, there was only the sound of a record needle skipping, followed by crackling static. There were no colours left on the palette of his mind either, only pale brown stains, like washed-out blood on cotton. His eyes, once mischievous and animated, were now bits of ground glass.

I began to believe it was no schizophrenic delusion, that an electrical current had indeed blasted part of my brother's brain that random July morning, a month before we turned sixteen.

Late at night, when his breathing was finally even and I was certain he was asleep, I tried to push beyond the reef of his pain, to decipher what, exactly, was happening to him, to us. I felt bad about the night I'd sat on him, and so I tried to access him subtly. I wanted him to know I wasn't angry, that I just wanted in.

Only, when I tried, there was nothing: just a white light so blinding it forced me back, with its heat and intensity, to my own small thought-world. Miserable, dejected, I'd stand by my brother's bed and try to read his mind, mumbling magical words from our childhood: *slacks, acorn, gambit, chippy*—there were so many words we'd invested with code. I'd play with his hands, smooth down his covers, demanding acknowledgment, entry.

Still, nothing.

Grouchy and hungover as a bartender, I sat at the kitchen table every morning over my oatmeal, unable to look at the vacuous creature posing as Yawnie.

One morning there was a small note on my bed. Dad had taken Yawnie to the hospital for another appointment. I pried open the paper, expecting a long letter of apology and explanation. It was covered in tiny scribbles, lines and lines of unreadable text running together until finally, near the end, was my message from my brother.

Cut it out.

10
rize

After load-out, and a quick stop at a New Jersey White Castle, Rize sneaks into the hotel-room washroom while the rest of the guys drink white Russians in the lobby and flirt with the college bartenders who recognize them from the newspapers. He does his business quickly and, just as he unplugs the needle, he falls, ripping the shower curtain as he goes down. Margo slips in just then, locks the door. She laughs.

"Shhh," she says. "Rize, it's okay."

He looks at her through his kaleidoscope vision.

"Margo, you've got to leave!"

"You want me to go?"

He feels cold, so he draws the shower curtain around his shoulders while she huffs and sniffles. Ah, Margo on a coke tear. She pulls out her own white powder, sniffs a large bump off a key, and her eyes turn into pools of reservoir water. Using a wad of toilet paper, she recovers his needle and buries it deep in the trash. There is something so intimate and generous about this act that he says, "Don't go."

As her eyes spill more black mascara, it occurs to him that he hasn't seen her cry like this in months, not since she lost her suitcase in Detroit last tour. The tears fall unintentionally, like detached parts of a star's buried light. Calmly, without sobbing, she takes a cotton ball and swabs Rize's arms with alcohol, clotting the small pinpricks. The sharp astringent pain perks him up and he realizes, through it, that Margo's the only one who now knows his secret. Secrets. He watches her clean his arm the way he used to watch June pack lunch or type letters on her green French-English typewriter.

As she perches close to him, on the edge of the tub, he can hear the guys outside in the hallway, smoking and talking. He can hear Kellogg's loud laugh and Jules pacing the halls. He imagines Jules smoothing out his shirt, hauling on a joint, and passing it back to Kellogg. He can see Jim at the bar with Guy, sipping her Cosmopolitan slowly and then switching off the phone her rich, mysterious boyfriend gave Jim so he could keep track of her. He thinks about the way she's acquired a new kind of sophistication in the last couple of weeks. Now her notes are always measured, never rushed, so he never even needs to cue her onstage. It's like she knows he's about to become unreliable, somehow out of sync. As if she doesn't need him any more.

At this moment, he just wants to sit with Margo, never go anywhere, never eat in a restaurant, tell a lie, shave, fuck, play, dress, ever again. Beyond Margo's mouth, and her knowledge of his worst self, he needs her this way, silent, unselfish, holding his hand on the edge of such uncertain darkness.

* * *

ON THE WAY to New York from Jersey, for the last series of shows, Rize lies on the floor of the van, immune to the gummy-rot smell of Jules's sneakers, immune to Margo's innocuous, fairy ankle-tattoo and Jim's sleepy, tuneless humming. He concentrates on an empty Coke can rolling between the door and the back bench, on disappearing entirely from view, from this set of people, his band, these people whom he has—apparently—aligned himself with.

Inside the small yet ample space of his bandmate's legs, he cocoons himself into his sleeping bag and tries to read an Archie comic book. Then he tries broaching Kellogg's ragged copy of *Siddhartha*, but it's not the same as being twelve and reading it, it's not even close.

He closes his eyes and thinks about how far away his birth was from the Buddha's, thinks about his eighth birthday, when Clay and June invited all his rich cousins from NDG and he puked blue icing into the sink.

When Clay nudges him and asks what he wished for when he blew out his candles, he says, "Less garbage, more squirrels." Then Clay smiles, puts his big hands on Rize's face, and tries to squash his son's head, until June gets in the way and shoves another present into his hands. She tells his father to get more beer, the imported kind, *not* 50.

Even at this age he is intrinsically sensitive to his mother's anxieties. He doesn't understand the specific contours of her disappointment—that she has married a Vietnam vet in the age of francophone emancipation, that they will never live in a house with a garden or a parking space on the island of Montreal. But at eight he does comprehend the shape of his mother's longing. It is round, throbbing, amorphous, and distinctly feminine, and he is able to gauge its girth and weight. When he bounces off it, it shrinks a little. So far, the monthly Irish Society newsletter, the days Clay manages to suture a grin onto his face, are the only things—as far as he can tell—that have lessened its presence.

Only later will he understand her sorrow fully, as his own life accrues and fattens against the shape of her sedentary monster. Later on, Rize will feed it with his musical talent, greasy long hair, hash burns in his jeans, and the lithe, unconscious pose of Clay's he has no control over.

What's the difference between an Irish mother and a Rottweiler?
What?
The Rottweiler eventually lets go.

But now, at eight, he understands only that it's important to his mother that he remain clean and that he does not throw up any more. So he pretends he's happy about the hot dogs and all the laughing, joke-telling uncles asking Clay about the Vietnam War. That he doesn't smell the odour of cabbage seeping in from the hallway.

He knows that his birthday party is important, somehow, to his mother. But he would rather be watching television with her, combing the knots out of her hair and asking her to explain the complicated plots of *Little House on the Prairie.* His favourite episode is when Mary Ingalls wakes up blind and starts screaming. He didn't need any explanation for that one. Pa, Michael Landon, looks like he's going to cry, while Mary's chucking things and stumbling around in her gingham nightgown, screaming at God the whole episode.

He wishes he could wake up blind one day. To be angry enough to scream at God. This is the secret side-wish he makes over his blue race-car cake, the one he doesn't tell Clay about. When he tells June he wants to be as angry as Mary one day, that he wants the drama and shame and vengeance of Mary's predicament, she opens her eyes really wide as if she is blind too, and says: "Don't worry, baby, there's time for that."

He'd rather be in the park, with Clay, while his father pushes him on the big-kid swings and smokes. But he isn't; he's in this stuffy three-and-a-half and Clay is the only man drinking 50s, crushing cans with his fists.

He's trying only to hold onto the memory of his father as he rushes in through New York's bridges.

He's lying on the floor of a speeding van with his back mashed up against flight cases and stolen hotel-room pillows. He's trying not to remember anything. He's not thinking about how the fire extinguished in his veins like coming, or falling. That feeling, of stumbling off a precipice with your legs intact while your arms get torn, he wants it.

When your body erases you for a moment.

He wants that again.

He is not driving into New York City with The Riots. They are not now entering the one place on earth that fills him with more dread than the results of an STD test. He is not an American citizen, he only plays one on TV. He is not a lead horn player and one of three guitar players with the biggest Canadian indie band in North America.

But he does manage to bawl out a solo every night despite the fact that Jules and Kellogg never tire of dismembering his ivory guitar in creative ways, leaving him with only three strings to play.

Despite evidence to the contrary, he does not wake up in the morning in love with two women. One: striking, shit-kicking Kit. With her oversized feet and raging eyes. Silent Kit, who knows more than half a dozen ways to undo a man's belt buckle and then kill him with it.

The second woman he loves travels with three suitcases of vitamins and face creams that she rarely uses. Margo's broken bird voice, once it hits the room, gives every man a tug in his groin and causes the women to deflate a little.

He tries not to think about how Margo has removed her wedding band. He imagines he hasn't witnessed her growing aversion to Jules, has not put her wedding ring in his mouth in his private washroom moments, tongued the hole of its metal centre lovingly, like a clit or a sorbet figurine surprise you used to get for a dollar at the corner depanneur. He hasn't betrayed his best friend, his lover, the band, June, or Margo by using the last of his American money to buy three dimebags of H.

When the van brakes jerk him out of his cancelling of time and the restless feet around him propel themselves out of the vehicle, he completes the first step of his mission. His vanishing act, his great demise.

It's incredible, he thinks, *to be here, finally, at last. That I was so smart to hide it in my shoe. That I concentrated and cleaned my horn in my last nod and restrung everyone's guitar, including mine.*

Rize claims the precision of his habit: the spoon burns black, the syringe opens up easily, filling up with his viscous blood. It's as easy as playing scales. He'd imagined having more trouble with it all and is proud of his skill. He's proud of his bulging arteries that allow him to be prone and efficient without going vertical.

What a natural junkie you are.

He has an affinity for both primitive and advanced mechanics. He loves machines and machines love him back. Entropic carburetors, motorcycle parts, computer motherboards, and guitar pedals jump into his hands and reconfigure their broken functions. And now, finally, he and the hypodermic are one, too.

At least we're in Harlem, he thinks, while he's perfecting his game of denial. He loves Harlem, it makes New York forgivable.

Pulling his arm out of the needle, he refolds his shirt and lies down again.

* * *

THAT NIGHT WHEN HE PLAYS with two other bands in Manhattan, his shakes become severe. He can't remember tuning, only the washroom lock, Margo smoking in the hallway and slugging Rolling Rock.

"Why the hell were you in there for so long?"

"What do you care?"

Something's turned around in her; it's she who comes to him now. In the van she jumps onto the back bench and plants herself next to his pilled blanket and crossword books. At night, when Jules is still at the bar doing interviews, it's she who crawls on top of his sleeping bag, trailing her fingers over his sunken chest. It's she who whispers "Now," and he who pushes her off.

He'd like to remind her that Kit is the type of best friend who'd give Margo anything she asked for: a drink, her favourite pair of lapis earrings, a ride downtown, her signed copy of *The English Patient.*

That Kit would give her anything, except him. But he doesn't say anything about Kit to Margo, as if Kit is just an uncomfortable dream they both had, not a real person whose heart and well-being they are responsible for.

He knows that thinking about Kit may just crush the last of his hope, along with everything else, and yet there's a momentum to this thing with Margo that's almost like being inside a song. Plus, he reminds himself, they still haven't done anything, so this comforts him in the way you are comforted when you're gambling drunk and holding nothing but singles.

Onstage, through Kellogg's bird's nest hair, he tries to find his mouth so that he can figure out what the hell he's singing about—no one ever really knows except that some of it's vulgar, some of it's about God. But mostly it's cryptic.

Everything moves quickly, no, slowly, decisively, the rushing through, the assembling of cords and cables. With Margo off his back for the night, he manages to get a nod in before the second set. The set goes long, triple encore. The crowd nothing but a roar of white noise as he buries his eyes in the pitted surface of the amps and pretends no one can hear him.

Jim's at the side of the stage, back straight, behind Guy's plastic drumming cage. Her big pine-coloured eyes follow him back and forth as he works the plunger with a terrific violence and quaking. Backstage, before the show, he stopped to let her place her rosined hands on his face and melted a little under her child-hands. "Rize, your mouth is bleeding. You've got cold sores, like, three." He closed his eyes for a minute under the chalky scent of her amber hands.

Ah yes, the cold sores, every morning a new one. But there's no time now! No time to keep track of all the bloody orifices in his needled body. From foot to head he counts fourteen holes and can keep only seven clean and under wraps. His mouth will have to wait.

Onstage, Jules pulls off his jacket to reveal a shirt that says I STILL LOVE YOU PEE WEE. Jules ties his red leather necktie around his wrists while Margo attacks him and the two have a mock lover's quarrel on stage. She kicks him while he lies on the floor, undressing himself as he croons like Johnny Rotten on Quaaludes in a distressed pinstripe suit.

The music is hard and metallic under Rize's skin. As his body slowly digests the junk, he experiences a quick frisson of joy. It sluices over his hands as he jerks his fingers up and down the brass ladders of the piece and disappears. It's a miracle he can even play, really; a miracle—these moments—he can forget the agony of ever having been born.

* * *

RIZE FEELS LUCKY to have inherited Clay's manual dexterity and to have absorbed a few precious lessons from his father. They include: how to knot a tie properly, how to swing a baseball bat, how to shine boots, and the importance of sharing your animal crackers.

The rest of his lessons are included in the note he finds inside his ripped teddy bear, Bo-Bo, five years after his dad leaves.

Son,
Buy flowers on your mother's birthday and sing her an Irish song, she loves Irish songs, even drinking ones, especially drinking ones. Always have your passport ready, don't forget to turn the burner off after making a grilled cheese.
Sorry we didn't make it to the zoo the other day.
So sorry,

c.
(Your old man)

Too bad it takes him five more years to figure out the note is a fake. A well-meaning but awful joke from Jules, who thought Rize should have something from his old man, even if it wasn't real.

Too bad he can't explain to anyone, not even and especially not June, why he broke Jules's left wrist and got suspended from school, plus thrown out of band, even though he is one of two trombonists and the only one who can play worth shit.

Too bad.

* * *

WHAT ARE WE?

He knows what he and Kit are. He knows it in the same sick, certain way he knows Clay is dead now and that in precisely forty-five minutes he will barf White Castle into his hotel-room toilet.

Because he cannot forget that night when, curled up beneath the red covers of her bed, Kit opened up her famous tangerine-smelling hands to him and said that she had to protect him from all the bad people. That he did not know it, did not even realize it, but there were too many variables, too many warped, suffering souls. Souls that liked to peel the skin off prostitutes and pee on you, or drive a car over your head.

It made her so crazy thinking about it. That's why she learned to use a gun. Became a cop.

It made her sick, really, the things people were capable of, she said, but she could be his moral bodyguard and, if someone touched him, she could have the guy hands-splayed on the floor in five seconds flat.

It hurt her heart, she said, all those shitty people doing shitty things to each other. She could tell him stories that would make his eyes pop out of their sockets. She'd explained all this holding her body over his, her dark hair falling into his face like mosquito netting.

She said she'd like to protect him. And he agreed, promised that he'd protect her too—from the Montreal cold, from her occasional but intense bouts of sadness that pared her body down.

I'll feed you spiced meat and keep my funniest jokes only for you, he'd sworn, pushing her hair off her eyes. Caught by her skin's glow, the pull of commitment swayed him.

One morning, he'd even promised her a child with her grey eyes, who'd be dexterous with tools and have perfect pitch. He described the child's pink flesh as he laughed and propped a pillow behind her head. Their smooth bodies seemed protected then, safe.

Now, wedged between the cold tiles of a bathroom wall with Margo's heel jammed into his spine, he tries to forget his glowing girlfriend, that fat, imaginary baby with its mother's eyes. He forgets what he and Margo rip away at in the ticking seconds that the act takes.

The severing happens quickly and, in one swift heave, he arrives and becomes one of those people. Blithely rolling an SUV over the softest part of Kit's heart.

11
jim

During my last summer on the farm I'd go to the fields with Judas, the cat. I'd bring my sleeping bag and guitar and lie down in a meadow just to watch night come. I'd strum Dad's guitar—which I'd recently restored—and watch Judas snipe mice, tracing the moon's movement across the sky. Maybe something in me knew, even then, that I would leave, because each time I went out there, to sleep and play and dream, I'd try to imprint the smell of dust and wheat on the wall of my senses. I'd kneel on the ground like a blind mole, waiting for the scent of dirt to permeate my clothes. This, I thought, was the smell of Mars.

Sometimes I took Yawnie out there. Mom didn't like this at first. I don't know if she thought it would trigger bad memories for him or what, but then, one night, I heard her talking about it with Dad in their bedroom. I crept up to the door so that I could hear their conversation better:

"I'm worried about those two."

"Why?" my father grunted. I could see him lying in bed, wearing a threadbare shirt and a pair of boxers, reading an article about whales in *National Geographic.*

"Jim's always trying to get Yawnie to do things, but he doesn't want to do anything any more."

My father harrumphed and adjusted his position in bed. There was a silent stretch and then I could hear my mother sobbing. I imagined her back turned toward my father, her flannel nightgown enclosing her body in a soft rectangular shell. I implanted my ear more firmly on their door. Hearing my mother cry reminded me that they had some decisions to make about Yawnie's future.

He refused to go to school, wash his hair, or eat. Eating was still a big issue. My mother—who'd come from a long line of carnivorous Ukrainians—made him odd vegetarian meals consisting of breadcrumbs and cauliflower, which he'd poke at lethargically. He'd lost a lot of weight and, since the accident, it was true, he didn't do much of anything any more. I heard my father's body creaking in bed as he reached out to wrap his arms around my mother's cocooned figure.

"I'm just afraid that he'll do something. Freak out," my mother said.

"He'd never hurt Jim," my father said firmly, "especially with the medication."

I knew then that I had to tell Mom that, sometimes, when I cleaned our room, I found Yawnie's diazepam pills lined up under his bed like mouse scat. I stayed at the door until I heard my father's precise snores. For the first time I understood what my mother feared: that she would grow old taking care of her schizophrenic son.

Yawnie was also heavily asleep. He'd taken his meds that day and they had successfully knocked him out. I went over to his side of the room where he had covered the walls with tinfoil mobiles and stars he'd constructed with his twitching hands.

Because Yawnie wasn't completely useless. He had started writing a book called *The History of Electromagnetic Universal Forces: A Treatise on Mind Control.* There were pictures of scientists and molecular structures on the wall cut from magazines and various library books on the subject of force fields. Like me, Yawnie had been good at music, sports, and arts, but now he was getting into physics and metaphysics and knew about concepts I didn't understand. I touched a metal star on one of his mobiles, examined the fingernail sliver of moon in the sky.

Again, I tried to send him a message: *The sky is silver tonight: talk to me, please.* But I got nothing, only the usual static buzz of a million mechanical wasps floating around in his head.

* * *

THE NEXT DAY when Yawnie, Judas, and I were walking back from the field, Simon came toward us with the guitar in his hands. He was wearing a Def Leppard T-shirt and a pair of rubber boots.

"Don't leave my guitar in the barn again," he began. His boots were covered with dirt, his face was red, and I could smell his sour, hopsy beer breath.

"It's Dad's and you don't even play," I said, teeth clenched.

Yawnie was hanging back a bit, his hands in his pockets. Then a funny thing happened. Simon grabbed my arm and pulled me to him:

"Move," he whispered.

Just then Mom came out to tell Yawnie that *Cops* was on. He started running toward the house with his odd gait. When he'd left us, I turned back to Simon.

"Look, I'm sorry about the guitar, if you want it I—"

"I don't care about that." He pulled my arm and the blanket in my arms fell. Thinking it was a game, Judas clawed at the balled centre.

Yawnie hadn't gone inside yet. He stood on the porch watching the clouds stretch across the sky like a human torso. I could feel his eyes; they so rarely focused now that, when they did, I could feel them gouging me, in the pit of my gut. He was watching us watching him, but then, finally, he went inside.

"I need to show you something. In the barn," Simon said plainly. "Come on." He kept an eye on the house as he spoke.

He took me into the stalls, where we kept the grain, and pointed to a cardboard box in the corner. I opened the top and looked: inside were five small black and brown kittens that were the property of our neighbours, the Olsens. Barn kittens, bludgeoned. Judas was all over them, mewling loudly and trying to pick them up with his teeth. He was licking them, trying to save them. Simon leaned over and, in one clean motion, threw Judas against the wall of the barn.

"The coyotes?"

"I found them in the tree house, Jim." Simon moved the blood-soddened box so that the ruined animals rolled to one side, then he picked it up. I followed him out the back entrance and handed him a spade. I held the tiny box of death while he dug.

Yawnie and I were nearly eighteen, long past the age of torturing small animals—something we had never done anyway. The old Yawnie, the before-Yawnie, couldn't even stand to watch Simon chase chickens, let alone be capable of something like this. A silent, hysterical laugh threatened to escape my throat.

"Should we tell them? About the coyotes?" I asked, leaning on the spade. My eyes had adjusted to the sudden night and I could see my brother's tired face. He looked at me with pity.

"Jim—"

"What? Yawnie didn't do that."

Simon sighed again and patted down the ground. He unearthed a cigarette from his pocket and struck a match.

It was all skewed. It wasn't supposed to be Simon and me against Yawnie, it was supposed to be, like it always was, Yawnie and me against Simon, against the world.

Memory filtered in: Yawnie and I jumping into the Olsens' pond together, attacking our brother with our tiny fist splashes, our fingers linked like prawns. Simon pries our hands open and forces us into underwater poses of surrender. Yawnie and I leaping on him, scaling the length of his long back. We land and seize skin, hair, any vulnerable spot we can attack in the most brutal way.

Waking Simon was our favourite morning activity because he always roared up like a shaggy wildebeest and threw us onto his headboard so hard we giggled at the cartoon stars that appeared above our heads. Oh! How we loved the breathless violence we could evince from our common enemy.

I thought about the limp bodies nestled in the ground, about going back to our room that night, about how each day there was more tinfoil on the wall and more pages of text in Yawnie's alien handwriting. I considered his dry, old-man breathing next to mine—the drugs made him parched, left white spittle at the corners of his lips—and then I felt impossibly tired.

If Yawnie wanted to, he could open his mind to me, he could glean that I knew about the kittens. But I wasn't really worried about that any more; he'd left my mind. Still, I had come to understand that he felt as though people were watching him, recording things. I, who'd always been one-half his intuition, I was *people* now.

Simon stroked a hand over his too-long bangs. "I moved my stuff into your room. You should have your own room now. Mom and Dad agree."

"No, it's okay. He needs me."

"Jim, look at yourself. You're—"

"I'm what?" I pushed Simon's shoulder, hard, wanting him to hit me, pinch me, as he'd spent so much of his life doing. Instead, he took a step back and looked over my head.

"You're not a girl any more," Simon said evenly, as if he were explaining some new kind of invention to me.

"Promise you won't say anything about the cats, Simon. Please. Anything, keep that forty bucks you owe me. The guitar, it's yours."

He stood there blowing smoke into the air, watching me, watching one-half of the bane of his existence begging for more time.

"Okay," he said finally. "But I don't care about the guitar. It's yours, you're the musician."

I stayed with Simon until a heron flew by and we couldn't see anything but the moths killing themselves against the barn light. And that first night, in Simon's room, one nightmare followed another.

I dreamt there was a huge yarn ball filled with barbs of steel rolling all over the barn. It bore down on the high walls, revealing rats and snakes below the floorboards. I dreamt of Yawnie's arm pinned beneath the tractor, the unnatural jaunt of his collarbone breaking up through his chest before the greased tractor heaved over him and nearly cracked him in two.

I dreamt of the bloodied cats. I saw their shredded insides that looked as if the purveyor of their death had been searching for something shiny locked inside their barely formed intestines.

And then I knew what he'd been looking for.

Although Yawnie no longer yielded to my mind he could still penetrate my thoughts. He had discovered my perfidy and was punishing me because, the next morning, when I sent out the small searching satellites to reach him, I found that even the static was gone. He'd dismantled every system of contact, buried the last one, perhaps, in those cats.

* * *

THE DAY BEFORE our eighteenth birthday our parents had a corn roast at the house. It had been a good year, a year of bumper crops and fine Almanac weather. For the first time my parents were flush, flush enough to hire a guy to help Dad, flush enough to buy a new coat of water-resistant stain for the barn. I'd won a province-wide music scholarship and was headed to McGill in two weeks. My parents had also given me money for school. So, in addition to celebrating our late August birthday, it was a send-off, a show-off farmer's party.

Everyone came, the Olsens, my school and music friends, all the neighbours in the fifty-k range. By this time Simon had taken a job as a mechanic one town over and moved out with Jen, a small woman with round apple cheeks who loved Led Zeppelin, children, and Simon, apparently.

Yawnie sat apart from everyone else at the party; he lounged in a flimsy patio chair close to the fence that bordered our land, lighting cigarette after cigarette. His hair was greasy and he glanced around at the fields suspiciously, as if he expected to be attacked by the electrical currents he so feared.

I hauled food out of the house, brought people beer, made punch, and caught up with my friends. I was smiling, dressed in a pink terry-cloth jumper, my hair pulled high in a ponytail. To look at me that day you wouldn't know that my insides were cut up and thrashing like too many eels in a small aquarium.

To see me smiling, hoisting plates of steaming potatoes and pouring ice into coolers, you wouldn't know that I was actually not present at that party. That in my mind I was locked in a room with Yawnie, trying to stare him down as he averted his gaze and twisted bits of wire together out of my broken violin strings. I already had a hundred or so of Yawnie's creations. I couldn't bear to throw them out, even though they smelled like dirty pennies, like blood. They were the only things he made, besides his star mobiles. Dad had even started to hang his stuff in the barn, which had begun to look more like the inside of a city installation gallery than a storage place for grain.

Since he had left my mind, Yawnie had done little except rock, stare, smoke, and write reams of unreadable notes. And, in a week and a half, Yawnie would be sent on a new life adventure: he'd been assessed and accepted as an in-patient at the mental health centre in the city. When our parents told him this, sitting in front of his chair as Simon and I stood in the background, he'd squinted briefly, loped one leg over another, and lit a cigarette. He'd said nothing, as usual. When I tried to talk to him about it, later that night when our parents were asleep, Yawnie handed me a large manuscript.

"How do they expect me to finish my book if I'm in the nuthouse, Jim?"

I flipped through the pages filled with diagrams and small notes.

"Yawnie, this is—"

"What? It's what? So now you're the artistic genius and I'm, what, the wacko? I just need more time," he whispered. "Can you make them understand that?" His eyes filled with white light before they glazed over again.

And it was true, I suppose, that Yawnie watched the race of time instead of moving with it. Maybe he was a writer, maybe we needed his protection, needed him as a witness, a backdrop to our busy little lives.

Later, when The Riots and The Divine Light were at the centre of the local music scene, I met a few writers and realized with an awful pang that they weren't that different from my dishevelled brother. Like Yawnie, they liked to be present, part of a larger social circle, but they also looked forward to retreating inward to think, to write. As a musician who practised at least three hours a day, I should have appreciated that my brother and I still shared something fundamental, a need for isolation.

All he'd needed was time, to sit in his chair in the parlour as he collected metal objects and catalogued the pressing of clouds. He needed us to pretend he wasn't crazy for just a little while longer, so that he in turn could protect us from the electricity, from the unnamed menaces trapped in wire and light.

* * *

DAD HAD HAULED OUT the trampoline from the barn. By the time it got dark the kids were so high from the store-bought angel-food cake that they were all jumping on the trampoline at once to Michael Jackson music. I left Jen there to watch in case one of them vaulted into the sky. She'd been drinking red wine and her dark lips now matched her red cheeks.

I approached the small fire pit where Dad was surrounded by his Legion buddies. They were drinking beer and listening to Mr. Olsen's story about a black bear that had almost sliced off his right arm during a camping trip to Alberta. I'd heard that story over a dozen times and I figured Dad must have too. So when he winked at me with both his blue eyes, I knew I was a welcome distraction. Dad wrapped his arms around my waist, pulled me to him, and I joined the circle of men around the fire. I leaned into the crisp smell of my father as he handed me a can of beer.

As Mr. Olsen droned on, I considered my birthday gifts: a new black velvet concert dress, a charm bracelet with my name on it from Mom and Dad, a fifty-dollar gift certificate for a CD store and a scratched-up record of the Rolling Stones' *Exile on Main Street* from Simon. Jen, who worked in a hair salon to pay for veterinarian school, had offered to cut and style my hair for free.

I thought about how no one—except Simon—had gotten Yawnie anything for his birthday, not because he was unloved, but because it seemed wasteful. Yawnie had no use for things, and our community understood this. Only Simon had bought Yawnie some gifts: needle-nose pliers for his jewellery and mobiles, and a carton of cigarettes.

After Mr. Olsen reached the end of his tale, Dad asked me to play a song.

The men focused their bleary eyes on me. I shook my head.

"Go on," he said, his eyes twinkling. "It's a party in your honour, the least you can do is entertain your guests." Dad was a little tipsy and glowing.

I shrugged. "Okay."

I walked to the house, where Simon and his friend Dan were not so discreetly rolling a joint on the bottom porch step.

"Hey," Simon said, sitting up a little straighter in his motorcycle jacket. Behind me the men's slow talk blended with the children's shrieks. I picked up paper plates and pieces of gnawed corncob from the lawn and headed for the kitchen.

"Want some of this?" Simon asked, offering up the twirled spire of the joint.

"Yeah, hold out for me, if you can."

"Sure thing. Jen'll probably want some, too."

I thought about how, ever since the night Simon had given me his room, almost everything about our dynamic had changed. It seemed so strange to me that Simon had once been personally offended by Yawnie's mental illness because, for the past two years, it was Simon who, after the first couple of weeks of shock, had carried Yawnie up the stairs when he wouldn't move. It was Simon who had the patience to sit next to him, a few hours every day, saying things like, "Are you there? Can you move your arm, buddy? Just move your arm, please, if you can hear me."

In the end, it was Simon, not me, who was the capable, present sibling. Instead of loving my silent brother, I could not pretend to give a shit that his bones were becoming as dry as the pieces of straw Dad trailed inside the house. Instead of coming up with creative new means of reaching inside Yawnie's still mind, I allowed his thoughts to spiral further and further from anything vaguely connected to reality. Ever since Simon showed me the barn cats, I only made sure he took his medicine and kept my distance.

Nobody blamed me, which was the worst part. Nobody saw anything abject about the fact that I had latched onto Simon like a needy dog. In fact, people thought it was good, thought it was healthy and proper that Simon and I had come out of this family crisis together, united by Yawnie's schizophrenia. And they felt sorry for me. He was my twin, after all. They pitied me, they understood that my accomplishments were compensation for the fact that one-half of my self was going rotten in the darkest room of our house.

And they were right.

And their pity made me sick.

Because now I counted on it: their pity, my success. I used every concert, every grade, as a way to supersede expectations. Any opportunity I had I showed the world that I was not locked in the prison of my brother's cradled hands, that I was free. But I wasn't.

Loss had corrupted me. And what my city friends would later call genius or precociousness was neither. It was simply that, by the age of eighteen, I'd logged double the information, lived a duplicated adolescence. I'd been born and I'd died. Twice.

part2winter

12
jim

Itinerary of Phenomena: America

3 vans. 18 shows. 4 guitar players. 2 drummers. 2 bass players. 1 trumpet. 1 French horn. 1 trombone. 1 euphonium. 1 cellist. 4 backup singers (who double as guitarists). 2 leads.

Requires: 6 hotel rooms per night. 2 vans. 1 Canadian flag. 2,754 bottles of water. 3,876 bottles of beer. 76 bottles of wine. 200 sunnyside-up eggs. 9,000 french fries. 15 interviews. 4 press photos. 29 hamburgers. 98 grilled cheeses. 5 photo shoots. 17 sweaters. 3 lumberjack jackets. 9 pairs of glasses (half of them broken). 25 pairs of jeans. 15 working visas. 95 T-shirts. 500 CDs. 20 ounces of pot. 9 novels. 1 Bible. 2 map books. 1 Rhodes. 2 samplers. 1 Triton. 15 guitar pedals. 1 package of birth control pills, sadly mislaid somewhere outside of Jersey. $1,400 worth of gas. 1 sound guy named Harry. 2 keyboards. 3 ounces of coke. 15 bottles of tequila. 1 thumbed copy of Frankenstein. 1 meditation prayer book. 4 cellphones. 1 video camera. 1 French–English dictionary, 1 Spanish–English. 4 bottles of vitamin C and lysine for cold sores. 8 regular cameras and 2 digital. 346 books of matches. 1 rosary. 2 jade Buddhas. 9 mismatched socks. 9 toques. 14 ball caps. 4 cartons of Benson & Hedges. 4 cartons of du Maurier Lights. 14 sets of medium-gauge steel strings. Over 3,500 kilometres. 2 acoustic guitars. 4 oil changes. 3 hash pipes. 7 packs of rolling papers, for Jules, who loses a fresh pack each time he rolls a blunt. 9 skirts. 24 suitcases. 13 tampons, and 1 burnt-out angel lying on the floor of a speeding van.

* * *

I'M NOT SURE what I expected life on the road to be like. I knew it wasn't going to be exactly glamorous, but I had no idea it was so tiring. That it consisted of so much van time and boy farts and nebulous vegetable dip and green-room booze.

After a long day of driving and then sound check there was usually time for walking around. I marked miles through the California hills where nobody walked and where convertibles and SUVs slowed down to see if I was an alien trapped in pedestrian form. I'd wave enthusiastically, like a crazy person, hoping to deter serial killers from stopping to pick me up or, conversely, hoping I wouldn't be reported as one. While the others slept off their hangovers or pursued them, pool- or bar side, I explored.

In New York I walked for hours, from Central Park to SoHo, from SoHo through Chinatown, falling in step among hundreds of bodies, looking at the street vendors' wares of pretty, useless things I couldn't afford or use. With my generous per diem, I bought yogurt, fruit, Winstons, and Rolling Rock beer. I ate and drank my purchases out of brown paper bags as I wandered. Of course, being eighteen, I couldn't buy my own beer, so I enlisted Rize or Kellogg for the task.

Everything in America seemed bigger, louder, more dangerous, and yet more bureaucratic. The food was richer, more ersatz, but the tobacco and beer tasted weaker. *Canada has its priorities straight,* I thought, draining a can of Rolling Rock and dropping it in the trash in Brooklyn. A handsome black man, with freckles and dreads, stared at me as I cracked a fresh beer and continued my pace. I gave him a thumbs-up. He bolted down the sidewalk.

I continually patted my pockets to make sure my passport and driver's licence were there. America seemed built on a checkpoint system that required I had my paperwork on hand at all times. I needed my papers to get my backstage pass and cigarettes. I needed them in case we were stopped, which we routinely were, on the highway. I needed them to get into clubs, where I was often denied entrance for being underage. The others felt bad. "Do you know who we *are*?" Kellogg would demand, stepping up to the three-hundred-pound doorman, using his rock 'n' roll royalty card to get me in. "We just played *the Bowery*."

"It's okay, K," I'd say, tugging on his jean jacket, "I'll just take a cab to the hotel."

I could see Margo, Jules, and Rize giving me sorry looks as my yellow cab pulled away. But secretly I was relieved. There was something comforting about being let off the hook, about not having to socialize any further. Besides, I already felt separate from everyone else, not because I was younger but because I felt older, and anyway I liked going back to my room to drink weak beer and watch cable.

Playing wasn't lame, though. Over the phone Isaac would often wonder, loudly and obnoxiously, why I did what I did when I complained about it all the time. In turn, I'd get frustrated with him. Poor Isaac. It seemed so obvious to me, like asking why writers wrote when it made them all lonely and suicidal. Or why painters put up with losing a million brain cells from the fumes just so their life's work could be undervalued by rich people who matched their paintings to their furniture.

Besides the fact that touring is really the only time the money rolls in consistently, it's an addictive lifestyle. Once they're back home a lot of musicians get all tweaked out by the everyday routine: they yell at their girlfriends when asked to take out the garbage because they're so used to being admired and applauded every night, they forget that life is mostly made up of the mundane. Some pack a small bag, clench their jaw, prepare to be sleep- and vitamin-deprived; they swear to keep themselves together and treat it like a regular job. I think I fall into this second category: not averse to the road, but not nuts about it either.

Still, those two hours every night made up for the excruciating drives, the bad food and beer, not to mention the distinct brand of American paranoia. Those hours compensated us for the arguments, headaches, and fatigue we endured during the days. At the beginning of success those two hours were enough to make it through the other twenty-two.

On this particular tour, one of the best things was watching the scale of the crowds get bigger with every show. I don't know exactly what Kellogg was doing to create a fan base, but with every city we toured we'd collect more and more bodies until the back rooms turned into main stages and the main stages turned into halls. People loved the music, but they also loved the idea of us: twenty or so musicians onstage all sleeping and fighting and playing together. We cut a romantic image, I suppose, for outsiders.

But inside it was different. For one thing, Margo and Jules fought like the animals they were. Even though I was apparently part boy and part genius, those two scared the shit out of me. I feared them more than broken backstage glass, Kellogg's scabby old track marks, and Isaac's disapproval. There's no question their dynamic was destructive—the push and pull of their onstage fights was part show, but mostly it was the public manifestation of the continual brutal lover's tug of war they lived, day in and day out. By my third Riots show I'd figured out the rules of engagement: an earring spat into a bad indie haircut was punishment for Margo's earlier flirtation with the bartender; Margo's quick left hook to Jules's actor's chin was retribution for his neglecting to salvage the last bottle of red wine from the rider the night before. It was exciting and unnerving to watch the two of them tumbling onstage, night after night, pulling each other's hair, flushing their wedding rings down the toilet, and then crying together all night in the locked van.

One night, high above the stage in the green room, I watched the band from behind a peeled-off piece of green Plexiglas, pretending I wasn't part of it. I wanted that feeling when you have a new haircut and catch a glimpse of your unrecognizable self in a store window; I wanted to get it, to see us as others did, as this big, functioning, sustainable entity, because all I could see sometimes were the seams ripping apart.

Underneath the red and white lights the silver in the kit shone like mercury, the brass in the horns was almost blinding. In an instant the group inhaled together and then transformed into a beast, half human, half technology, and the keening wall of guitars and drums dragged the audience to a sacred place where nothing mattered except this fever pitch.

I understood Kellogg's accomplishment then: he'd created an all-star band. Plus, what a cast of miscreants! The kids ate up his own drunken, Vegas-meets-Buddhist stage banter as if he were Jim Jones. Besides the Margo and Jules domestic circus, they loved Rize, who wended around the stage like a tranquilized horse, proving he could delay his overdose by cranking out horn lines that would move even the deaf.

Kellogg looked up at that moment and caught my eye. He winked as if to say *Check it out. I promised you this, didn't I?* Yes. He had. But I couldn't help thinking about how, for all his meditation and self-proclaimed solitude, Kellogg needed an entourage for the simplest private affairs, from buying underwear to taking a bath. When I picture him he's always surrounded by others asking him for something: money, advice, or both. Even if somehow, miraculously, everyone from this closed-circle entourage evaporated, Kellogg would still be surrounded by fans, journalists, or new friends made earlier that day at the bar. You could never have a coffee or lunch with just Kellogg unless you specifically made an appointment and gave him a concrete reason; hanging out with Kellogg always turned into a big social affair.

A second later the song ended, the lights went blue, and the band dissipated into a bunch of tired, burnt-out individuals. They were no longer one massive Hydra, they had their own bodies and instruments and problems. Later, when I'd been shuttled home in my cab, alone again, I sat on my bed drinking from the bottle of Jim Beam Kellogg had given me. He was always buying us things. I suddenly felt very worried about Kellogg and how he could maintain this, this—I didn't even know what to call it any more. All I knew was that I felt an acute uneasiness, my own and Kellogg's. I couldn't explain it. I was afraid of his being afraid. I was afraid of what he might do when he got to think for a minute, when his inevitably human, un-Zen self took over. The band was no longer just a bunch of *flâneurs* romping around Mile End, killing time.

A strange, sacrilegious thought formed in my head: he wasn't a Buddhist at all. He was just mouthing the words. He was collecting us, using us. I drank and paced and smoked and tried to reason with myself: Kellogg wasn't evil, I was just paranoid. He was generous, his charisma had built our careers, and I'd be an idiot to pull away. But the same question rolled around in my head until I was forced to answer it.

"What does he want?" I asked my empty hotel room.

He wants success, I thought, my pulse quickening. *He wants Jules under his right thumb and Rize on top of his hand. He wants Margo so drunk and desperate that she keeps singing in that soulless, sugary way. He wants the best-looking indie kids in the front row, three different kinds of tequila backstage, and rails until morning.* And he wanted us to love him even as he ordered us around, criticized our playing, cut our paycheques, built and unravelled our lives. He always had to be the good guy.

The next morning I got woken up by the phone. It was Kellogg; he sounded psychotically happy.

"Jim, it's me. Listen, it's official: I'm going to start a label. The Riots and Divine Light are, of course, a big part of this."

"How much coke have you done?" I asked, taking a quick hit from the bourbon for courage, for patience.

"Aren't you going to thank me?"

"Uh huh," I said, choking back the burn of the whiskey. "Thanks a lot."

13
rize

Margo is giving Rize a bath. She has poured one of those miniature hotel shampoo bottles into his burgeoning tub. Slowly the warm water covers his legs.

"Show me again," Rize whispers, barely able to hold his head up. The room fills with water; he sees flashes of magenta. Goldfish! He can't remember the last time he saw goldfish, maybe in the artificial pond inside June's favourite Chinese restaurant.

"Show you what?" Margo giggles, trying to pull herself up to the sink.

"Your feets!"

"Feets!" Margo shrieks.

It's been this way for hours: Margo and Rize's nod morphing into a game of who can be more outrageous, who can drink more Aqua Velva mixed with Jim Beam—"A new cocktail! Bleamy!"—who can eat more soap and blow bigger bubbles out of his or her nose.

Rize has the occasional flash of why sitting naked in a bathtub, high, with Margo, for four hours straight, might be a bad idea, but then he remembers he can catch goldfish in his mouth and ducks under for another mouthful.

When he surfaces Margo draws a curly trail of whiskers on his face, then sits on the bath mat and holds her feet up to him. "See!" She has written his name on the bottom of one and CANADA on the other.

"Remember Canada, Rize? Remember Quebec?"

They have been speaking of the homeland. Of poutine, and how the French say *la la* ("It's there!"), and cops that mostly leave you alone, and bars open till three, and their beds, and how this is almost the last night. How they will sleep with their bodies cloistered next to their respective lovers and watch movies and eat good food and not feel tired or strung-out or unlaundered—for a while anyway, until the next tour. They'll set things right in Canada and be friends forever but, okay, just this night, before redemption. Because, look, there's one last line, one last tie-up, one last glug of Bleamy, one last everything—before America spits them out and back to the homeland where no one gives a shit about The Riots.

Underwater it's at least quiet and there Rize gets the chance to catch his breath with Margo. Lately he's been unable to assemble his memories and fantasies correctly. He looks into the eyes of a pop-eyed fish, who looks back at him plangently. He comes to the crest of a bubble-wave, grabs her arm.

"Margo!"

"What?"

"This is fucking awful. We can't—"

Margo's eyes expand as the pounding on the door increases.

And this is how Jules, hotel security, and the band find them: Margo, skirt up, ass flat on the floor, face streaked with makeup; Rize, naked in the bath.

"Lovely scene," Jules says, crossing his arms with a rigid kind of calm.

Rize fixates on Margo's mouth. Jules's calm lasts exactly two and a half seconds and then Jules is on top of him and Jim's on top of Jules, trying to harness them both with her unnaturally long arms. He thinks of Margo's private, deranged mouth again, but it doesn't help.

Underwater, Jules pounds his head against the bathtub, while above him the 250-pound security guard pulls Jim and Jules off the bathtub pileup. Amid all this, he swallows the last goldfish. It swims away down his throat, taking with it a flashing bit of gold metal.

* * *

SHE SITS ACROSS FROM HIM in a busy café that serves terrible pastries but good coffee. She's wearing a purple chiffon scarf to cover the hickeys Jules gave her two nights ago, before the bathtub incident. *An interesting choice,* Rize thinks, critically. He considers telling her that purple is an unflattering shade but then stops himself.

A stolen moment, the two of them alone: Jules is out with Kellogg, buying music gear and getting coke, while Jim's out with the rest of the boys in a Brooklyn arcade. No one knows they're together: everyone believes Rize to be sleeping off the last of his nod, and Margo has fabricated a mani-pedi appointment.

The scene has the ominous quality of a final encounter that's compounded by Margo's nervousness, the slatted midmorning light, and the rude waitress who eyes them while she pops her fruity gum. Rize focuses on the strained lure of Margo's eyes. Buzzed from two cups of coffee and exhaustion, he bursts out:

"So, there's going to be a video?"

"Who told you about the video?"

"Kellogg."

Margo straightens her scarf, wipes her mouth, and picks a fleck of polish off her cracked nails, then says slowly, "You want to talk about the video, now, Rize? Is that it?" She peers at him, pale under her makeup. Though the two look nothing alike, she suddenly reminds him of Kit. Margo has learned to pitch her voice in the same high, accusing way as Kit does. Or is it Kit who's learned this from Margo?

"In case you didn't notice, I have been under lock and key for the past twelve hours being interrogated by my husband."

He thinks about how Kit once told him that love and hate were separated by only a corrugated piece of tin. It's cheesy, but he can't stop thinking about how she said that. Then he's accosted by the memory of Jules stomping a mic to a pulp of metal wires three nights ago. Jules has not said a word to him since he almost mulched his brains to the bottom of the bathtub. Rize, too, has been secreted in private chambers—*private* being a relative term for sharing a room with Kellogg, who dealt with Rize by throwing him into a freezing shower, whistling low, and calling him a lying sack of shit. Margo reaches over to Rize and tucks his long bangs behind his ears.

"You're sweating, you need a haircut. You look like a member of Sloan, dear."

"I'm scared of what you're going to tell me."

"Don't be, everything's fine. I told him we got a little crazy with the drugs, that's all."

"We did. That's exactly what happened."

"Rize, have you seen my wedding ring?" Margo says as she tugs a bloody hangnail off her thumb.

He feels as if his mouth has been stung by a dozen bees. They throb in his throat with malice.

"I have no idea where it is, and you know all about Jules and his symbolism and stuff, I don't have to tell you."

"That night, I—"

"Look, you and I, but especially you, are on probation here, I'm serious, Rize. I am in the doghouse, and so are you when Kit gets wind of this. So, if you have any idea where my ring is you—"

Rize clears his throat as the bees seize up, one by one. They shake furiously in his esophagus.

How did this get turned around?

He digs into the cardigan Kellogg gave him and tosses her wedding band onto her coffee-pooled saucer. They both stare at it.

"Where?"

Rize waves his hands at her. "You don't want to know." In Kellogg's room, at six a.m., after standing by the bathroom sink feeling the last of the junk wash through him, he vomited red hibiscus, blue Aqua Velva, and, finally, the wedding band.

"How did I suddenly become the asshole in all this?" he asks himself loudly.

Margo shrugs. The vague thought that she is a sociopath floats across his mind as he taps his hands together.

"Margo, say something. You agree that this has to end, right?"

Another dead silence in which she sneers over his shoulder at some invisible enemy. "Listen up," she says with a burst of energy, "you're going back to Montreal while we shoot this video. You, the blond kid, and Kellogg can arrange the launch. That's what we've decided."

"We? As in the royal you-we, or as in Royal Jules, king-of-the-drama-queens we?"

A slant of sun descends on Margo; she winces before turning toward it. She looks at Rize with light dancing off her retina.

"Don't you think that, after our little spectacle last night, Jules has the right to do just about whatever he wants? Including kick your ass out? Can you stop thinking about yourself, and whether or not you're an asshole, for just one minute, and think about what it might take to win back his trust?"

He tries to think of the last time he had a conversation with a woman other than Margo and summons a yelling phone conversation with Kit, almost three weeks ago, on a club owner's phone.

Margo's got her game face on now; she snarls openly at the waitress. Rize is abruptly transported to one of Kit's monologues. She's smoking in bed, wearing men's pyjamas, her long legs entwined.

"Trouble. I mean, I love the girl to death, she's my best friend, but god, Rize, have you noticed? Every time something breaks, or catches fire, physically or metaphorically, Margo's always at the centre of the action."

Indeed, that same week Margo had dented the van's rear bumper, caused a fire in the rehearsal space, and broken a pair of Jules's dead mother's gold earrings.

Though similar in voice and gesture, as best friends tend to be, Kit and Margo are also polarized. As surely as Margo can be found at the centre of a show or party, immersed in some argument, Kit will just as likely be hanging back, smoking moodily, watching Margo with one wary eye to make sure she doesn't break too many beer bottles or lose her wallet.

He feels a pang for Kit, misses her sturdy sorrow, her slighted confidence. He wishes she were here right now to dismiss the whole lot of them with one raised eyebrow and a plume of smoke. The very idea of her existence makes his cheeks burn with shame.

Then he considers how he and Margo have lived like brother and sister for so long that he can barely even see her. They've become so close, physically and emotionally, that he doesn't even understand her role in his heart any more. They've shared van floors, cooked eggs together in dingy motel kitchenettes, hounded crusty clubs for water bottles and ashtrays. All at once he feels ashamed for being one of the reasons Margo looks plump and harassed, her face too shiny, hands too shaky, her pink-mauve lipstick bleeding off her lips.

And he feels ashamed for falling for it, for her. He's embarrassed by his love, his hate, his powerlessness over this moment. Because he knows that, asshole or not, he's in the middle of Margo's latest mess and he has to follow whatever she tells him to do.

"I'm sorry, you're right," he says, experimentally.

"We're not bad people, Rize, we just did a bad thing."

She waits for him to agree while he fights the impulse to slap her face. Then Margo transforms into what Jules calls her Queen-Bee-interview-mode, and as she slips her wedding band back onto her finger he sees that she's neither his sister nor his lover. For a moment, he sees it clearly: she's his ruin.

* * *

DISINGENUOUS.

Kellogg drives through the New York City snowstorm while Rize bastes his cracked lips with Vaseline and Jim sits in the backseat listening to her new iPod, kicking the back of Rize's seat at regular intervals with her rangy legs.

"What are you? A fucking teenaged girl?" Rize snaps, biliously, turning around and almost smacking her on the side of the head like a stooge.

"Um, yeah, I am, actually," she replies, unflinching, before she sinks back into her seat and disappears into herself for the next twelve hours. Rize shivers and backs off, the ice in her pupils colder than whatever threat is outside. *That girl,* he thinks, *is not afraid of anything.*

"Now, children, we have a long ride home so let's not start, shall we?" Kellogg says in his most queenly voice.

To calm Rize, Kellogg begins to talk about the work he'll be doing in the next two weeks for the new label. But Rize already misses Jules's sinuses, Margo's early-morning, pre-coffee insults. A cuff on the head from Jules and an unmanicured finger on his arm from Margo have left him feeling traded, like a second-string defence player.

Rize inspects Kellogg, who's wearing a too-small green sweater vest. His friend is a slightly horsy-faced young man with long girlish lashes and blue periwinkle eyes who likes to look at people too long, until he detects a slight discomfort in his subject. This subject, lately, is Rize. "Are you okay, man, you sure? You need anything?"

The antidote to Jules's friendship is Kellogg's, Rize thinks. Sort of. His tall, charming friend speaks as if everything he says is an accident; his soft voice turns upward, like a question. But if Rize separates the sound from the content, he finds Kellogg's voice is disharmonious, often at odds with what he's expressing.

"Between the goddamn holes in your arms and the ones in your face you look like a leper," he informs Rize, enunciating every syllable as if he's quoting Shakespeare. It strikes Rize that, actually, Jules and Kellogg are quite similar in their painful, ass-biting honesty. Only Kellogg is more solicitous, is able to disguise his awful revelations with his nice voice. Also, he's a good listener and has an ability to anticipate what you're about to say. He plays drums the same way, listening acutely and aware of every sound around him.

His drumming, like the swabbed, desperate sound of long-ago fucking in a car; his dry, quiet insistence that he will not tolerate Rize doing any heavy drug, save cocaine; and his periwinkle eyes all convince Rize that Kellogg will do everything he predicts. Kellogg will launch Autumn Records, manage both The Angel Riots and Divine Light, as well as get the three of them across the border and back to Montreal in a literal and metaphorical snowstorm. He's already whipped up enough hype around the bands to create a full-scale American invasion. Kellogg has put bodies into clubs, packed more asses into more seats than any promoter or manager ever could. Hasn't he?

He has.

Rize smacks his sore lips and removes Kellogg's scarf for him in the slowly warming car.

"Jules despises me. He doesn't want me in the video."

"Are you worried about the video? There's much more at stake here. First—and this is something I've been meaning to discuss with you—the music industry is sorely lacking loving-kindness."

"But this isn't the music industry, this is Jules."

Kellogg puts a wonky cigarette in his mouth and wiggles his eyebrows, the indication for Rize to give him a light. Rize lights it, then opens his passenger window to let a cold blast of air in.

"You know, I take your side, usually, in all this band stuff, but it's disingenuous of you to say that about Jules, man," Kellogg says, sliding his eyes toward Rize, who pulls his toque down. Kellogg grates the stick into fifth.

"What do you mean?"

"Quit being an idiot. What do you think I mean?"

"Are you referring to the bathtub scene?"

"Yes, Rize, I am referring to the night before last when you and Margo decided to sail away in a bathtub and security had to pull you, half-naked, off her. What's wrong with you?"

Rize frames his hands around his face as if the accusation will merely bounce off the force field of his flesh.

"So, pardon me for informing you that this is not about any video. As if you didn't know. He's had Margo's full Christian name tattooed to his *spine* since he was eighteen. They are married! He's your best—"

"I know! I know!"

There's a binding silence in the car as Rize curls his hands into fists and presses them into his eyes. Till he sees orange psychedelic blobs clinging to his corneas. He can hear Jim singing along to a Fleetwood Mac song in her tiny baby voice, can feel her sneaker jammed into the centre of his spine, offering a kind of support. He feels bad, suddenly, for losing his temper with her. His throat clutches up at the thought that he's alienated his last ally.

Kellogg taps his cigarette into the ashtray and touches Rize's knee.

"Look, buddy, all I'm saying is boundaries. Okay? And it's not just you, it's all of us. All of us tangled up in this, this thing, this band, ach. So messy. So it's important to stay intact. This will blow over, I mean it's not like anything happened, right?"

"Right."

"Give those two some time to reconnect. See your old lady when you're in town."

"If I have one."

"Of course you have one, and you'll be busy. You're going to help me put together this band of egoless guitar freaks, a brass section, some beautiful, rotten, revolutionary Riots fare. All of us officially making music together. It'll be fun. What say you?"

"It's not very revolutionary at all, it's fucking exhausting, dude, and I don't know where you think you're going to find an egoless guitarist, or an egoless anyone—not everyone's into your dharma loving-kindness vibe."

Kellogg pulls himself closer to the wheel. The snow is coming down heavier now. He slows the car, and it wobbles slightly as he turns onto the highway that takes them due north. Rize grasps the armrest between them and tries to steady the car with his weight while Kellogg sings "American Woman" in his gentle, twangy voice.

"But you're into my vibe, right? You're feeling me with this collective, am I right?"

"Sure, K, sure I am."

"And you trust me as your manager, right?" Kellogg turns to look at Rize as the white highway curls under them.

"I am feeling you," Rize says, in order to get his friend's eyes off him and back on the road.

"Because I can get you any horn player you want to work with, any guitar prick, any drummer."

"Ah, come on, you're the shit-hottest drummer in town."

Rize knows Kellogg's bravado is only half-serious, that Kellogg is the only Buddhist rock star who cares not at all that he has the keys to the city. Knowing that K uses this angle with him only when he truly wants something, he acquiesces. "Okay."

"Good. So, when we get back, you're going to—"

"Oh my god, K. Will you please, please, please stop telling me what to do? I got it from Margo this morning. I'll be good. Okay? I get it. I fucking get it: no H, no Margo, watch boundaries. Shut up and play, Rize."

"And take something for those cold sores, dude, your whole head looks infected."

* * *

INSIDE KIT'S APARTMENT, dust bunnies collect on the hardwood floors like tumbleweeds and it still smells faintly of a curry dinner they had in November. Rize tosses his leather bag and his horn on her bed and heads straight to the refrigerator. After dropping a very tired and grumpy Jim off at her dismal-looking apartment, a long hug from Kellogg, and much emoting and talk, Rize is overwhelmed by the task before him. He can think only of a King can he left at Kit's months before.

Hallelujah, rejoice, it's there! Rize cracks it and gulps until he begins to cough. He looks around her kitchen, decorated with hanging spider plants and purple wandering Jews, she'd called them. She taught him the word for Jew in French: *Juif.* They hang about him in tentacles of longing. He holds one up to his face and smells: nothing. *Purple is the smell of nothing.* He examines the bare bulb reflecting off the blue tiled walls, the dishes neatly stacked on a chrome drainer.

This is the chapter called "Kit and All the Beautiful Things You Left Behind," he thinks, tapping his fingers along the counter.

Like me. It's your fault, Kit, you shouldn't leave me. You should have protected me, like you promised, from the shitty people. From myself.

He turns another light on and inspects the tiny pen drawings of each queen in a playing-card deck and a framed photograph of Edgar Allan Poe. Kit's tastes: austere, with a hint of gothic and romantic sensibility. He sips his beer and studies a small black-ink sketch of a long-limbed woman, elfin but sensual, like Kit.

He traces his finger over the dusty frame of her graduation picture from the RCMP academy. Smiling a little smugly, she's wearing those ridiculous jodhpurs, along with the broad-brimmed hat and the red jacket tailored down her waist. Behind her, the Canadian flag looks limp and out of focus. He stares at her determined, almost defiant smile, and kisses the top of her hat.

Come back. I know I'm the asshole, but please, come back. I'll make it right.

In her room, on the low futon bed, he notices there isn't the usual collection of clothes and papers on the floor. The red bedspread is unrumpled and pulled tight. After ten hours of keeping his eyes open and snorting up all the coke before arriving at the border, he feels a sharp pain in his nasal cavity. And oh, all the cocaine plans that he and Kellogg have made! To overtake the music industry with a set of slick, giant indie hits.

To raise Divine Light out of the incestuous local scene and completely integrate them with The Riots, to undermine Starbucks and McDonald's in the process, to stay mentally balanced. *Intact.*

So, he crawls, after one last sip from his beer, at exactly 9:41 a.m., according to Kit's digital clock, under her cool, scentless sheets. He feels the drugs rattle off his skull as he chomps at the edgeless pain in his head. He feels his guilty angel heart and then, pulling her favourite black blazer over his eyes, he sinks into sleep, and feels nothing at all.

* * *

WHY AM I doing this, again?

Without an immediate present, he dreams of the past: Kit in a black dress with a white rose in her hair waiting for him to get paid in the green room. Kicking her heels together like an Oz-bound Dorothy, her grey eyes roll heavenward. She announces her displeasure at the wait.

"Just one more minute, Kit, they're counting the door. Wanna beer?" He hands her a Stella and she grabs a fistful of Margo's hair and puts it into her mouth. Margo laughs, and the two go hand in hand out to the fire escape while he, Jules, and Kellogg load the van.

Later, in the cold street, with the wind seeping through their leather coats, Kit steals his cigarette and puffs on it thoughtfully.

"What do you call it?"

"What? The show?"

"The music, Rize."

He shrugs, holsters his guitar on one side, hands Kit his trombone, and snatches his cigarette back. He kisses the edge of her lip as if he is catching a word slipping out.

"Art-rock, porn-pop, ambient-indie."

"That's what the papers call it, but I want to know what you think it is."

Rize smiles. Kit's drunk, weaving slightly; he slips his arm through hers to balance out her step.

"Shouldn't you be out in Ville St-Laurent, catching crooks or something?"

"Now, now, be nice."

"No, seriously, I dunno, it starts and then all I know is that I'm in the middle of it."

Inside his dream he starts to float while Kit claps her gloved hands and giggles—then the phone, the exigent wail of a car alarm blaring into the street. Rize reels up. "Hello?"

"Glad you're up, asswipe."

In between sleep and arousal, Rize wonders why, for the millionth time, he cannot let a ringing phone alone, even though he knows it's only Jules. He suspects he must secretly believe someone is trying to call to tell him that he's dying from a long-term wasting disease.

"I spoke to Kellogg and, listen, Rize, if you think you're going to go to the Metro today to jam with that homeless guy for sandwiches and smokes, let me tell you something—"

"Jules."

"Yeah, man."

"I'm sorry."

Rize can hear his friend sucking at his ever-present joint and looks at the clock: 11:40 a.m. It's early, even for Jules's self-medication.

"Did you hear what I said? I said I was sorry. Like, if you think about it, the word 'sorry' comes from sorrow and that's how I feel. I'm sorrow."

"Spare me the etymological lecture, you dumb ass. For god's sake, it's not even noon yet and you're giving me a migraine."

A very long pause in which Rize bites his cracked mouth and winces. "Besides, I'm curious about what, exactly, you're sorry for."

"How's Margo?" Rize asks, hoping the weed and question will distract Jules.

"Don't start with me now," Jules says, his voice detached. "I have business to discuss with you at this precise moment, and I can't get into this other shit. I'm just calling to tell you that you have to get some equipment, hook up with K, and set some dates up."

"So, how's New York?"

"Expensive. Boring. I just need you to act like a real musician and a normal human being for a change. Think you can handle that?"

"Yeah," he says, sulking.

"Good. There's some money coming down the pipe, some old publishing money came through, Kellogg will give it to you. Plus, we made a ton of cash on U.S. merch."

"Really?" Rize is awake suddenly.

"Yeah, really."

Rize looks into the sunny parking lot, devoid of action save for one blue Chrysler. He ducks under the window.

"I gots to go, man, I think I'm being stalked. Hey, what's the date today?"

"December twenty-second," Jules says, lighting something else on fire.

"I think it's my mom's birthday today," Rize says into the dial tone.

* * *

"DIDN'T YOU FEEL ANYTHING?" Kit had asked him, in real life, in the street behind the club, bringing him down to earth. She was examining his bloody hands and lips in the orange alley light, clotting his mouth with pads of Kleenex. It was then that he felt the phantom grooves of the strings cutting into the tips of his fingers, the taste of brass, of poison, in his mouth. His fingers had been calloused, numbed since playing some kind of string instrument since age thirteen, so none of it made sense. Odd that, a sort of dubious miracle, all that blood pouring out of his hands. He'd felt like one of those ceramic Virgin Mary statues, leaking vermilion tears, and he wouldn't have even noticed without Kit there.

Later, in the hospital, he'll learn his blood produces dangerously high amounts of iron, that his steady diet of red meat and booze is actually the worst thing for this condition. Yet another gift from Clay's genes, along with the streaks of paranoia, perfect pitch, and a penchant for junk.

He winced from the cold, the contact, as she wiped his mouth and fingers clean. Then she tucked his left hand into her coat pocket.

"I know you are so rock 'n' roll, but tell me, can you feel anything?" she'd begged, dropping the bloodied wads of tissue onto the white snow. "Can't you feel yourself bleeding? Even with that sheet of steel wound so tight round your heart?"

* * *

RIZE THINKS ABOUT that conversation with Kit for some time afterward, about how to describe the music, if he were ever in a position to talk about it. Only Kit asks him questions about what he thinks, so he doesn't have to worry. Still, he has no idea what he'd say. Even with all the clippings rolling in, even with the abstractions in the music magazines that contain phrases like "serendipitous shamble" and "Canadian obscurantism," he finds it brings him no closer to any solid definition. Articles like that, that are supposed to be reviews of something he knows as intimately as his own body, actually just give him a headache and make him feel as if he has a learning disability.

Anthemic. Feedback rock. Jam-band cacophony with a hefty dose of messy mystique. Or else, in plain English, Kellogg's blurred lyrics simmering alongside military-style horn solos. All Rize understands is that only when he plays does he feel in sync with anything happening in the whole world; it's the only time his life makes sense.

He doesn't know what kind of words to put around that feeling, just that people like to see them playing together as much as they like putting words on top of it. And now all those words piled up on top of each other in stacked newspapers have changed them.

But Rize recognizes that when Kellogg started to take an interest in managing them, everyone else got interested too. Rize knows only that something clicked for Kellogg, with The

Riots, when he shared a room in New York with him and Jules. Rize had made an A with his legs, one foot on each of their twin beds. Wearing a faded pair of Corona boxers, he'd started playing Jules's trumpet over his friends' heads while they lay in bed passing a joint between them.

They watched Rize as he came back, again and again, to an old Chet line. As he improvised around it he saw their stoned eyes widen; he saw their surprise that there was such sound in him. As he set his horn into the rim of his mouth, something defiant and bold rose in quiet, dull Rize, with the too-small nose and inelegant hands.

Elbows out, he'd dropped the trumpet and snatched the trombone from the dresser, his own true instrument. He flexed his arm and continued, pulling the sound out of the tarnished brass in a yawning segue of need. Mesmerized, his friends watched as Rize's spit dripped on their toes. He tightened his own toes, purchasing himself on the mattress, and continued. It was the first time he played for Kellogg, really played, what he could never hear in the world or come close to naming. When he thinks about it now, he realizes he was showing them his real self. His shattered collection of disappointments lined themselves up like baby ducks in those notes. They contained everything he wanted to express, and nothing he could say: the dirge, the waste, the triumph, and the playfulness of his life. His own silly sense of humour that could never quite come across with someone as witty and wry as Jules around all the time.

He remembers when he stopped and looked at them, how something slid into place, aligned itself.

"That's Chet, right?" Kellogg had asked, his long fingers dropping over his eyes for a moment. He saw Kellogg calculating how he could take this wayward tempo in Rize, capitalize on the wet breath and the endless hope in his lungs.

"Sure," Rize shrugged, tucking a cigarette into his mouth and taking a seat at Jules's feet on the bed.

The gulf of his talent opened wide, gave him a momentary distance from the two. It closed, of course, when Jules bounced a hotel ashtray off his head. But he knows that was the beginning of Kellogg's plan. That he looked for that same desperate talent in everyone who would eventually be invited into the band. Also, after that, Kellogg started getting really organized about shows and plans and Jules stopped shoving any old instrument at him like he was a monkey. Sure, they sabotaged his guitar, but they also put him in charge of organizing a horn section, scoring parts and arrangements. Of course, he knows there were other important components: Jules's lyrics, his aggro-charming stage presence, Kellogg's pace-maker drumming and smooth management, Margo's ghosted voice, not to mention the air-tight orchestra run like a German car factory.

So to him, sometimes it sounds like the end of the world, the music. And the beginning of his life. Because for some reason everybody now believes he is no longer a nobody. Almost everybody, except Rize.

* * *

ONE METRO RIDE and two buses later, Rize arrives at June's place in Verdun. The tulips and chocolates he bought, costing him a third of the American hundred Kellogg shoved in his pocket, are near-frozen. In the lobby, while waiting to be buzzed in, he breathes on the petal of a white tulip, trying to revive it.

Instead it goes transparent and hangs off the side of the stem like blistered skin. Half an hour late, freezing in his thin leather jacket, he walks into what appears to be a Tahiti-inspired Christmas nightmare.

His mom has the living room decorated tiki style, with Christmas lights hanging over the fake fireplace. Ted, his mom's husband, who is completely bald and somehow too tall in the low-ceilinged room, takes his jacket and hands Rize a lei.

"Hullo, Rize."

"Aloha. Thanks, Ted. Sorry I'm late."

June rushes in, wearing a red frilly apron covered with a holly design. She places a casserole dish on the table and, upon seeing Rize, puts her hands together, Egyptian style, to assess her freezing-cold son.

"Hi, Mummy." He kisses her cheeks and hugs her; the smell of roasted meat and chamomile fills his face.

"Sweetie." She holds his head for a minute and looks at his eyes, checking if he's high. June thinks he and his friends are always high on marijuana, like it's the sixties and everyone's running around with flower wreaths on their head, stoned to the gills. He breathes his nicotine breath on her and hands her the flowers.

"Happy birthday," he says, pulling away and picking up a piña colada in a coconut. She laughs, folds the bouquet into her arms. Ted begins chewing the tip of an almond in a way that is vaguely annoying. On the mantelpiece, he notices about five postcards he'd forgotten he'd sent her from the road.

The small image of a palm tree on one of the cards in the middle of her tropical paradise ignites an insufferable sadness in him. At the end of the row of cards is a school photograph of

Rize wearing a white cowboy shirt and a blue bandana. His nose is plastered with a Band-Aid and there's a large scratch on his chin. Why June chose to display this particular photo eludes him. He remembers falling that day, in his white cowboy boots, in grade seven, exactly twenty minutes before the photo was taken. And how, that time, it was Jules who took Rize to the nurse's station. He even remembers what Jules was wearing: a blue velvet bowtie with a matching vest and frilled white shirt, as if he'd just touched down from Vegas.

"Some storm, eh?"

"Yeah."

Rize can hear the sound of Ted's toenails scratching the inside of his polyester blend socks as his stepdad walks across the room.

"You might have to stay here, honey, if the snow keeps up," June says, hopefully.

"Ma, it's Canada, we're used to snow, remember? There's a bus at 10:45, I checked the schedule, I'll take that. Besides, I have a rehearsal tomorrow."

"With Jules?"

"No, with this orchestra thing."

"Orchestra?" Ted pipes in, holding his own coconut cup, which looks like a brown animal-testicle in his huge hands.

"Yeah. We're going to merge with this other band, sort of a rock-orchestra thing, I guess. Plus, we're starting a label." Rize sits down at the table, inspecting the fake poinsettia plant.

"Hey, Ma, do you have any tequila?" She produces a bottle of Sauza and pours him half a glass without comment. "Hey, how come you're cooking on your own birthday? We should've got takeout or something."

His mother stands in the kitchen doorway holding a steaming plate of scalloped potatoes and exchanges a look with Ted.

"Well, technically, sweetie, it was my birthday two days ago."

"Sorry, I was still in the States."

"That's okay, sweetie. Ted took me out to a nice Eyetalian place. We're just glad you could come, with your schedule and everything. I'm just glad we could have some sort of Christmas together."

"What your mother is saying, Rize, is that we're happy to have you for a meal."

Rize examines Ted's narrow, dough-white face, and thinks of his stepdad's long toenails scratching his mother's slim ankles. He wants to tell him that one of the luxuries of being the child of a single mother is that he's never needed a translator for June's emotions or thoughts. He wants to tell Ted that the sole benefit of spending twenty-six years on this planet with only one adult who gives a shit about you is that you're granted the ability to telegraph pain and joy to each other in whatever fashion you wish. You can do this in dreams or in harried, drunken phone calls from anytown USA. You can come home, blitzed out of your mind off a particularly bad tour, and collapse into your mother's bed sobbing and she'll rub your back even though you're twenty-four and supposedly long past the age of such things. But Ted is smiling at him good-naturedly so Rize closes his eyes and thinks about the words *stepfather* and *tequila*.

"Excuse me." Rize goes to the bathroom to blow his nose and inspect his image. Long, jet-black hair, average height, lean but muscled, and decidedly ethnic-looking if only vaguely handsome, he's reassured by the fact that he looks nothing like Ted. He inspects his mouth sores, washes his hands, and hums Bach.

When he returns there are various lumps of steaming white food plus roast beef on his plate. Rize looks at the cheese casserole and scalloped potatoes and watches June and Ted eating quietly, only grunting appreciatively between bites.

He sips his rum-coconut and asks, "Did you make all the food white on purpose?" With a few bites of nourishment in him, he feels better, calmer.

His mom peers at him over her glasses, which, apparently, she needs to wear all the time now. "What'd you mean Rize?" The faint Irish lilt in her slightly drunken voice bolsters Rize.

"Nothing, it's just funny, it's all white."

"It's all very festive," Ted says, pushing the dough-food into his dough lips and smiling, "The lights. The coconuts. We just got a new Gauguin book at the library, your mother was inspired by the art, I guess."

Rize raises his nut in cheers and thinks he could almost like Ted, especially after another drink.

After dinner, he and his mother light up du Mauriers while Ted clears the dishes and puts on a Bee Gees CD.

"Ted got me a stereo for my birthday. Now we can listen to all your music, Rize."

"Sounds good." Rize looks at the second-rate JVC system and nods as "Jive Talkin'" starts in.

"I'm doing a concert in two weeks. I can put you guys on the guest list."

His mom nods and takes a drag on her cigarette. Then she tilts her head and pushes her chair back. "You lot usually start playing at eleven and I have to be at work by nine, I don't know if—"

"Well, whatever, I'm just saying, I'm doing this thing. Jules will be there, I know you like him."

"Of course I like him, he's been like a brother to you," she says, pushing an envelope toward Rize. He peers into it, counts three hundred-dollar bills.

"Geez, Mom."

"S'nothing, s'Christmas." She leans across the table and kisses him full on the lips while Ted stands at the back of his chair, wiping his hands on a dishtowel.

At 10:40, Rize puts on a too-small pair of his mother's leather gloves, a Guatemalan hand-knit scarf—his Christmas present from Ted, who had one "exactly like it" in the sixties. He's holding two yogurt containers full of the white-mess dinner and has a serious tequila buzz on. He stands at the bus stop in the middle of Verdun with snow collecting on his leather collar.

His hands nearly frostbitten, Rize's nose begins to bleed, a remnant from his coke fest with Kellogg.

"Fuck." He folds the Guatemalan scarf over his nose and thinks about how cold Jules's voice was when he hung up on him in the morning. He can't remember the last time Jules hung up on him. Usually Rize hangs up on Jules. Instead of worrying about what Jules knows or doesn't know, Rize decides to concentrate on the fact that one of the things he loves most about his best friend is that at any given time he can reel off at least half a dozen things that are depressing him. The list is always changing and is not to be confused with the list of things he hates—which is also a prolific work-in-progress.

On the last leg of last year's East Coast tour, Rize copied down a partial version of Jules's list. He keeps it in his pocket next to an old condom and a voucher for two-for-one pizza at Mike's, which expired in 1996.

So it goes: music journalists; the president of the United States; pugs; pug owners; Elton John glasses; people who are not British but who use British expressions like "cheers" and "snog"; people who call themselves friends but who wait for you behind a wall and then jump out and scare you and then laugh 'cause they think it's funny; Rize's muscles; Margo's flirting; Kellogg's ability to tune everyone out and eat twenty-five buffalo wings in one sitting; the fact that Rize broke his wrist and then left Montreal after getting suspended from secondary; mouldy avocadoes; the band's old manager, a rich puppeteer from Michigan named Hersh, who has threatened to sue The Riots for the past five years and whom he blames for giving him the lump behind his ear, which he is confident is brain cancer; The Inner-City Zionists (the Montreal band, not the movement); broken glasses; driving in the rain.

Sometimes, like tonight, with a bloody nose and his fingers curled in and almost frostbitten, when he thinks he has finally done it, that he's finally lost his fingers, his only link to making a living, Rize remembers Jules's list and the message from him scrawled on the back, where he misspelled *gather.*

He thinks of the photo Jules has tucked into his bedroom mirror of the two of them nuzzling each other's necks, done in one of those Metro photo booths in the early days of The Riots. When they were just a duo, before Kellogg, and Margo, and Guy, and all the rest.

In the picture they're wearing floppy women's hats and mascara and Rize wonders, while stuffing the scarf further into his nose, how he could have done such a thing to Jules. Who, besides June, is the closest thing he's ever had to family. Who's only ever beaten on Rize with the intimate violence of a brother, and loved him with the fierce, wolflike devotion of a brain-damaged child.

Lets gaether forces.
Lets make our mistakes.

Standing in the snow, with no sign of a coming bus, he tilts his nose up. He feels Ted's gift turn black with blood and then, gradually, he lets it all filter up through his lungs, from his heart to his head. Deep, wretched sobs. He lets them warm his shattered brain.

* * *

JULES CALLS FROM an anti-poverty protest to remind Rize not to say anything stupid to the press in case they make a mistake and phone Rize and not Kellogg. Like a lover who's heartbroken yet cannot bring herself to physically leave her ex, Jules calls Rize out of habit rather than intent. The morning ritual's familiar now: Rize scratches his sleepy morning bum, grinds coffee in Kit's kitchen while he listens to the sound of Jules's amphetamine voice, or his silence, as he flicks on the CBC. The soothing voice of the announcer assures him that, indeed, he is not imagining it, there is a metre and a half of snow on the ground.

He sits in Kit's closet while Jules drones on. This is also a new habit: he likes being near her clothes, he likes looking at her shoes. Some are heeled, some aren't and, wow, a sequinned pair of genie slippers! *How long can this go on? How long can I live like a spirit among your things?* He feels safe, surrounded by these husks of her smell, her dirty laundry.

"They're burning a big picture of the president now," Jules says flatly. Rize hears Jules take a huff off his miniature pipe.

"You know, you better watch that habit of yours over there. They're not as understanding as they are here."

"Don't worry, I'm inconspicuous."

Rize falls back into Kit's laundry, laughing.

"You're about as inconspicuous as VD."

"Listen, Margo's hungry, I got my own anti-poverty brigade here trying to keep her fed." Rize hears Margo asking Jules something in the background, amid the sound of cheers.

"There's, like, four thousand people here."

As Rize knocks a box of tagged items over, Jules's voice cuts out.

He pores through the brand-new objects. They smell guarded, perfumed, like a department store. Gloves, wallets, knee socks, last month's magazines, a jar of pickled garlic, a fat loaf of dried salami, vitamins, sealed makeup . . .

Then, a funny memory of Kit head-down in a department store while Rize sprayed her with perfume. Her arms are clenched against her sides and she's not listening to Rize, who's threatening to charge a green bolero jacket to her Visa. She all but runs out.

How many secrets do we all have?

Oh Kit, Kat, the kleptomaniac.

* * *

ON HIS WAY BACK from the studio with Jim, after a long evening of rehearsal, beer, and the methadone K has procured for him from one of his private health-care contacts, Rize's cracked leather boots narrowly avoid an ice puddle. Near Kit's, there's a raucous street protest. Rize turns on his heel abruptly, in the opposite direction, and knocks a slight squeegee boy into a pile of garbage.

"Oof. Je m'excuse," the boy squeaks as Rize and Jim pick the kid out of the garbage and seat him on the curb.

Cops and paramedics descend on them, firing questions in French. Jim bares her teeth at the cops, which lands them in a 1970s STM bus the police have apparently reserved for this riff-raff sweep.

Rize doesn't fight it. At this point it seems the natural subsequent act: go on tour; accidentally sleep with your best friend's wife; get fucked up on junk; clean your horn; stretch your last five bucks as far as it will go; find the spare key to your girlfriend's place that you stole and copied; take a yoga class with Kellogg; sob for five minutes through a methadone headache every morning; get famous; get drunk and then, oh yeah, get yourself on a bus with several hundred outraged, anti-violence French hippies.

"At least the bus is warm. Ish. Warmish," Jim says, grinning like an idiot doll, ever the ray of sunshine.

Rize looks out at the old city, the impossibly beautiful European-Canadian structure that is nothing much to look at from the river. *Well-hidden,* he thinks, its gothic pillars nearly buried by snow.

Old Montreal is choked between the cold St. Lawrence, Ste-Catherine sex parlours, and Belle Province hamburger joints. At night, when the businesspeople leave, the old city is a tomb. Fat secretaries swish away in their cheap boots, taking their Tupperware and lunch bags away onto buses heading to the South Shore. Young businessmen talk on cells and then get into their Jags to meet their friends in fusion Plateau bistros.

They leave the overpriced cafés and the kitschy, beaded-moccasin window displays for their sprawling suburban homes. They leave it to the homeless, the insane, who have been rejected from the highway missions for being too drunk or high. The ones left behind feel the St. Lawrence wind whip through them; the protective, iconic cherubs and lion faces etched in rock offer no protection. Icy wind sweeps up from the river's bottom, where whales swam once, and mutates the men's fingers and feet into purple lumps of flesh.

Outside there is shouting, plumes of tear-gas smoke, the roar of German shepherds barking.

From his bus-seat view he can see the perfect, cloudless night sky. It's the shade of blue that means it will be freeze-your-snot-to-your-face cold tomorrow. He stares at the clean-shaven, blue-eyed cop before him; they make eye contact. The boy-man is his age, his eyes are tough but manage to say *If I met you anywhere else but here, tonight, who knows, we might be friends.* Rize nods and looks back out the window, relieved that he's left his modest but incriminating stash at home. Jim searches endlessly through her humongous purse for something, ChapStick, he hopes. She finally finds half an orange covered with flakes of tobacco and offers it to him. He shakes his head.

Despite his battered French, the curiosity is overwhelming, so he turns to a pair of hippie girls behind them and asks: *"Cette proteste. C'est pourquoi?"*

He can feel Jim looking at him with a surprised expression.

"La brutalité de la police," the girls reply in unison, giggling.

* * *

LATE AT NIGHT, in Kit's big bed, he imagines his mind is a great boat and he buries the memory deep in its caisson, where no water or feeling or ship-moored rat can scurry over it. He does this because he cannot keep it above board, high up on the horizon, he can't look at it every day, can't live like this any more.

If he locks it away, he reasons, he won't be able to draw upon it; it won't be available to him. He won't see it when he looks at Jules, he won't have it at his disposal when she uncorks a fresh bottle and beckons him to the green room to help her choose an outfit. It won't figure as some part of his living when Kit eventually returns to forgive him—if and when it ever all comes out. Kit, he believes, of all people, with her understanding, tolerance, and sophisticated French views, might just be able to forgive such a transgression. But it won't even be there, he swears, when she returns.

Everyone has secrets. His father had secrets that he packed away, though Clay's were like horses gone wild in the bottom of a ship and, when he was asleep or angry, they'd fall out the bottom of his mind, trying not to drown him.

Margo and Rize didn't kill anyone, after all, unlike his dad, who killed a whole mess of people in Vietnam. But now that he's sober for long periods of time, what he recalls seem like killers' quick flashes. He remembers: her leg cocked out at a strange angle across the bathroom wall as they undid their clothes like exhausted soldiers, desperate for animal touch.

"Just because we're psychopaths doesn't mean we can't be nice to each other," she'd said, her face closing in on his. And he said something back to her, his voice oddly calm, intelligent. He sounded almost like Jules, in fact, though he can't remember what he said, exactly, because her hips twisted over his and he was too focused on believing her softness could be left behind.

He remembers it wasn't even loaded with the cloying bonds of passion, but rather that it was simply something they had to communicate to each other, something they had to say about the gap between them all. They did it slow and purposefully, enjoying the minutes of it, but knowing it wouldn't be repeated.

He remembers, now, the sinking in, the tears he made in her stockings, and how they reminded him of the holes in his cheap suitcase. He remembers that wonderful/awful feeling of falling off board, off promise, while he held onto someone tight. There was something so final about it; they were saying goodbye.

But they were murderers; they cut up each other's body parts and lay them on the ground near the Dumpster. They borrowed pieces of Kit's and Jules's hands and eyes and took strange instruments of torture to their memory every time they touched each other.

He tries to vault it so it doesn't leak out but it doesn't always work. He dreams a surgeon's dream: every night bits of nail, hunks of bone, grizzled sinew crest the edge of white-capped waves; it floats on.

* * *

THE NEXT MORNING he sits up early, feeling the cold seep in through the high windows, waiting for Kit to come back, waiting for Jules's morning call, even if Jules is still just mean to him. Finally, it comes: Rize, who is alert for once, picks up the phone mid-ring. "Hey, Merry Christmas."

"Rize."

"I was just thinking about the set list and wondering if there'd been any new additions. Oh, and dude, you have to see what my stepfather got me, it's, well it's covered with blood right now but—"

"Rize." Through the clipped, automatic moment of transmission between them, Rize hears something he has rarely heard in Jules's rich, Black Adder voice: fear.

"Margo's pregnant. Are you sitting down, man?"

"Call me when you get in."

14
jim

On our way back to Montreal I move to the back of the van, ignoring Kellogg and Rize who are too busy talking shit and getting high to bother with me anyway. I can't look at them. I can't really think about my new feelings regarding Kellogg, and if I have to talk to him I'll betray myself. So I lie there listening to seventies music, which makes me feel sad and nostalgic for a time I don't even remember. And I do what I always do when I can't handle the present: I return to the past.

I remember driving.

I remember packing a bag full of my brother's clothes—button-down plaid shirts and jeans he hadn't worn in years. Taking a fistful of music scores, my violin, my father's old guitar. Grabbing a set of keys from the hallway desk. I remember seeing the cluster of Seven Sisters stars high above the plains and following them east.

When the dividers of the highway speared out in all directions I stopped, choosing a dank Manitoba motel room.

That night I caught the last item of news on *The National*, which happened to be about Saskatchewan farmers. The morning after I left, August 21 to be exact, there had been frost. The weather predicted rain, possibly snow, moving in fast. According to the report, farmers were working non-stop to harvest in these freaky weather conditions. High school kids were being enlisted to drive trucks, the older ones being taught how to operate combines. A year's worth of wages had to be earned in a matter of hours. This was the kind of work that etched out lines of dust and mud on a farmer's face until it seemed he was wearing a clay mask.

I thought of the way sweat crept into a silhouetted line on my father's grey ball cap, how red his eyes turned from his allergies when he had to pull in the wheat—though he always denied being allergic to anything. Simon would have phoned in to cancel on the garage for a week. He would have exchanged his white-sleeved rocker shirts for the soft flannels he'd grown to loathe. Mom would be driving people around and cooking massive meals. Jen was probably helping her, calling on her friends' husbands for a chance to make some quick cash.

They would have had to bury him in a scant matter of hours after they discovered the body, or else they would have to wait.

In the motel room I piled all the pillows and towels and even a patio chair, with one broken leg, on top of the bed. Then I put on all his clothes and lay down, crawling underneath the motel coverlet that smelled like feet. I was thinking of symmetry, the Seven Sisters.

Maybe they could bury him quickly, eighteen years and one day to his birthday. But the earth, crusted with a fine layer of freeze, would make it difficult for a shovel to get through.

I lay there with all those things on top of me, with my eyes wide open, all night. Even though it was the first real night I'd been away from my family I wasn't scared, only very awake. When the last signal on the TV threw out its rainbow of colours over the room, I didn't move. I hummed along to the off-air monotone because it reminded me of Yawnie and I watched my brother's dense, soupy shadow play off the curtains and waited for him to instruct me. But, as in the last years of his life, he said nothing. Asshole.

No, Jim. You're the asshole.

It seemed unfair to me, to be born with someone else and have him die the night of our birthday. And it was just like Yawnie, who appreciated well-rounded stories and airtight finales. It was just like him. His story had ended and I had no story at all.

No story yet, you mean.

It was just like him to die without me and then start talking again.

* * *

KENORA, ONTARIO:

"Jim? Jim, honey, is that you? Dad says it's time you come home now."

(The clatter of dishes, a muffled swear word, the sound of stomping men in the background. Like buffaloes. My mother with a bunch of buffaloes and me pinned high up by Lake Superior, drinking Southern Comfort and Dr Pepper.)

"Okay, well, if you won't talk, I'm gonna tell you about Dad: he's got a hernia. Yup, he had an operation. But he's doing just fine and, in case you been following it out there—"

(Out There. The words echo in that artificial long-distance way.)

"We got most of it and the rest, well, we just have to cut our losses, I guess."

(The crops. She's talking about the crops.)

My scratchy voice: "Mom?"

"Yes, honey."

"I'm sorry."

(Sighing. Footsteps. Whispers. A dog barking a long way off.)

"Anderson is kind of wondering about his car, sweetie."

(Grand auto theft of the priest's car. Will drive it into a ditch in Magog. Hitch my way in.)

"He'll get it back."

(The sound of air moving through my mother like a tall, worshipped tree. What the hell is she doing?)

"There are so many flowers here, Jim. I've never seen so many flowers in one place in my entire life."

"I'm glad, Ma."

"I'm glad, too. He's resting now."

(Caring for my father's prone figure in bed, my mother has started regurgitating the words of her faith group. She is seduced by the floral arrangements, the high of having to cook and clean for four days straight. My mother has turned into a complete zombie. She hasn't even had time to mourn him but, then again, what is there to mourn, really? Haven't we been mourning him for the past two years?)

"I think he couldn't stand it, you know," she says, apropos of nothing, as if we are gossiping about a local farmhand we'd glimpse once or twice at the Safeway. "Like, he just *knew* you were going."

(*But he left first,* I want to say, as if I am still a child, invested in assigning blame to the correct party.) Her silent sniffing—

"I can't tell if you're smelling or crying, Mom," I say, my voice angry and stiff.

(I can see them: the roses, carnations, and lilies, piled high on our dining room table in various Mason jars and seldom-used crystal vases. They are so surreal, their flattened heads, their carnival colours, like something out of a television show, not real life. I can see Dad lying in bed, all stoic, weeping gently into his pillow over a piece of my mother's old blond hair. I can see all of them, working and sweating and then falling to the ground as they tear off their mud-heavy clothes to rest like hurt jackrabbits gone grey from running and fear. I can see my family in that clear, rarified air that continues to pump in my lungs.)

"You still there, Ma?"

"I am."

* * *

ITINERARY OF PHENOMENA: Homecoming

27 broken guitar strings. 2 charges of misdemeanour in Virginia that fail to stick. 3 cracked lamps. 1 drunken swan-dive off a motel roof into the deep end of a Miami pool. 5 speeding tickets in the Midwest. 1 encounter with Lou Reed that ended in tears in a New York City café. 7 tantrums. 2 blown amps. 2 hospitalizations due to alcohol poisoning. 3 flats. 1 broken speedometer. 1 torn brassiere. 2 lost shaving kits. 45 misplaced picks. 19 lost lighters. 1 case of crabs. 18 arguments about the set list. 1 missing guitar tuner. 13 lost hotel-room keys. 1 swallowed champagne cork. 1 use of the Heimlich manoeuvre. 1 cracked bass. 2 sucker-punched journalists. 3 cancelled shows. 5 meltdowns. 45 death threats to other musicians. $35 worth of library fines. 14 unmailed letters to wives and girlfriends. 267 sightings of road kill on the Interstate. 12 nightmares. 1 power outage. Innumerable stolen towels and pillows. $600 worth of outstanding room service charges that no one is claiming responsibility for. 1 wedding band lost and found. 1 $900 phone bill. 1 new set of track marks. 1 methadone habit. 3 bags of pot that *had to be thrown out during a spontaneous California highway check. 2 lost first-aid kits. 1 half-hearted suicide attempt with a butter knife at a Kansas City diner. 4 fist fights. 7 drunken Frisbee games. 4 minor head injuries. 1 full moon. 3 cases of tendonitis. 19 broken beer bottles. 15 stained carpets. 13 incidences of black-outs. 6 bottles of ibuprofen. 3 lost pair of jeans. 3 colds. 1 cocktail-shrimp-related incident of food poisoning. 4 busted-up hearts and 2 angels at the top of Mount Royal.*

* * *

IN A BIG GROUP, nothing happens in isolation. Events cluster like glutinous frog eggs in March swamps. If one person makes a bad choice others have to deal, quite simply, or leave. In a big social dynamic you're forced to choose sides, whether you like to admit it or not. And your choice isn't always based on some higher ethical or moral stance; it's more like a lemming or sheep mentality, an instinct that can lead to your destruction or survival.

I guess I chose Rize's side, for my own mental and emotional health, not because I agreed with what he'd done, not because I thought aligning myself with him helped me secure some kind of tenure (it probably did the opposite), but because by the time we got back from the road Rize was the only person in the band I could stand to be around for more than half an hour. So, I guess, from that perspective it appeared that I'd chosen his side. Not Margo's, not Jules's—though in a way I felt worse for Jules: I knew what it meant to love someone who was always on the verge of spinning away.

There was also something in Jules that vaguely reminded me of Yawnie. Maybe it was the fact that Jules was blond like my brother. Maybe it was because Jules was usually the smartest person in the room and found this fact paralyzing. I could see that Jules blunted his mind by constantly smoking dope: he thought it would help him avoid saying things that would sound assholish, or upset Margo. Jules's self-medicating tactic made me wonder if Yawnie hadn't perfected his own variation on this detachment theme.

Rize and I became the kind of friends who skulked around in alleys looking for garbage to paint or fix up. Once, we found a broken five-hundred-dollar juicer that Rize restored in about five minutes after a joint and a stiff cup of coffee. We could sit together watching shitty TV, or we could drink beer and play pool for hours without speaking. If the weather warmed up for an afternoon, in one of those freakish warm-winter spells, we'd sit on the wall at the old port, laughing at the scourge of humanity—Rollerbladers in spandex or, as Rize called them, Fruit Booters. We'd pay for a matinee and then sneak into film after film until we'd seen every crappy new Hollywood release and our eyes were glossed with electricity, our mouths spewing one-liners. That's not to say we didn't talk, because we did, we just never talked about the stuff everyone else wanted to talk about with him: band gossip, gear, and what had happened on the road.

When we got home Rize seemed different. Better somehow, more confident. Maybe the methadone was evening him out, or maybe it was the fact that he was away from Margo, who wasn't always the greatest influence on people.

As for me, I was shattered. I had a kind of unshakeable fatigue, an ache that extended from my skull to my lungs. I felt old, but not old-mature, not like before; it was more as if I'd lived too long. Before I left I knew life on the road took a toll, that all the clichés about its being rough on the interior and exterior were true, but I didn't know it would be this bad. It was as though someone had taken a Shop-Vac to my insides and sucked out all the blood and energy. Plus, the insomnia made me so tired I'd lost the distinction between days and nights; it seemed to me we all lived the same boring beer-filled day, over and over, without a tear in the fabric of our two-dimensional reality.

If Margo and I were close, she would have told me I was depressed, that it was winter. She would have advised me to go into therapy—Margo loved telling people they needed therapy, and the fact that she herself went only sporadically didn't seem to register for anyone. But Margo and I hadn't spoken since that bathtub incident on tour.

I told Rize about it one night when we were drinking brandy from a flask on the mountain, lobbing snowballs down at the trees and avoiding calls from Kellogg and Margo.

"Sorry you're so messed up," Rize said, packing an enormous slush ball full of dirt and sticks.

"Please don't throw that at me." I hoisted my fist up, showing him I meant business.

He laughed and pitched it down the path. "Explain it," he said, pulling up his coat collar and lighting a cigarette.

"Sometimes my life terrifies me more than night but still I say nothing," I blurted.

Rize nodded. "I know what you mean. I get it in my chest."

"Right," I said softly, "the panic." I wasn't used to this degree of lucidity from Rize. While I felt more tired, more frayed every day, he seemed to get more even-keeled, like some kind of *Freaky Friday* thing where we were swapping roles. I wondered what the others thought of the fact that Rize was no longer their whipping boy, no longer the clown.

We were at the lookout point where you can see downtown to Peel Street, across both bridges and beyond the silvery blue river. We sat on the cold flagstone ledge, our faces so close to the bare trees that if we leaned over far enough they'd leave long scratches down our necks. It was quiet above the city but you could still hear random car horns, the constant swell of traffic never too far away.

I wondered if Rize was worried about Kit coming back. She'd be back from her business trip soon. Isaac was about to return from Hong Kong, too. I thought about mentioning all this to Rize, about asking him what he thought might happen next with Kit, with the band, but then I realized that even though we were friends I didn't care.

There'd be time enough to answer the non-stop phone calls from Kellogg and worry about the future. Looking at the dirty clouds suspended above the city, with winter nearly half-nelsoned, I knew we didn't have much time to enjoy the cold, our senseless hope. And when Rize tipped his toqued head toward me and kicked off down the steepest part of the hill, I knew I'd never learned to hold on fiercely enough to the people and moments that were really important. As I ran behind him through brown slush and ice, my scream a thin-echoed ribbon across the dark, I promised myself I'd try harder.

15
rize

Rize sits on the bed with his horn at his heels, focused on the bottom latch, the one Kit can undo with her toes. He glances at the mirror on the closet door and congratulates himself on shaving. When he shaves, the lines of his face are less round and blurry. He traces his finger over his straight sideburns, which are black against the startling white of his skin. His jeans are clean, boots shined, cigarettes tucked in his T-shirt, fifties style.

He has a rare sense of his own magnetism. *Almost handsome.* When he hears the metal lock clicking, he's grateful for the sight of his strong image: only it refuses to betray him. Two hands throw a briefcase and a black bag into the hallway. He turns his head slowly.

Kit starts, holding herself against the doorframe. She wears a new grey winter coat, one he's never seen. He can't look at her face; already the force of her body—so close to his—is causing a reaction in his stomach. He looks back to the mirror to draw strength but sees only his endless brown eyes, too eager, too sad.

Already he remembers his guilt. He remembers that he's ten minutes late to meet Kellogg to discuss the set list and that, in half an hour, he has to lead the brass section and then call Jules to see when he and Margo arrive home.

And for the first time he remembers it, the baby, forming in Margo's womb. He thinks of its cells gathering, fuelling itself on her body.

"Look at me, Rize."

"Can't."

He puts his fingers to his head, teepee style.

"What's wrong?"

Then he does it, he looks straight into her face and something in him bends over like a leaf heavy with rain.

"Where were you?" he spits.

She stretches her long body out and kicks off her boots.

"I can't tell you, it's confidential."

"Oh, I see. A matter of national security?"

"Something like that."

He grabs at her dress, roughly. Patches of red appear on her face but she doesn't protest as he pulls her to him. She smells of lonely gin and tonics on airplanes and public washrooms. Kit folds herself to the floor at the foot of the bed.

"I'm sorry, Rize, there was nothing I could do."

"Who are you—James Bond?"

"Do I really have to explain this to you right now? I'm exhausted. Besides, your job takes you away for weeks at a time—"

"Not for nearly two months at a time. You didn't even call me once!"

He knows he's being unreasonable. But he can't help it. She begins to peel off her work clothes, pulls out a pair of jeans and redresses herself, as if he isn't even there.

"I've been living in your apartment for the past couple of weeks, snooping through your things."

"I see that. Rize?" She looks at his flight case, the cut of his perfect profile.

"What?"

"Come back. I mean later, after your rehearsal. Let's talk."

The top button of her jeans is still undone. Her finger strays to her navel, it gapes at him like a little mouth. He imagines telling it *I love you* and its yakking the words back at him in a helium voice.

"Okay," he says, thinking of the sad lament of the word. He picks up his jacket and his horn and walks out, but not before grabbing her shoulders and biting down on the soft flesh of her neck. So that she will remember, if only in a flash of pain, what it feels like.

This is what it feels like to always be making love to you later.

* * *

IN THE SOUTH AMERICAN cultural centre the pipes have frozen, the new trumpet player is ripped, and everyone is so cold they're wearing toques.

"Christ," Kellogg says, taking a sip of his frozen beer and tying his scarf tighter. "This is some serious hoser shit."

Rize nods and makes an announcement:

"The kind people in the tapas restaurant next door have a Ladies washroom. Men will have to relieve themselves outside."

Rize huddles with the horns in the green room and plies the inebriated trumpeter—whose name he has deduced is Martin—with hot chocolate and cigarettes. Amid this chaos some Peruvians have descended and are unloading plumbing tools. Rize watches Jim saw off a riff in the wings; the high notes splinter in his eardrum. He approaches her from behind as if she were a small animal likely to scare easily.

"Hey," he says, patting her soft blond hair awkwardly, "You're here."

Jim turns and slowly grins her gap-toothed smile. There's something about her that's almost five years old, he thinks, but also an over-intelligence that's disarming.

"Of course I'm here. Why wouldn't I be?"

She stares at him, confused, as the sounds of Martin coughing up his esophagus mixes in with the sounds of tuning.

"Well," Jim begins, as if she's embarrassed for him, "I have to go. I'll see you later."

"Okay," he says, not convinced.

"She back?" Jim asks suddenly, between her teeth, her eyes focused on something beyond the stage.

"Yeah."

"Good. You be good, now. I know you'll make it right." Jim's eyes light up, and suddenly Rize feels he's someone else, someone capable of making pretty, gap-toothed girls smile, someone who's the organizing principle and not the mess in the washroom, someone worthy of a fierce companion soul, like Kit's. He allows himself to feel a moment of pride as she hugs him. Then a stocky man carrying an electrical heater bumbles between them.

"Keep the morale up, eh?"

"Oh, the girls are dancing and drinking rum," she laughs.

"Good."

Then he pushes Jim through the hole in the curtain onto the stage.

* * *

LATER, after rehearsal, three pitchers of sangria, and uncountable shots and beer, Rize sits in a tattoo parlour thinking about the gap in Jim's teeth and how there's something missing from her eyes.

When he gets home he remembers only glimpses of events: tiny drops of blood on his face, Kellogg's laughter.

"Small, tasteful," the tattoo artist says, her red lips doubling up in his vision. A small Band-Aid under his eye, then a cab to Kit's, paid for by Kellogg.

She's asleep when he rolls in next to her body. He'd like to be inside her, not necessarily in a sexual way, he'd just like to crawl up under her eyebrow or into her throat and get in on some of that deep, restful sleep she's so committed to. Even when she's awake there's something in her that feels like it's always asleep, and it's there he wants to rest.

She's naked and welcomes him. And then it's all gone, the cold, the worry, the anger. There's only the sudden shaking in his veins as his toes unclasp in the warm grip of her flesh.

The next morning he dreams The Angel Riots are playing to ten thousand people and he couldn't screw up a note if he tried. Jules doesn't hate him and, for a moment, it's perfect. Margo's dancing on stage, her heavy belly swaying low. Kellogg's eyes are closed and he's not laughing at him. His guitar is not broken, it's perfectly tuned. Jules turns to Margo, reciting his apocryphal manifesto:

Because I like you raw in this cold city pulled up against the blue light. Because your father is gone and my mother is dead and all the bad guys can't wait to chop us into pieces and turn us into oil.

You guessing, your world all sweaty ties and more autographs, please. Keeping your manners together.

Because we were born in unbelieving, both you and I.

Do you know what it's like to have your gods already dead in the wet mouths of Republican swine?

Well, we do. We are The Angel Riots. Now, weep with me. Because your gods are liars and your friends are whores. Weep with me, now: all that's good is gone.

* * *

IN THE MORNING, she peels off the bandage while he's still asleep. "There's something on your face."

"I know. It's a teardrop."

She looks at him, her dark hair falling into her eyes. Horrified, she whispers, "What did you do, Rize?"

But he can't answer her because his head hurts too much.

When he wakes again, it's noon and Kit's in the doorway dressed in a blouse, skirt, and heels.

"Where are you going?"

"I have to go again." She sits on the edge of the bed, inserts silver hoop earrings and changes her shoes. "I have a meeting."

"Sunday."

"What's Sunday?"

"Come to Lima on Sunday. We're launching the new label and Divine Light are playing with us."

"Of course, I remember now."

Rize sits up and looks out under the blinds. It's started snowing again. He looks at the desolate streets, at the piles of garbage bags shored up against snowbanks.

"You can't wear heels, Kit, it's crazy out there."

"And you have to get that thing off your face. It makes you look like a total loser."

"Kellogg says I look like a Maori warrior."

A suffering sigh from Kit. "Oh, please. Kellogg says a lot of things, Rize. You look like a convict."

Rize gives her a childish smile to hide his disappointment. No matter what, he always screws up; now, nobody will ever take him seriously again. "Okay. I'll talk to Jules's uncle, he's a plastic surgeon. Hey, have you spoken to Margo lately? I was supposed to talk to those two last night but couldn't get through."

She looks at him worriedly and hands him a folded piece of newspaper.

Montreal Indie Singer Fingered as Protest Leader in NYC

New York City police swarmed more than 100 anti-poverty protesters after they raided the breakfast buffet table at the Grand Hyatt hotel in Manhattan yesterday morning.

Police arrested Montreal singer Jules T. Bay, citing him as a principal inciter as protesters threw scones and scrambled eggs at NYPD officers. He was detained for 48 hours in a New York City jail. Bay is the lead singer of The Angel Riots, a local Montreal pop group, and was filming a video in Brooklyn with his wife, Margo Bay, at the time of his arrest.

The charges were dropped after Bay threatened to sue the NYPD for assault. Bay, however, is being extradited to Canada, where authorities are waiting to arrest him for public mischief charges connected to a 2001 fire, where a mob burned down a new luxury apartment development in Saint-Henri. Despite his public persona, Bay has managed to elude arrest for years by arguing that the federal government violated his privacy.

Bay is also a public defender of marijuana decriminalization and a founding member of Shelter not Condos, a housing organization that opposes the gentrification of low-income areas in Montreal.

* * *

KIT WAITS FOR RIZE by the apartment door, jingling her keys. As he pulls on his boots and puts a fresh Band-Aid under his eye he notices a flash of silver on her wrist, a bracelet he's never seen before. Then he remembers her closet stash of stolen goods.

"His father's got some pricey lawyer lined up for him, right?" she asks, adjusting his collar.

"Absolutely, the Bays have a team of lawyers."

"I'll try to see if there's anything I can do, with the police angle, I mean, but I'm sure I can't."

He nods and straightens himself up, taking her wrist.

"Nice accessory, where'd you get it?"

Kit flushes red, unlocks the door, and pulls up her coat collar. "What are you trying to say, Rize? That I shouldn't buy myself expensive jewellery?"

"No, I'm not saying that at all. I'm just admiring all your new stuff."

"Are you worried about Jules? Is that what this is about? 'Cause you should be, he won't be allowed back to the States for ages."

"Give it back!" Rize hisses, holding her wrist.

"What are you talking about?"

"I mean it, give it back to wherever you got it. It's a nasty habit. Stealing."

"So, tell me, what's a good habit? Getting trashy tattoos? What about a group of rich kids who pretend to save the world with a bunch of mediocre pop songs? What are their bad habits?"

"I'm not rich," he says, before he lets go of her hand and walks down the three flights of stairs. The frigid streets smell like ice and blood.

Why is everyone I love a crook?

* * *

OUTSIDE THE POLICE STATION, Rize tries to remember a time when the city was warm. When tar baked between his flip-flopped toes, when the tall heads of sunflowers stooped low to worship the sky. When a Montreal summer goddess was on every corner, wrapped tight in a sarong. He knows he should go inside, like a normal person, and slap down the 140 dollars he withdrew from the bank toward Jules's bail, that he shouldn't be waiting in the cold. But somehow he can't make his way into the grim, windowless building; plus, he doesn't even know if bail is a real Canadian procedure, or if it's something only from American television. He thinks about all the things he doesn't know as he smokes his cigarette down to the filter, crushes it with his boot, and huddles next to Jules's father's slush-encrusted Beamer. He notices a cop watching him.

Finally, when his pinky turns completely white, Jules is hustled outside by his father. As they approach the car, Rize sees a bright slash against Jules's cheek that has barely begun to scab. He steps out from behind the car.

"Hey, man," Jules says, wiping snot on his mitten as his father nods at Rize and says, "Come to emancipate our little freedom fighter?"

"Something like that. How are you, buddy?"

"What is this? Reconnaissance?"

Jules pulls his hood up and gets into the front seat of the car. No one says anything during the ride home.

At the Bays' Westmount residence, Rize climbs up the long stairway and follows Jules into his room where they remove their coats, light cigarettes, then sit in Jules's closet, like they did when they were sixteen.

Jules cracks his head both ways and moves a pair of tuxedo shoes to the side.

"Did you bring it?"

"Of course." Rize crumbles the hash and begins rolling a joint. "Courtesy of Kellogg."

Jules laughs bitterly. "Isn't everything these days?"

"What do you mean?"

"I mean, I feel like he owns us."

"He's producing our album. He does own us."

"I can't talk business now. Sorry I brought it up." Jules blinks twice. "How's everyone?"

"Everyone? You mean Margo? I dunno, Kit went to Margo's folks' house—we went on separate recon missions tonight."

As he licks the spliff closed, Jules picks up a ball cap from the floor and puts it on.

"What's with the face gash, Jules?"

"Aimed too high."

"Fuck off with that suicide shit." He passes Jules the joint and offers a light.

"Nah, shaving accident. Is *that* a shaving accident?"

"What?"

"That teardrop, is that what it is? Is that a teardrop on your face?"

"Yeah, Kellogg, tequila. I dunno, it seemed like the right idea at the time, but now I'm not so sure. Kit wants it gone."

"I don't blame her, you look like a skid. So, now Kellogg's branding you?"

"What do you mean?"

"I don't know about that guy, man."

"What are you saying? It's too late to be talking like this."

"I think he set me up. Who else—besides you, but you probably forgot—who else knew I was planning that mini-riot in the city? Kellogg. Kellogg, man. I get there and the place is swarming with undercover pigs. Not that that stopped me from grabbing a couple of scones and whipping them at the cops."

"I really don't think he'd want to get you into a situation like this," Rize says, tying one of Jules's sneaker shoelaces into a triple knot.

"Are you kidding? He wants to get rid of me, man."

When there's no reaction from Rize, Jules shrugs and slides his eyes away. Rize thinks again about all the things he doesn't know, things he could have learned about but was too busy watching Jules's mind unravel with drugs. Helium, the function of insects, how the American Congress works, the definition of *surcease, specious,* and *epicene.* Cubism, the native food of Brazil, black American beat poets, chaos theory and its effect on weather and irregular heartbeats. There are so many things to know.

Rize reaches out for Jules's arm. "What's jail like?"

"Sucks," Jules says, as two parallel streams of tears roll down his face and he shrinks away from Rize's reach. "Tell me about the show."

"You can make it, right? It's Sunday night."

Jules pulls the cap over his eyes.

"Court. Monday at ten."

"Are you serious?"

"Yeah. Ma Chris', these Feds don't mess around."

"But you're the main attraction." Rize grins, trying to keep it light.

Looking amused, Jules relights the joint and offers Rize a drag, but he refuses. He's already sky-high from Jules's second-hand smoke.

"Yeah, so talk to me."

"There's stories in both weeklies. A minor mention in the French ones. You know, we're getting big with the French now, right? They're loving all this revolutionary shit. Still no word from the *Gazette*, but I'm sure they'll have your mug shot by Monday."

"You're kidding me."

"I'm not. They're calling you a radical activist."

"I hate fucking activists. Besides, the old man won't let me out. I'm twenty-four years old and grounded for Chrissakes."

"So, we'll jailbreak you."

"Dude, I'm really not into this cloak and dagger shit."

They sit in silence, listening to the paper crinkling on Jules's spliff, the electric heaters clicking on and off. Jules peers up, his eyes are bloodshot. "I can't play this game for much longer—I'm going to be a father, Rize," he says casually, ashing the joint in an Adidas sneaker.

The click of the heaters goes off as Jules reaches out and slowly grasps Rize by the neck. He pinches his Adam's apple with his other hand. For such a small man, Jules has remarkably large hands, Rize thinks, as he tries to take a deep breath. Jules pulls himself so close to Rize's face he can see the open slash under his friend's eye in all its gory detail. The wound is clean but pressed open. Beneath the surface scab Rize sees a strip of blood laced through like a placenta thread.

"Tell me what happened between you and Margo," Jules says, clenching Rize's throat.

A half-gasp escapes as his windpipe shrinks. "Nothing." He can look nowhere else except at the wound near Jules's eye, which happens to be shaped like an accusing mouth.

"I don't even know who I detest more these days," Jules says, his non-strangulating hand karate-chopping the air through the pongy hash smoke, "Kellogg, your lying ass, that crazy bitch"—the stench of jail-piss rises from Jules's pores as his adrenalin peaks—"or myself."

16
jim

There are nights in this city when, deep in the core of winter, people need to escape the indoors. Despite the minus-thirty wind chill, despite the flaking of dry skin and a belly full of wine, winter's frustration becomes enough and these soldiers of spring layer on their hats, socks, and coats and leave their apartments. They desert dinner parties; they leave wooden tables covered with candle wax and cheese plates, abandoning rosy-cheeked friends in mid air-guitar solos. They leave these rooms filled with stunned laughter to see a show.

Are you going to the show?

When this collective desire to end hibernation overtakes, they flood into rooms of dimmed light, wrestle over a position at the bar to catch the bartender's attention. Everyone wants the same thing: to be anonymous, to see their skin sweat under red stage lights, to listen to the conversation of a stranger. They peel off their layers, pile their coats in a mountain of winter gear, and get ready to feel the pull of a single, pulsing mob. Everybody needs to forget there's three more months of winter, or at least deny it for one night.

Kellogg has timed it perfectly: the city is hungry for just such an event, and the press has been buzzing about the new Montreal label and the scandal in New York. No matter that the last time The Riots played Montreal it was to a room of twenty-five people, most of them friends. No matter that the only recognition they've received from the press in the past five years is a nomination for Most Pretentious Local Act. All is forgiven.

Kellogg—as Rize tells me backstage, emptying gob out of his horn pipe—has the Midas touch: "That guy turns shit into gold. Or gold into shit, depending on your perspective."

And it shows, because this shit shines. All groups are represented in spades: there, the two music writers sulk at the bar; here, the hardened, yawning weekend regulars. Over there, McGill students pretend to be Concordia students; fresh-faced and curious, decked out in eighties-style T's and trashed jeans, they try to hide their Christmas tans with baby powder.

Then there are the true Riots fans: gay guys with black glasses and tight black T-shirts, nerdy girls, cynical and knee-socked, angling to catch sight of Kellogg or Jules. They press their heads up against the speakers, giggle too loudly, drink ginger ale and shots. Even the enemies are present: downstairs The Inner-City Zionists eat ceviche, drink Boréale, roll cigarettes. Due to their worldwide success, The Zions own this town while The Riots only rent apartments in it. The Zions have purchased half the city's deteriorating spaces on the north side and turned them into clubs and recording studios to be used by bands from Tennessee to Nunavut.

Also, the requisite Franco fans: a handful of drop-dead gorgeous girls dressed to the height of European fashion, with legs that lope right down to hell.

Even Isaac, who's back from his Hong Kong business excursion, has promised to come out, curious about what I've been doing for the past couple of months. When I asked him if he'd come, he surprised me by kissing the top of my head and saying, "Of course."

I search the crowd for him but he hasn't arrived yet, so I settle into a seat near the stage where Rize is stirring his sangria furiously, oblivious to the clustered bodies around him.

"Pretty good crowd, don't you think?" He looks up at me as a middle-aged woman and a large bald man approach us.

"Are you nervous, darling?" the woman asks in a faint Irish accent.

"Not really, Ma, I've been touring and playing for fifteen years now."

"But it's your hometown."

"Jesus, Ma, do you *want* me to get nervous?" He hands her some beer tickets and introduces us. "June, Ted, this is Jim, she's in The Divine Light."

"Hi, June!"

"Hi, ah, Jim. Rize, Ted and I are going to the bar."

"Okay, Ma, I'll see you guys later, after the show."

The woman grips the soft underside of Rize's arm before leading Ted away from the table.

"I think the only thing I've ever given my mother, besides a headache, is beer tickets."

"You look like her, a little," I lie.

"Really? Everyone says I look like my dad."

"Was that him?"

"No, that's my stepdad. Dad's Missing in Action. Total cliché: went out for a pack of smokes, never came back."

I pause. I've heard a lot of things about Rize's dad, that he was an amazing trumpet player who got strung out on junk and died when Rize was a kid. I'm not sure if the stories are true, because Rize has never talked about him to me.

"Hey, you get cut or something?"

Rize flushes, then peels off the Band-Aid under his eye to reveal a really tacky tear tattoo.

"Oh my god. Are you kidding me with that thing or what?"

"Wish I was," he says as he readjusts the plastic. But the Band-Aid doesn't stick and ends up sagging, so you can see the outline of the scabby ink beneath his eye. It's so sad and ridiculous it's all I can do not to crack up.

"Go on, mock me. Just like the rest of them."

"I'm sorry."

"You know that kid in school that the bullies and cool kids forced to pull the fire alarm? The one that ate dogshit? That's me. I'm that stupid kid, forever. Everyone else is getting As in science labs and kissing cheerleaders and I'm always the one eating shit."

"Everyone else is not kissing cheerleaders. You're not eating shit. Look, maybe it gives you character?"

Rize shrugs like he really couldn't care less. "Whatever. Maybe I will keep it just to spite everyone."

Then he peers over to the side of the stage, where Martin is trying to get his beer tickets. Kellogg shakes his head and points in our direction.

"Lean over me, I don't want Martin to see me. He can't drink before the show, I need to keep him sober."

"Don't worry, he has plenty of time to get drunk after the gig," I say, blocking out Martin's view of Rize by draping a coat over his head.

I smile at Rize under the coat.

"You know, Jim, you're a goddamn good-natured girl. Do you want his beer tickets?"

"No, thanks."

Rize keeps looking to the back of the hall, looking for Kit probably. His face alters as he watches her and a snow-drenched Margo make their way to the bar.

"I wanted to say," Rize begins, keeping one eye on the girls, "that I'm sorry about being so messed up on tour and everything. If you don't know already—"

"The Riots, I know."

"You know, what?"

"I just know it can't be easy."

"Still, it's no excuse." Rize seems so dejected I put my hand on his knee. He looks up at me, startled.

"Hey, it's okay, you and me, we're the same."

A small bomb goes off in his eyes. "What do you mean?"

"I mean, there's this, all this." I gesture to a geeky kid wearing an old Riots T-shirt, hugging Martin, trying to work his way backstage. Behind them, the green-room curtain draws open to reveal Kellogg, who's now yelling at the orchestra. Rize and I watch him as if it has nothing to do with us.

"I mean, you and I, we just want to play, be a part of something. We're players, not leaders."

Rize takes a sip and nods, facing the empty stage.

"I want you to meet someone after the show," I say, just as Kit comes up to us.

"Okay."

"Hey, babe," Kit says, planting a kiss on Rize's head and giving me a small nod. "The fugitive here yet?" she asks, tugging at his hair in a sexy way.

"Ow." Rize pulls away from her, instinctively putting his hand to his mouth like she's about to punch him in the jaw. Then he looks at me, as if I shouldn't be witnessing this brutal affection. I have a flash of Rize covered in bubbles and magic marker—in "the bathtub incident," as the band has now begun to refer to that night. I wonder if this new cowed attitude is his penance to Kit. I wonder, too, how much she knows.

* * *

AFTER I FINISH MY SET, I stand by the curtains to watch Rize. His cheeks inflate and he charges into his solo as if he isn't afraid of anything, not even death. I think about what Rize told me once, how the trombone is like an elephant: on its own it is magnificent, but its awkward and unpredictable beauty alongside other instruments isn't always immediately clear; it needs to find its own way into the music.

"Mesdames et messieurs," Jules whines when Rize comes up for air, "I'm coming to you tonight from a jail cell which I shared with Bruce Springsteen's deaf half-brother and a sycophantic whore."

Kellogg's playing Rize's four-string guitar, absorbed by the beginning of these cracked, winding sounds where there are no safe corners, no soft places to rest his head.

"Ladies and gentlemen, members of the press, you may have heard the rumours that our band was dead, that they'd captured me and were all ready to throw away the key."

Above the swelling of keyboards, the bombastic horns, Jules climbs to the top of the biggest amp and raises his arms.

"They will try to bury you with false manifestos, inscribe you in wars against false enemies, and then charge you with treason if you have not committed murder for them."

Rize's horn fills with liquid light that enters the stomach of everyone in the club. The sound lifts the crowd, slightly, from its skin into a falsetto war march.

"And how I fucking hate them."

Cheers, whistles, foot stomping, as Jules winds the microphone around his neck in a noose.

Time morphs, four hundred people clutch their belt buckles, their collarbones, their heads as the swell of saliva from mouths travels to the waiting, golden piece inside their guts. The tide of the song keeps rising, rolling in the crowd's organs like a small earthquake tremor while Rize clutches at time, reaches out for that magnetic space where air meets his own gargoyle voice. He couldn't make a mistake, couldn't hit a false note if he tried.

Jules rips his shirt off, reveals his bruise-covered chest. The crowd hisses. The bright slash across his face begins to bleed. Jules has been marijuana-free for a day and acting more rock 'n' roll than anyone, throwing beer cans at Rize backstage and kicking holes in the green-room walls. Jules is now having an onstage meltdown, and the crowd is his. "Enemies," Jules screams, throwing a quick look at Rize, "enemies of faith and love." He points to the brass section and Rize ducks low, as if he thinks Jules will throw the mic at him. He does.

Tangled in cords, Jules leaps, nearly impaling himself on the mic stand while Margo stands at the back of the stage, barely moving, as if she has accidentally found herself onstage with a bunch of grade-nine lip-synchers and has no idea where the exit is.

Then Kellogg mangles the mic from Jules's hand and slaps him twice, hard, like in fifties movies when women become hysterical. He stuns the crowd for a moment with this sudden, real, violence. But they're gone, the crowd. They're all Kellogg's now and they don't care that he's just bitch-slapped Jules, discarded the band's lead singer like a piece of used Kleenex.

Because when Kellogg steps into the light everything that's gone wrong goes right: shit to gold, as Rize said, gold to shit, depending on where you sit.

"Ladies and gentlemen, what my colleague is trying to say is that we are The Angel Riots, and we are not for sale."

* * *

THAT NIGHT, in Isaac's arms, I still can't get rid of the image of Jules's half-naked body spasming in pain as the band played on and on. And something else: the look of shock on Isaac's face when he saw Kit, as if he recognized her from somewhere. In bed, Isaac's breathing is slow and comforting. I pull on his arm. "Did you know that woman?"

Isaac feigning sleep, his warm butt pressed against my pelvis.

"Hey, I know you're awake, faker." I shake him again.

"Hmmm?"

"Did you know her?"

"Who?"

"Kit, the black-haired woman. Rize's girlfriend."

Isaac sits up, takes a long sip of water, and sighs. "I think I met her, maybe once or twice, through you."

"You never met her through me, but she seemed to want to know *you*."

"Yeah, I guess I have that effect on women."

I edge closer to Isaac, tracing the hair on his belly down to his crotch.

"Yeah, I'll bet you do."

* * *

TWO DAYS LATER I go to the hotel room where Isaac is staying and knock repeatedly, but there's no answer. Then I walk half an hour to Westmount and try to look into his house, but all the blinds are drawn. I stay there until dark, even though it's minus a hundred and my hands nearly freeze off, hoping to catch a glimpse of either him or his wife—whose sudden presence would explain his departure from my life—but no one appears.

On my way home I think about how Isaac had stayed up all night after I woke him, as if he was nervous, as if he was waiting for something to happen. How he smoked all my cigarettes and paced the suite.

When I get back to my apartment there's a large manila envelope full of over five thousand dollars, as well as a note from Isaac.

Darling girl,
Sorry, I had to go. Hold onto this or spend it as you see fit. Thank you for everything.

Love always,
xx
-I

17
rize

Since the launch, he can't walk the streets any more with Kellogg, who, at every turn, has to stop to congratulate someone on the birth of their child, invite them to a show, or commiserate on the loss of a job. It's mind-boggling to Rize, Kellogg's Rolodex social skills, for K cannot spell the word *giraffe* and yet is able to recall a girl named Selia who spells her name with an *S*.

Photo shoots have become so numerous and tedious now that Rize, Guy, and Martin wear tutus and spike their beards with hair wax. They climb into shopping carts and race them down wonky Plateau streets to keep themselves amused. Music journalists quote Kellogg saying, "If you really want to know the truth about us, we're always self-combusting, recreating ourselves. Like butterflies."

Butterflies, for crying out loud.

He doesn't crouch in his room any more in the needful meditation sessions when he tried to carve out money and his own name. There's no quiet time any more, every moment is filled and every bit of information is shared. He can't think about the stunned, separate part of himself that's always asleep with Kit. When he tries to reach for that essential part not colonized by the band, talk of the band, or talk of talk of the band, he can't find anything that belongs to him except a crushed set of fake eyelashes and an overflowing ashtray. The studio, which used to be empty save for Jules and Guy's occasional jams, is now filled with strangers, ringing cellphones, and Kellogg barking orders.

These days he stays at Kit's most of the time simply because he's fallen out of the habit of being alone.

What do you call a musician without a girlfriend?
Homeless.

* * *

"I THINK WE'VE finally cornered this guy," Kit says, pouring Rize another glass of wine at dinner.

"Who? That fraud guy you tracked to Hong Kong?"

"Yes," she says, sneaking one of his last cigarettes.

He invests his voice with a concern he does not feel as he asks: "So, what's up next, then, for you?"

"Well, there're a couple of new cases open, but I want to finalize this." Kit flares her nostrils and wiggles her black brows. Her square bangs and painted-on Asian eyes make her look like a big-boned Japanese girl.

"I'm sure you do. That poor bastard."

"What about you, how's life as a big famouz rock-starr?" she asks, doing her best Québécois accent, which is easy for Kit as she is French-fluent. She tosses him a music magazine: on the cover is Kellogg, with a turban on his head and his arms wrapped around Margo. The rest of the band is at his feet, clinging to his cloak.

"Why isn't Jules in this picture?" Kit wonders.

Rize shrugs. "I'm really not sure, especially when he's the one who comes up with all the best sound bites." He tells her about Guy, who has lost patches of his hair because of stress, and Martin, who's been drunk for two and a half weeks.

"Guy's under a lot of stress. Drummers are like the goalies of music: they have a lot to keep track of."

"That's very insightful, in a hoser sort of way," Kit laughs, turning up a Glenn Gould number on the radio. As she drones along to the virtuoso's humming, Rize leans back, feeling the muscles and tendons in his arms relax after a long day of rehearsing.

Oddly, they have become physically closer than ever. Kit barely lets him out of her sight now. She waits for him in the smoking room at the studio, she talks with Jules and reads everybody their horoscopes out loud. They cook sensible meals together, when he's home, and make slow love every single night. It's the kind of sex that undoes the hard, clustered knots inside the hole within him where the fake eyelashes are, but there is also something impersonal about it.

He listens to Kit tell him that she knows the perfect homeopathic doctor for Guy's alopecia. Her voice instills confidence in him; judging by her tone, his friend's hair will grow back if he inhales some lavender and talks to a moon and crystal doctor. He tucks the word *success* on the back steps of his mind as Kit reads him one of Kellogg's quotes from the magazine: "'Fame is like being pawed at by a girl with bad skin, good body, and no sense of adventure.' I think that sounds an awful lot like Jules, not Kellogg."

"That's because it is Jules: Kellogg just gets him high and repeats parts of his monologues to the press."

"Oh," she says, disappointed.

On the heels of this sudden popularity, plans are emerging for a second, larger American tour and two possible European ones. Since the launch, membership in the band has risen, though Kellogg has decided to lock the group down to eighteen floating members.

At night they break up into packs: some nights they all practise, some nights they simply trawl the Main for smoked meat and attention.

Two blocks and a cab ride away, The Professor of Synchronicity launches his new album: *The Progress of Stars.* Scarred, and beautiful in a terrifying way, The Professor is myopic and is the devoted lover of the illustrious Genevieve, a young, promiscuous French chanteuse and Kellogg's latest ingénue. Purportedly half Mexican, half Anglo, The Professor croons like a cabaret ghost in his battered gringo Spanish.

Marry me, professor, dude, you rocked my underpants last night—pleas such as these appear on The Riots' chatroom the next day. So, The Professor is asked to become the nineteenth member and third guitar player for The Divine Light/Riots. He's also requested to open for both bands along the way.

The Professor accepts.

Ultimately, this is Kellogg's gift: his ability to assemble talent and palliate egos and rage, most of the time. Since the launch Jules has been mostly absent, and usually catatonic when he is around the social unit of the expanding band. Jules's face has healed but he is not the same; he barely sings any more and no one, except for Rize and some hard-core Riots fans, seems to notice that Margo does all the singing now, Kellogg cheering her on with his drumsticks tapping the curtains at the side of the stage.

At divided representations across town, The Riots and Divine Light cross-sect, exchanging members, phone numbers, gossip, and places to crash. Some stay too long and drink all the free booze at art openings. Some go for pizza, and some are left behind on park benches—in a rare warm-winter spell—to sleep it off. These few, among them Jim, cannot resist the drummers in the park and are lost to the francophone hippies.

The band wives have organized a clothing swap and a wine and cheese. Later, after a battery of calls, they all hook up at the Flora to drink Stella and eat calamari. Everyone's eyes are tinged with a little drunkenness and shock after being in tight, B.O.-smelling rooms and trying a little too hard to impress strangers. Finally free of the world's demands, The Riots and Divine Light fall back on themselves.

Rize and Kit stumble back to her place every night, hanging onto each other's leather jackets, not saying much. Both of them worry about Jules's second trial date. Rize doesn't talk about the new tour plans and she doesn't ask.

Holding her hand in the thawing night, he thinks about the new morning ritual that has evolved. When Kit has already left for work, Rize wakes up with Mr. Mittens on his chest. Doublez-M, as Rize calls him, is Kit's new cat she found in a marijuana barn-raid.

Though only a kitten, Doublez-M is a grey and black ball of pure energy whose gentle if intense wake-up call leaves Rize's chest a little emptier than usual for the rest of the day. The first morning the cat sat on his chest, Rize thought he'd been stabbed. Sweating and cursing, he could feel the sensation in his left arm fade and be replaced by a tingling numbness. In that last drawn-out moment of dreaming, before his eyes flew open, he had a very clear thought in his head: *Oh my god, Kit's stabbed me. Dying doesn't hurt.*

"You've got empty-chest syndrome," Kit says, smiling, poking a finger into his ribcage. "I wouldn't stab you, though. Never. Too messy and obvious."

She punctures his chest with her ever-ready finger gun.

Part two of the morning ritual is when Rize lies down, *sans* Doublez-M, after feeding him. On the bed, with his eyes closed, he tries to stop his shuddering heart from beating out of his chest. DTs, panic attacks, internal combustion—he searches his lexicon, believes that if he can place a word atop this feeling it will surely go away. The previous night's drinks pass before his eyes in a cartoon montage: two Caesars in the studio; one martini in a slick bar with a suspiciously silent Jules—out for an hour or so only—who tinkered at the Steinway between sets; and then, finally, four Stellas at the local.

What is it? What's wrong with you?

A craving for H? No. He's been clean for weeks. He thinks of H nostalgically. Like a sentimental ex-wife, she's always there, waiting for him to close the door and attack her with a kind of sad, perverse desire. But she can wait, it's not *she* he wants. Strangely, his head is clear; only his torso feels like an excavated piece of pottery. Just as he feels well enough to open his eyes, another blight of crushing panic seizes his chest. He wheezes and the new truth of things settles in his mind like the visceral memory of a gory, vice-filled nightmare.

It's like a cult. We travel together, play together, drink, eat, pray, and shit together. All the time now, all the time.

Now in any city after a show they can accrue at least twenty to thirty people on any given night. Surrounded and helmed by their fans, friends, and fellow musicians, they can rest here, talk about guitars and equipment and that time on the road when—

The phone rings, he hears Kit's sonorous outgoing message, knows immediately that it's for him, that it's Margo.

Vous avez rejoint le cinq, deux, huit . . .

No message.

Margo's in a state of retreat. She is sequestered in her and Jules's former apartment listening only to country music, Mahler, and television. He imagines Margo making love to Jules's ragged body every night to reverse the damage of the past five weeks. Rize has a sudden urge to call her back, to tell her about his stupid eye tattoo, about Doublez-M. To ask about the baby, but he knows he can't call her. He can't even breathe properly.

He thinks of Kit, hanging on the edge of this scene, rolling her eyes at the little indie girls in skinny jeans and feathered earrings who miraculously appear now, adding confusion and youth to their mob. He thinks of her at the Autumn Records launch, leaving before the encore with a stolen beer in her pocket for the cold walk home. Then he remembers finding her handwritten message to him just two days before, the note she failed to give him. But he found it, crumpled amid Kleenex, Q-tips, and pencil shavings:

Dear R.,
I don't know what happened to you, who you are. You have no sense of humour any more.

P.S. How I hate your bands.

His chest seizes again, locks, and then his heart continues beating, faster, till he reaches over to the ashtray to light half a cigarette. It's true. He doesn't have it any more, the ability to wake with a top-forty wiggle. It's pathetic, really. He can't summon the energy to slap his bare ass into her morning shower.

He can't mash a soft yam into his mouth to save his life or play guess-who-I'm-thinking-about-wearing-nothing-but-a-pair-of-leather-chaps-and-a-blue-boa, just to please her. He's tired. He bristles at her descriptions of Margo's messiness. It pains, not amuses him, that Kit has to go over there, every couple of days or so, to clean out her fridge, to make sure she's not smoking. Or drinking. Her slight disdain for The Riots, which once bolstered him, is now full-fledged resentment and it depresses and embarrasses him. Because he has to take the band seriously even if to Kit they're all a joke. *Because I'm inside now, Kit, and this life is mine.*

This life is Kellogg coked to the nines all the time now, his hand bandaged after slamming a pint on a glass table, sweat beading his brow as he overtips cab drivers and coat-check girls like he's goddamn Hemingway; is paranoid, anxiety-ridden Jules locked in his father's house and consulting his bulldog lawyer as he plans his divorce; is the patches of skin that appear on Guy's head like leopard spots; is Margo, who keeps missing the lines on her face when she tries to apply makeup and hasn't stopped drinking despite her pregnancy.

I don't know what happened. No sense of humour.

How can it be that thousands of people want to hear them? That *Spin* and *Entertainment Weekly* are calling Jules up to arrange interviews about their Meteoric Rise to Fame. Not funny, not ironic, not this.

"So, why are you doing it if everyone's so unhappy?" Kit asks him, tossing the dishtowel over her shoulder and folding her arms over her breasts. He can't answer her, not with a simple "Because we've worked so hard for this." She won't understand. There's no time for hashing it out with her in the solid edges of light, or afterward, in the drunk, throbbing boredom of other people's dramas that have become their problems.

How I hate your—

But all they do not say is always there, lurching The Riots into the next stage of wonder, America, and regret.

Still, he and Kit keep it tight. They present a united front, and wherever they go they appear as a team, dressed in matching leather jackets. They are quiet, serene in their collaborative depression. They crane their cigaretted hands to their mouths in unison and share the same eerie glow of suffocated defeat. They pretend they're not anxious about Jules's follow-up trial date, about the next stage of The Riots' career.

At night, in bed, they lie there, tethered to each other's secret lives as they think about Kit's garbage truths.

P.P.S. This, my love, is success.

* * *

IN THE COURTROOM, Jules looks small and young in his grey suit. Without a steady supply of marijuana he seems drained of all his fight and has the bearing of a man who believes he is in deep shit. He rolls his eyes and puts his head on the table. The judge calls a fifteen-minute recess. Jules borrows his lawyer's cell to call Margo, who's home sick.

Outside in the corridor, Kit and Rize share a salty hot chocolate and rub the sleep from their eyes. He feels feverish, his hot-cold head is ready to implode.

"Kit, we need to talk."

She shakes her coat for a cigarette and leaps off the bench, nodding at the security desk attendant on her way out the marble doorway. Rize follows the echo of her heels. She perches on a step halfway down the old stone staircase. It's snowing lightly; a horse and buggy go by as she lights up.

"Go on, then," she says, nodding toward the door. "Get back in there. To your family."

He gulps at the air.

"Oh, quit it, Kit."

"Isn't that what you're going to do? So, just get to it, Rize. Skip the talk."

His head throbs as he watches a piece of her black hair get caught up in the wind and fly upward. Some rightful-thinking inner voice tells him to walk away and yet he can't seem to tear himself from her side.

"I need to explain something," he says. "About leaving."

"Go on," she smirks, "I'm listening." She raises her hood over her head. She waits and waits as he examines his boots. Finally, she extinguishes her cigarette. "Okay, well, thanks for the explanation. You've been very clear. You can get your shit out of my place in the next forty-eight hours."

He forms his mouth in a way that threatens speech.

She smiles as if she is going to be sick. "Better yet, I can ask Margo to come get your stuff, if you'd like, or I'll just run in and explain it all to Jules, I'm sure he'll—"

"What are you talking about?"

A fake expression of concern passes over her face.

"Come on, Rize," she whispers, tilting her head. "You think I'm an idiot? I'm a detective. It's my job to know everyone's secrets."

She waves her hand at the gothic building, dismisses him. A white horse with a dirty tail and blinders trips on its shoes and sneezes in the street below and Rize feels as if his face is turning into a huge question mark. Kit descends another step.

Head spinning, he reaches across the space between them and grabs her arm.

"If you knew about Margo, why didn't you say anything?"

A glitter of a tear crests in her eye. Rize makes a move to wipe it away but she cuffs his arm. "Because you're not in love with Margo, Rize, you're just used to having her around, it's convenient. You two are so lazy and unimaginative, I can't even believe it."

Rize coughs.

"But maybe I'm wrong. Maybe you and Margo are just trying to put Jules and me in our place."

"In your place?"

"Is this talking, Rize? You repeating the last thing I say? Okay, I'll talk, you listen. I chose you. I chose to love you and only you." She shakes her head. "My best friend? *Your* best friend. Do you have any sense of human decency? Do you?"

No, he supposes he doesn't. *You're the decent one, Kit, remember? You and Jules.* He tries to say this but instead silence fills him like cement. They stand there like that, the knowledge that Kit knew his lies and took him into her bed and fed him dinner anyway makes his legs quiver. But they remain there, for frozen minutes that feel like eras, with Rize gripping her arm, his index finger jutting into her bone intimately, and Kit crying in the wind. They look at each other like grey stone lions until she says, quietly but fiercely, "Let go."

But he can't. He wants to follow her home and watch her fall asleep, without pain, in her bed, through the night, the way he did in the beginning. In the beginning of love he knew what a promise was and that keeping it meant he had to choose her nightmares, her fears, her beauty over his own wretched place in this world. It seems easy: he understands his mistake. He wants to make it right. He can. He can press Restart and take them both back to the beginning, back to the roof, when they laughed with their big mouths open, unashamed, and her collarbones shone like thin spears in the autumn light. When her hands held his cold face like he was someone good, someone special, someone worthy of simple human decency. Maybe he can—

"Let go of me. You loser, you psycho. Go on and get her, I'd like to see that. The junkie high school dropout and the drunk. Go on."

Why won't she stop talking? Why can't he let her go? Why is he shaking her arm like he's going to snap it in half? And why is he banging his own head into the stone wall, over and over? Like he *is* a psycho. Why isn't she breaking or bleeding along with him? And why, why god, why won't she take out that gun and take him out—get it all over with—like she's always wanted to do?

Then, oh. Two security guards tackle him and smash his jaw to the ground. But she's silent, finally. He can't hear anything except the guards screaming in French, along with the sweet, welcome sound of ebbing adrenalin in his ears.

Blood, on his hands. His mouth full of teeth, his own, just like the old dreams about losing them, just like that.

part3spring

18
jim

I was in a dingy motel, one that Isaac and I used to frequent sometimes when we felt like being trashy. I don't know what I was doing there, counting the cars in the parking lot, lighting cigarettes, watching the rain pound the asphalt. I'd even brought my violin and set up a practice stand to mitigate my boredom.

Out East, the dubious reward for surviving winter is two months of rain. Each year floods rampage river towns as the St. Lawrence melts into lives, ruins basements, and whooshes mice away.

Life stops. The news plays clips of people canoeing from neighbour to neighbour, collecting children and old folks as the foundations of their lives absorb water and ice. Walls that seemed so high, so solid, give way to the impermanence of season's end. In the city, grey nights and days repeat themselves over and over, from March to April. Trying to go outside is a perpetual struggle as bones freeze, then thaw, then freeze again.

In Montreal, gutters belch and streets become liquid asphalt, mixing gasoline and water. Warped bicycles cling to wrought-iron fences like mangled fossils of transport. Any Montrealer knows the familiar reek of dog shit released in the first warming weeks of April. Yes, this is a taste of Europe too, the forgotten debris in snowbanks now awash in the medley of organic and not so organic fluid. It's the stench of loneliness, of exposure. Spring reveals the filth we've hidden from ourselves, everything we've buried for six long months. The garbage, like our insides, is mixed up, strange: a doll's head, spaghetti, wool socks, chicken skin, a broken humidifier.

I turned away from the rain and looked at the empty bed where only weeks before Isaac had sprawled, his dark athletic legs poking out of the sheets. For a moment I imagined he was there, that he was watching me, his gaze warming my skin through the outside chill.

I'd left the West to come East in drought, when every breath pulled through my lungs ached with dry heat. When the earth seemed too close to the sun. Where I was born the sky was too wide, to eager to plummet straight into the dirt road, like me. But I guess I hadn't really wanted to plummet; in the end I'd wanted to run. To trade my blue and yellow clothes for white, black, and grey, the colour of everyone's else's clothes here.

Because now you fit in.

I did fit. My loud, childish clothes were wrapped in garbage bags and tucked in the back of my closet, just like my memories of the earth's plain scent. Now I wore black clothes, smoked a pack a day, and could nearly keep up with Margo's Chardonnay and Merlot habit. I contemplated my new sophisticated self as I finished my cigarette.

Standing there in that shitty motel room, communing with Isaac's long-gone sexy spirit, it struck me that I'd traded my life. I'd come all this way, for what?

For music?

I'd replaced my family with Rize, Kellogg, the band, but who were they, really?

The Angel Riots?

What kind of angels chew each other up, throw glass, and snort up their talent? What kind of people screwed each other's wives, poured champagne on perfectly well-made beds, and then threw themselves into half-empty swimming pools? These same people would then turn their smiles on for the cameras and say they were a family.

I could hardly blame everyone else; I was the most spectacular fraud of all. Suddenly, watching the rain come down, I had an urge to run. Run backwards over the clouds to where I could root my feet and look down at the sea of land below me, ten miles off in all directions. I wanted to trace the journey of a butterfly for half an hour, to watch life instead of being caught up in it. But I was paralyzed, I was stuck here now.

"Why don't you come to bed?" Isaac wooed, in my memory. I could imagine his thick lashes, half-closing.

The rain was falling harder now, it was torrential. The last time I'd seen rain like this was more than a year ago; it had swept over our fields while my father cheered it on. He'd stood at the threshold of the house, just as I stood now, pumping his fists in the air like some bucolic Zeus. He didn't know the rain would well in the corners of the fields and dry up in one short afternoon.

I opened the aluminum door to the balcony, pushed aside a heap of newspapers and stepped out. The wet cement was freezing on my bare feet and I could see my breath as I hugged my body for warmth. I needed, suddenly, to race back to my parents' warped yellow farmhouse, to leap off the balcony and leave Isaac's memory in that grimy motel room with my grey clothes.

Here the rain never stops; there, it never comes.

I gripped the rail and watched the churning clouds, the relentless damp seep into the ashen earth. Though I was an expert at running away just before the shit hit, this time I could only wait. I went inside and practised some more.

* * *

THERE IS SOMETHING humiliating and impersonal about surviving tragedy. I don't care what anyone says about its being heroic and life-enriching. All you get, all you really get out of it, let's face it, is the ability to be cynical in a confident, grownup way. I knew terrible things transpired in the world: people blew each other's heads off, threw their newborns in the garbage. Brothers went crazy. I knew that now, but to have to stand around and grieve and mourn and then go to the kitchen and make yourself a tuna fish sandwich? That killed me.

It killed me that I held onto the instinct to survive despite Yawnie's schizophrenia. I hated that I rode my bike, took tests, played concerts, when all I wanted was to become immersed in him again. We'd promised to be different, to remain one. But I was just me now: normal, not part of some telepathic super team who liked to fling loaded, cryptic objects around the literal and metaphoric universe.

But I couldn't be with Yawnie any more, either. And I hadn't been patient and kind as Simon had. I could barely stand to look at my twin sitting there silently, or rocking, or doing some other crazy-person thing like talking into his nicotine-stained hands. And now I didn't know who I hated more, that zombie with his head full of wet decaying hay or me as I flew into every obstacle like a newly widowed swallow, enraged by the indignity of death's small solitudes.

* * *

AFTER MY DAD asked me to play by the bonfire I weaved through the house searching for the last place I'd left my violin. On my way upstairs I stopped in the kitchen where the priest, a jovial man named Anderson, was having coffee and helping the women clean up. At the sink my mother was elbow-high in suds. She was talking to Eva, her best friend, who dried dishes and wrapped Cellophane around plates of food.

At the sight of me, both women stopped talking.

"What?"

"Oh, nothing dear," my mom said, vigorously scrubbing a roasting pan.

I knew they had been talking about Yawnie, about what kind of new doctors he'd have in the city and the new drugs those city doctors would prescribe. If anyone shared my guilt about not doing enough for Yawnie it was Mom, who'd spent two days in bed crying after my parents had decided to institutionalize him.

Mom had aged ten years in five. The price of doing farm work, domestic work, and caring for Yawnie showed in her beaten hands, her slow limp. Her hair, which had been exactly the same shade of blond as mine, was now all grey.

"I'm getting my violin. I'm going to play by the fire, if anyone's interested," I said, putting the paper plates in the garbage and wiping my hands on my mother's apron.

Mom nodded distractedly while Eva and Anderson nudged platters of food into the overflowing fridge.

"We'll be there in a second, honey," Mom said, still scrubbing at invisible grease on the pan. This was another new symptom of Mom's depression about Yawnie: her compulsive cleaning. Sometimes in the middle of the night you could hear her downstairs vacuuming, or else she would wash and re-dust all the sideboard china she'd cleaned just the day before.

She no longer scolded our father for bringing dirt in; she was only too happy to mop it up. While our house had never been particularly messy, it was old, and reflected the usual wear and tear of a family of five. But since Yawnie had stopped talking it had become as pristine and uncluttered as a five-star hotel room.

She emptied Yawnie's overflowing ashtrays without complaint and rotated him around in his seat, lifting his stiff legs so she could swipe a cloth over the bottom rung of the chair. Maybe she thought that if she scrubbed hard enough she could clear the fog away from his mind.

Before heading up the stairs, I stopped to look into the parlour. Yawnie's chair was empty but I could smell the lemon polish Mom had used to remove his fingerprints from the seat earlier that day.

Walking down the hallway toward my room, I was crushed by the onslaught of memory: Yawnie and me at twelve, lying in a field, our ankles hooked over our scratched-up knees. We wore cut-off jeans, mismatched sneakers. We were busy making plans. We'd decided that, at eighteen, we would get an apartment together and move far away. We hadn't decided on the exact location, but we knew we wanted to be in a city, either to the extreme east or west of the choked flatness of our youth.

"What about Vancouver?"

I wrinkled my nose and tugged on Yawnie's shirt, which had a number 2 on it.

"It rains too much."

"But Jim, we love rain, remember? You could join the Vancouver symphony and we could swim in the ocean every day."

"What would you do?"

Yawnie's eyes focused on a slow-moving smear of cloud. "I could be an architect." His eyes lit up at the revelation. Only two months ago we had won first prize in the regional science-fair competition by ignoring the rules and constructing a miniature replica of our farm. We covered it with an "eco-dome," which controlled the weather, but don't ask me how. It was all Yawnie's idea and it made no sense to me. My role had been purely manual: I glued bits of wood together and wrote out some mumbo-jumbo about weather systems and erosion because my penmanship was better than his.

Everyone had been so impressed by the miniature world, not to mention the sheer patience required to construct such a thing, that we'd won hands down, beating even the colour-coordinated project on radio waves and one compelling if abstract project by another pair of twins, from Regina, on how dogs really see.

"Um, I think you have to be good at math to be an architect."

"No problem. I can take it at university."

"What about Toronto?"

This was our usual quandary: while Yawnie was drawn to the waxy West Coast foliage, the promise of mountains breaking up the sky, I had a fascination with Eastern cities like Montreal and Toronto. I imagined myself playing violin in the bowels of a subway system. I saw myself drinking café au laits with like-minded artists, my hands dirty with newsprint and hardened from practice.

"What if we spent our winters in Vancouver and our summers in Montreal?"

Ever compromising when it came to me, Yawnie was eager to work out a firm plan. He seemed to think our possibilities were limitless. That we could run back and forth between the coasts, stopping in occasionally to shower our wealth upon our parents. According to Yawnie, we would eventually convince them to move with us, leave the farm behind.

My brother had already conceived of a palatial ranch in the B.C. interior where our parents could be the farmers they deserved to be. His dream estate contained five rooms, cattle, horses, a hot tub, a manmade pond. Yawnie knew he couldn't discourage our parents from being farmers, but at least he could convince them to be great, rich ones, high in the mountains, not flattened by a landscape of glacial erosion, of longing. They could hire ranch hands, dudes, and enjoy an endless supply of the precisely timed sun and rain required for the steady running of a modern ranch.

The two beers I'd drunk were making my head hurt. I undid my ponytail and put my forehead on Yawnie's closed door, which I hadn't opened since I'd moved into Simon's room. Here I was, eighteen now and my mind still hanging off the scaffolds of all my brother's great plans. And then I felt it: an abrupt stab on the left side of my skull.

Get away from the door, Jim, please.

The cable connected, the wires conducted at once, at last. I ripped the door open.

And there, from a hook in the ceiling, like some awful mock-up of death, hung Yawnie. The yellow twine rope Dad used for almost every fix-up task corralled his silhouette. His body moved back and forth, slowly, in front of the moonlit window.

He was gurgling, still alive. I wondered whose voice it was inside the room, filling it. It was so formal, I almost didn't recognize it.

"It's important that I not be moved."

"I understand," I said, taking a step toward the lolling figure that blocked out the near-midnight moon.

I was now standing on his bed. My hand struck out.

Don't.

I nodded, but once again ignored him. My limber violin fingers wedged themselves between the taut rope, against his skin. They cracked from the weight, but I didn't feel any pain, except for the one in my head.

I said, leave me alone.

I watched the whites of his eyes roll. My fingers stayed clenched between his neck and the rope as they grappled for more space.

Yawnie clawed my arms with his long fingernails. But my arms remained stiff, unmoving as tree limbs steeling themselves against a thunderstorm. I watched blood trickle down as he carved the scars in my arm Isaac would later interrogate me about in his Westmount mansion. I watched and listened as my heart shifted and then stopped beating for a second. Then my fingers snapped away; I couldn't hold on any more.

"So, this is it then?" I asked calmly, my warped fingers bending between us like worms. For an instant the old Yawnie—the playful and macabre boy I'd grown into and alongside—reappeared and grinned at me heartily.

God almighty, Jim, you make it hard for a man to die alone.

And then he was gone again.

19
rize

Back teeth: soft, corrosive, but still present. Except for two incisors, frontal units are nonexistent.

The muddy green of outside slowly leaks into his room. There are white sheets on the bed and his window faces a small backyard with piles of slush. Beneath that are lumps of brown earth, grass. The black fire escape winds around the window like a yawning ribcage. When he wakes he cowers for a moment, examining the stairs, not understanding their function. He imagines he's been swallowed by some beast, like a horse, or a whale. But how could it be raining inside a whale?

I'm like Pinocchio, only my teeth fall out when I tell lies.

His throat is surfeited with pain, it clears the top of his palate. There's a retainer in his mouth and when he moves his head toward the window he feels it again, the throbbing in his cankered and bruised mouth. He is grateful for it. He lets himself be pulled under by the tides of sleep that leave him without dreams, without time, without the separation of days.

Surfing this reef between pain and sleep, he begins to suspect there are things he has forgotten, but the leaves on the soaked trees outside tell him that it's all right. It's okay, kid, sometimes we have to acquiesce to falling, to forgetting, some odd inner voice tells him.

He forgets that he sees Margo by the bedside, looking chunky and strange in a blue dress with a white collar. She tells him spring is coming.

What's she doing? Knitting. Is she knitting? She puts down her needles to tell him that Jules is waiting for him, that they've all started a new life. But he knows she's lying.

The only thing she doesn't lie about is that the album is doing well; they've sold over a thousand in just under two weeks. He knows this should mean something to him, but along with the pain and the remembering, he's having trouble comprehending the significance of certain expressions like "We need you." And then and then and then. And then there are the questions. Like:

Will the baby have to go on tour with us?

Is Jules in jail?

Did you even really love me, Margo? Or was it—

Kit?

But as soon as he remembers he forgets again. Forgets that once, on the road, in Kentucky, they all slept in an eighteenth-century attic room across from a country bar, and he found a book of spells there that he gave to Margo for her birthday. He forgets how she held his long hair when he barfed on her lap after eating nine fireflies for one of the spells. He knew it was his penance for stealing the book in the first place. He forgets that he was once dumb enough to eat the cat food that Jules said was pâté and that he's the only one of his friends who isn't afraid of spiders.

Feeling the dull crush of pain as it releases him once more into sleep, he forgets his mother's name. But, before he goes under, he reels up for one last gulp of air. In this brief respite between memory and pain he remembers everything, and screams his mother's name through his bloody embouchure.

20
jim

My first Eastern winter was spent being cradled by Isaac, toting my garbage-bag-covered violin case home from auditions, weeping for sun, for a break from the daily sight of garbage piled high. In the heart of winter, Isaac had promised me a week in Mexico. But we would never take our trip. Like so many promises Isaac made, the vacation south was just something he'd said to distract me from the fact that he was leaving on another business trip.

This new season, I'm not so fearful of the elements. Now I crave the endless cold and rain, have grown used to it. In some ways, there's nothing worse than beautiful days when you're depressed. At least a lagging winter mirrors your terrible mood. I wouldn't know what to do if the season turned, if I had to be trapped in blocks of sunshine and witness green vines on walkups. This year, some grit in me tells me to stay here, that to watch this cold spring unfold without my lover, my brother, is my punishment.

Now, with Isaac disappeared, I'm compelled to face the filth in my life coming to the surface. Loneliness is contradictory: it makes you hard, yet contemplative. There are a lot of silent hours to fill, and so you play reels of the past. Things come up in these images. Yellow rope and owl holes. Sneakered feet and buried watercolour paintings. Given enough loneliness, you can excavate almost any sunken memory. *But I'm not alone,* I try to convince myself. *I have the band,* I chant, as I pack up my violin, put on my dull entertainer's uniform, and brave the sleet. I get to the basement early, to practise. I grab a café au lait from upstairs and sip it slowly to warm my hands.

Some others are already at rehearsal, setting up stands, talking. I rosin my bow and tune. Kellogg breezes in wearing a brick-red muslin and a silver necklace. He's greeted with applause, whistles. Fresh from a week-long meditation retreat in California, Kellogg looks unnaturally brown and healthy next to the rest of us. He pulls me aside.

"You look great, Kellogg. How was La La?"

"He won't talk to anybody."

"Who? Hey, nice dress."

"Rize. It's not a dress, I prefer 'robe.'"

"I know about it, I heard, it's awful. His mouth's full of infection, he's—"

"He's asking for you."

"Me?"

"Yeah." Kellogg studies me.

"Take a cab to his place after rehearsal. You got cash?"

"Yeah."

Kellogg pulls me to him and gives me a fifty.

"I don't need money, really, Bodhisattva. Why does he want to see me?"

"Dunno, but Margo got him a chalkboard and he keeps writing 'Jim' on it. At first we thought he wanted his Hendrix records, or one of his crazy Irish uncles, but, turns out, it's you he wants. Any idea why?"

"Rize and I are friends, I guess he just wants to see me."

Someone knocks over a cello and Kellogg starts yelling.

"Ten days of silence, with nothing but lentils and yoga, and not half an hour back in this town and I'm swearing and smoking like a sailor. Jesus." Then he grabs me by the arm again and says in a low whisper, "Tell him this toothless business is played out. Tell him it's time to stick his dentures in and get his ass back in the game. Tour is less than a month away." He pulls my hood over my head and squints at me. "Tell him whatever he needs to hear, my little messenger."

* * *

RIZE'S ROOM IS DARK and the blue curtains are pulled against the oncoming night. Boy-sweat and some other slightly musky odour hangs in the air. It's the smell of neglect, reckless sleep. It reminds me of Simon and Yawnie's room.

His eyes are closed when I come in and there's a small notepad hanging loosely from his hand. I find a jar for the daisies I brought and prop them precariously on his bedside. Then I pull up a chair and wait, not wanting to wake him. When I look up Rize's eyes are open; he hands the pad to me.

Daisies. My favourite. Thnxs.

"Mine too. How you feeling?"

Rize shrugs and tries to cough.

Don't look so scared. I look worse then I feel. Or the other way around. anyway, its not so bad.

"How many teeth? There are all kinds of rumours floating around. Some people say your whole bridge, some say—" Then I realize I'm babbling. "Shit. Sorry, Rize."

He scratches on the pad.

Incapable of bullshit. Small talk. You. 4. 2 top, 2 bottom. 1 was a fake, anyway, so, 3, actually.

"Kellogg sent me."

He flips a page over: *I know.*

"Listen, he wants me to tell you to think about coming back. He says—"

FUCK KELLOGG, Rize writes, taking care to make the letters all the same size.

"Okay, then." Not knowing what to say, I pluck petals off a daisy, examine the pile of books and music magazines next to Rize's bed. Then I remember his last night onstage, how he glowed out from the corner, his cheeks filled with air as he struggled for that fragile, plaintive tone of his. I recall his shiny black hair—that now looks so dry—falling around his face. I stare at his chubby hands that look tiny and swollen, incapable of making any noise or trouble at all. I sit there, patiently, with Rize. Just sit there, as I never did with Yawnie.

We stare outside and listen to the wind gurgling like a starving stomach until I break the quiet with, "You know, Jules was acquitted. They said there wasn't enough evidence for a conviction."

Rize nods as if to say, *That's good.*

"It is good. Could you imagine the hysteria if Jules had a real criminal record and not just a bunch of speeding tickets?"

Don't. It still hurts to laugh, he scribbles.

"He started the divorce proceedings, you know. Right after she, ah, lost the baby."

Rize turns away, giving me his back. There's a small transistor on his bedside table, which he flicks on. The radio blasts out a wail of jazz. Rize flicks it off, knowing that a blare of horns will not make it right this time. Even though we've devoted our lives to music, we both know that the most important things happen without a soundtrack. His back shudders for a moment and then he goes still.

"Rize," I say, rubbing his back. I say it in a soft voice because, even though it's hard, I want him to know I'm actually with Kellogg on this one, that I don't think he should feel sorry for himself and lie there all broken up and crying.

"I know you're mad at him right now, but Kellogg says to tell you, and I quote, 'You ain't no Chet Baker just 'cause your teeth and mouth are officially all rotted out now.'"

Rize turns to face me and beams, like a toothless baby, as he weeps. He laughs with knowing sadness; a man who finally understands the truth about something that's eluded him for a long time. He reaches out to me then, with his chubby hand, and takes my arm before turning back to stare out the window. I sit with him under the shadows of early night, listening to big-band radio. I hold his hand till it feels like a flat dull object and the day goes away.

* * *

THE NEXT MORNING there's a stock photo of Isaac on the cover of *The Gazette.* In it, he's wearing a too-small tux, holding a cigar in one hand and a martini in the other.

Pearle Dead After Near Arrest

Isaac Pearle, a prominent businessman, is dead after suffering a heart attack when RCMP officers entered his home to arrest him on charges of fraud.

After a lengthy RCMP investigation, Pearle, the CEO of Pearle Imports, was charged with having embezzled over $4 million from various corporate accounts. "Obviously Internal Affairs is looking *into the extenuating circumstances of this tragic incident," said Katherine Lemay, the lead investigator on Pearle's case.*

Pearle went into cardiac arrest shortly after RCMP officers entered his home last night with a warrant for his arrest. Officers were unable to revive Pearle, who died almost instantly.

Known as a playboy, bon vivant, and supporter of the arts, Pearle, 45, is survived by his estranged wife, Lily Pearle.

Maybe the mystics are right: it's a total free-for-all and you're on your own.

Having crushed a living being, my own brother, in our mother's womb with our umbilical cord, my own karma was set from the start. I had been wrong to believe otherwise. I'd already broken the cardinal rule of not hurting another living being, and without even the benefit of direct oxygen.

Yawnie was born choking, and after the accident he always seemed to be throttled by something—cookies, water, air—so maybe it made sense to leave him there, tangled on that cord.

I was born loving a man or, rather, an acorn of a man. I'd had that love and held it in my hands and then I crushed it like a pink-skinned bird when it got too hard to take care of. I never deluded myself into believing my love was anything other than damage. I never told Isaac I loved him, as I knew it would curse him, so I committed my body, and my actions, to relay the message.

I'm only eighteen and it's already too late for me, I see that now. I've already harmed my soulmate, taken his name, abandoned him, so I've no right to talk about soulmates, or any of that. Because even if you're lucky enough to have one it doesn't mean you can be together.

I try to string my thoughts into some kind of logical order, but it's useless. After drinking half a bottle of Jim Beam and holding my head in my hands for four straight hours, trying to feel something other than numb, I decide it's better to go to rehearsal than stay in and watch the eleven o'clock report on Isaac. So, garbed in distressed leather armour and black gloves, with my case in tow, I head out into the endless April rain.

My cellphone starts ringing. Instinctively, I know it's more bad news, that it's Kellogg. I know this because it doesn't stop ringing. I can hear it jangling away inside my purse as I unlock my bike and hoist my case on my back like some hobo.

When I get to the brand-new rehearsal space in Old Montreal, a cramped room up five flights of industrial stairs, it's dark in the studio. There are candles all around, as if Kellogg's in the middle of a séance. The only artificial light is the blue glow of his laptop lighting up his clean face.

"You shaved your beard," I say. "What? You going all corporate on us now?"

He rolls his eyes and winces as I turn on the overhead light.

"I've been calling you," he says, flicking off the light.

"I know."

Kellogg has his manic, cocaine lisp, the one he gets when things are happening too fast for even him to keep up with. He taps out a number on his cellphone as I sit on a guitar amp and look around.

"What's up, K?"

He waves his hand at me distractedly and discusses plane tickets to Amsterdam on the phone. Watching Kellogg clench his jaw like a nervous monkey makes me uneasy, so I look at my silver fingernails that I recently had manicured for Isaac's pleasure.

He liked my body plucked and shaved to a seal-like texture. It's ironic, I think, that Isaac will never see my nails, or any other part of me, ever again. Especially since I've gone through the effort of getting everything waxed and painted. The thought that I'll never again lay eyes on him makes me feel as though I've been punched in the head, so I put my face in my hands to breathe properly. It's the first time the reality of his absence from the world has occurred to me and, in order to process this, I trace every change in my physical appearance since I last saw him: a new undershirt, my manicured hands, a new toe ring for my left foot. As I catalogue my recent changes, I wonder if this is the familiar morbid and mundane song of the one who's been left behind. *You piece of shit, you will never see how great I look in this new yellow sweater.*

To calm myself, I think of how Isaac's body might have changed too. This isn't a disgusting thought. In fact, it comforts me to think that he's altered. As a country girl, I'm comfortable around dead, loamy things. Bones and earth aren't gross, it's my buffed nails that are disgusting. Vulgar, in fact. Suddenly, my whole put-together, clean, crisp look feels obscene.

Although it seems an hour has gone by since Kellogg picked up the phone, I've likely spent only about five minutes contemplating life, death, and nail polish. Finally, fed up with the agent's slovenly English, Kellogg hangs up, locks the door of the studio, and sits on the floor in front of me, embracing my violin case, his long fingers moving over it in exaggerated strokes.

Outside the studio, Martin and Jules are watching bad TV in the smoking lounge. "So, where is everybody?" I ask. "This place looks too small to hold us all."

Kellogg nods, then pulls his chin to his chest.

"Hi!" I wave my hands in his face, trying to get a reaction. "Can you at least speak to me, dude? I rode my bike in the rain from the Plateau to get here!"

"Jim—"

"What?"

"We're going to Europe."

"I know."

"Jim, we're downsizing. We're getting Parisian musicians to cover the tour."

I crack my knuckles in the silence and watch Kellogg cradling my case.

"I'm sorry."

I hold out my hands out. "Give it."

"You'll get money, Jim. For your time, your contribution. Plus, you have some points."

"Everyone's throwing money at me these days."

"There's plenty of it now."

"Sure. What else is there?" I get up from the amp and kick the case from Kellogg's hands. I have a sudden desire to rip through the studio, mangle wires, pour his beer on the control panel, throw wax on his precious hands. But my innate respect for musical space restrains me, and so instead I grab his beer bottle and fling it against the door. It cracks and spills across the entrance pathetically.

I can hear Martin and Jules laughing in the lounge, Jules's big warm voice smearing the moment with a taste of what's lost. I miss Jules already, his humming jokes buried in his half-day beard. I miss the way he sings castrato in a British accent till we're all on the floor, peeing our pants.

So many voices of people you love in the other room drowned out by these broken promises, how this scene breaks us apart. Kellogg looks up at me with his sorry eyelashes, his blue eyes filled with sparks.

"I can't believe this. You're ditching us?"

"You don't know what it's like. It's like breaking up with ten people, Jim."

"Are they next? Those two in there?" I hitch my fingers toward the lounge.

Kellogg nods and takes a swig from a mickey he produces from his jacket pocket. "Look, I had a drink with Sam from The Zionists last night, he says they want you. They're recording a new album and they need—"

"Fuck The Zionists. Fuck you and your bands. Fuck your loving-kindness, and fuck your money."

"Jim, I—"

"We aren't just stand-ins, asshole, we're *it*."

And then I realize that what I said to Rize that last night we all played together, that he and I were just players, just followers of a kind, was wrong. I realize, too, that what Kellogg's saying, that it's cheaper to hire European musicians, is all wrong. Everybody knows the obnoxious amounts the French unions demand. It's a joke, it's got to be. There's more to all this, to Kellogg's wanting to be rid of his minions, more than I want to know. Still, I don't feel done with Kellogg, so I step in front of his imposing figure and poke him in the shoulder.

"Hey, you don't get off that easy. You're supposed to be our leader, so why don't you lead us. Why don't you stand up for us?"

Kellogg grabs my lapels and pulls his face to mine as he looks down into my hair, the way he did that first night I met him in the school gymnasium. "Quell that self-righteous tone for a second, little one. And don't preach about leadership, okay? None of these clowns knows the first thing about leadership."

"Except you," I sneer.

"Except me," Kellogg says, releasing my coat, arms spread in a benevolent Don gesture. "You came to me looking for an experience, for some success, and I gave that to you, so leave me the fuck alone."

"If I was so pathetic, you should have left me where you found me. You should have left The Riots alone, too."

"To what?" he laughs, exhaling cigarette smoke from his lungs. "To implode on themselves?"

And then it hits me that I was right, that I saw it all that night in the New York City green room. It's all been some sped-up human experiment with rewarding results; Kellogg just wanted to see what would happen.

"Yes, Kellogg, to implode. So what? What's the difference? What was the point of uniting the bands, making a label, just so you could fire everyone? Just to see if you could?"

"If that's what you think, that it's all money and I'm on some bullshit ego trip—if you want to reduce it in your inimical I'm-only-twelve-but-I've-got-fucking-ghosts-in-my-eyes Jim way, then what can I say?" Expansive with anger and drink, Kellogg is beyond reasoning, beyond figuring out: he's beyond us all now.

For a second I think of Rize and me in his room, breathing in the silence around us as if we were small sparrows puffing up our feathers to shield ourselves from the windy blare of a spring storm. I walk to the door, looking back once more at Kellogg, sitting on the floor with all his props: his cellphone, his beer, his baggie of coke, his tiny laptop glowing bright blue. Suddenly

I see black snakes flicking around his head in silhouette as he turns toward me.

"Jim, listen—"

"What? What do you want from me? You want me to pretend it's okay that you've just cut me loose like baggage the minute your 'concept band' is successful? What?"

Kellogg gets up unsteadily and weaves toward me; I can see that he's much drunker than I thought.

I look at him calmly. "I quit school for this bullshit, K."

"You didn't."

"It's okay, you didn't know."

And then I see them again, the snakes. Cut off at the roots, they're trying to survive without his head. One wild snare winding murderously around another, like broken lightning, snapped guitar strings, worldly entrapments, bad dreams, clingy American girls, all his worst fears.

He places his hands on my shoulders and looks into my spine.

"What do you want from me?" I ask again, wanting so much to be away from him. Realizing that what I thought was magic in his eyes, something special from him to me, was only another exercise in manipulation.

And then I know exactly what he wants. Forgiveness and freedom. It's what I wanted too, that last night when I held Yawnie's head and my fingers twitched down and failed to save him.

It's what everyone wants when they're breaking someone's heart: to be rid of the person and yet absolved of guilt, of the unhappiness they've caused. They want their rationalizations heard and gulped up by the wronged, and then they want their victims to go away, peacefully. To never be haunted again.

* * *

THE LAST TIME I see Margo she is standing outside the studio building looking like a stitched-together doll, an imitation of a girl. She has the fake composure of the very drunk, as though everything inside her is about to spill out. I sigh as she offers her hand out to me.

"Sorry, Jim."

"Didn't make the cut, Mar."

"Can I buy you a drink?" she asks, looking over my shoulder as if she actually expects to see heads rolling down the marble steps. I shake my head. "Nah, I've got to ride home, in this—" I swing my arm out into the rain, slapping her waiting hand out of the way by accident. It sends her stumbling on her red heels.

"I can talk to him, you know," she says quietly, finding her balance and straightening up slowly. "He's all—"

"Coked up and freaked out?"

She smiles as if I am speaking a different language and she wants to agree but has no idea what I'm actually saying. "Please let me buy you dinner, drinks, Jim."

I step back, prop Margo up on the curb as if she were some tiny delicate thing instead of a chubby rocker girl three sheets gone. I'm wasted from all the sneering and fighting and struggling and just need to get home. Besides, I've meted out enough forgiveness today and there's nothing left, sadly, for old Margo with her movie-star sadness and wine-stained mouth.

"I just need to get home, Mar, I'm tired, I—"

"I can get you back into the band, Jim. I love you," she adds, without a trace of irony. I laugh. Ah, the good old Angel Riots

"I love you" card. It's used to trump any betrayal, big or small. Though I know I should just leave it, turn on my heel and ride on home, it's just too rich to resist: Margo talking to me about love.

"You love me, Mar? The way you love Kit?"

She swoons on her red shoes at the mention of Kit. "This has nothing to do with her."

"Sure it does. You don't even know me. All you want is to replace her. All you want is for me to stick around so you have a female audience for more of your antics."

Margo glowers. "Antics? You have no right to judge me. I know about your dead brother, about Isaac, he's married, you know—"

"He's dead, too. Did you know that?" Staring into Margo's sodden eyes, I see my own hollowed irises reflected in hers. I see myself becoming someone else in her eyes. My guilt, my sordid trail of men have made me valuable: at last she knows, I *am* a true contender, after all. "So, you do know me. How'd you find all that out?"

"Kit," she spits. "Kit knows everything about everyone."

"Knew. I guess you'll miss her not only as your best friend but also as your prime source. Besides, if I'm such a shitty person, why do you need me? Please, Margo, let's just call this goodbye."

"I'll pay for dinner, I'll get you back in," she pleads, holding onto my handlebars as I unlock my bike. "Listen to me. This band is huge. You're an idiot to walk away."

I shrug. "Then I'm an idiot. Let go of my bike."

"No!" she screams, commanding the attention of every stray pigeon and soul on the street who happens to be left out in this awful night. She lodges her legs around my front wheel and yanks the bars toward her chest. "Listen to me, I need to get away from all I have. You don't understand, it's like, I want something, so bad, and then I get it! So, what do I do? I go and fucking destroy it. It's scary. I need to explain it to you, I need someone—"

I wrench my bike away from her grasp and push her gently toward the wall. "Really?" I say, my angry, atavistic, pre-Montreal self returning. The one that chucked rocks at coyotes and drank homemade chokecherry wine from my father's stash, the one that climbed the tanned shoulders of rambling Native boys and clawed at the good hot earth with blistered hands.

"It sounds terrifying. What's it like to be Margo Bay?" I say, clapping my hands together in mock wonder. "To get everything you want and yet never be satisfied?"

"It's fucking horrible!" A big crocodile tear slips from her famous eyes. Eyes that have been blackened for the covers of magazines. Eyes that cajole and will and seduce and sob on demand. Empty starving eyes that explain four broken teeth and no more girlfriends for anybody, despite Margo's theatrics and I love you's.

"You're right, you always get what you want. You wanted Kit and Jules gone, so they left. You wanted me out—goodbye. You having second thoughts about alienating us? Well, talk to Kellogg about the fact that you've changed your mind. But I'm not a part of this charade any more. You don't get me. I'm out."

* * *

IT'S RAINING HARD as I ride my bike up the potholed streets. I remember Isaac after the launch, propped up on all four hotel-room pillows, tapping his glass of cognac with his pinkie ring, warning me:

"Wait till it blows, Jim. These things always do. Trust me, you can't mix business and friendship."

"What are you talking about?" I was lying on the floor, trying to fall asleep under the cigarette clouds.

"You're the cultured one, the artiste," he'd said, laughing.

I rested my legs on the bed, pushed him with my heels until he rolled off on top of me, still holding his glass. But I didn't laugh with him, for once.

"I'm just your sucker millionaire, I know. I know you don't take me seriously, that you just use me for sex and entertainment ..."

"Shut up."

"No, listen to me, Jim." His fingers trawled to my neck. I flinched away. I hated it when Isaac got all paternal and intense on me; he rarely did, but it was infuriating nonetheless. He gripped my neck, took a long slow sip of his drink, and released me, counting off on his fingers. "One, that ridiculous, drug-addled horn player is sleeping with the singer's wife, that's obvious."

"He's not drugged, he's been clean since—"

"Whatever, something's going on with that kid. Two, that Kellogg is a good businessman, damn good."

"So?"

"So, like me, the guy's a megalomaniac."

"Kellogg's a prince."

He held up his hands defensively. "I concur: I just spent the last two hours snorting coke with the guy in his office."

"You did? You guys were in the van the whole time?"

"Yes, he's a charming son of a bitch. But what I'm saying is that rock music is bad business. Between egos, drugs, and fights about girls, well, no matter how good the music is, it all ends in tears."

"Oh, you. So cynical. Can't you just be happy for me?"

"I am. I just want to protect you. But you have to know this won't last, right?"

Right.

Breezing my way through a red light, blinded by the rain, I realize in one easy moment that it's my own fault. That there were warnings but I didn't listen.

On impulse, my hands seize the brakes as a car stops short in front of me, horn and headlights blazing.

You silly fool, whatever made you think you were bigger than disappointment? Bigger than life?

Nothing, I guess, Yawnie, nothing at all. Only *you* were too big for life.

Straightening my bike out and waving at the driver that I'm okay, I think of all their faulty parts: Yawnie's static mind, Kellogg's insatiable curiosity and greed, Rize's unformed will, Margo's broken eyes, Isaac's stuttering heart. I see my fingers grip my brother's throat uselessly; I watch them drop up and down the neck of my violin mechanically as Kellogg yells at us to play faster; I observe my head cocked against Isaac's barrel chest as he sighs and shifts in his sleep.

And then it hits me: I'm free. Of Yawnie's madness, of Isaac's games, of Kellogg's and Margo's lies.

It strikes me, too, that I've been conducting my own social and spiritual experiment, seeing how long I could live with the dead in my heart and the lost in my bed. Like Kellogg, I guess, I wanted to see how long I could coast, how long it would take until my old life exploded in my face. There's a kind of relief when it finally happens, when it's all over and you have no choice but to let go.

It's a kind of dying, to say goodbye, to see the last bit of poison drain from your infected union. *Dead to me,* I think, *you're all dead to me.* I repeat it over and over. Then I consider what those words really mean: that you have murdered inside your heart.

I ride up the Plateau streets, vaguely aware of the blaring horns behind me. I take the long way home, pedalling fast in the rain, away from their songs and murmured conceits. Away from the press clippings and blogs telling me how great it all is and was to be part of such a thing.

Others can believe we were once a group of lovers, a family who wrapped up our seasons in loud bars with swallow feathers sewn to our sleeves in the fragile solidarity of rhythm. *I* know we were just a bunch of children hooked on free hotel rooms and feedback loops. *I* know it was pure until we swallowed our own hype and it soured our guts, turning our private joys into bile. Other people can believe those myths—they aren't our stories or songs any more.

Up, up, the Plateau hill, knees cracking, tires slicked, face wet, I clutch my splintering chest, hold onto the last shreds of my identity. Then I am filled with something larger and more unpredictable than sorrow or loss. It's bigger than words or music and belongs only to me. It's so quiet and real I almost miss it. I dare not say my new name, my first one. It's enough to remember.

part4summer

Tonight the downtown marquee reads:

Autumn Records presents

The New Angel Riots

With Special Guests: I Have Replaced You

21
rize

When he emerges from the air-conditioned, puke-coloured walls of the dentist's office, it's summer, the season of his dreams. Around him people on the streets melt, and, from third-storey balconies, he can hear French songs being played on badly tuned guitars. Jubilant but sluggish, the voices carve out a space between exhaust sputter and shifting gears. He spies tight-jeaned girls tugging at their snug bras and tripping into dark bars and watches bike couriers weave through traffic like hummingbirds. An ice cream slips off a girl's cone and a golden retriever laps up the pistachio in staccato rhythm.

Outside, Jules is waiting for him with a package of clove cigarettes, his horn, and a smoked meat sandwich. Jules shudders at the sight of Rize, whose face is slightly collapsed. Rize shakes his head when Jules offers him a bite of the sandwich. He takes off his jacket and lights a cigarette, manoeuvring it in his mouth carefully.

"You can't even stand to look at me, can you?"

Jules meets his eye briefly, and then stares at a beefy couple Rollerblading by. "I came to visit you once. What? Don't remember?"

Rize shakes his head.

"I forgot about that bloody eye tattoo."

"One cosmetic procedure at a time," Rize says, giving him a gummy smile to show off his new dentures.

Jules rolls his eyes at him. "Why do you have to be such a disaster?" he asks rhetorically as he shoulders Rize's horn and begins to walk away, creeping after the Rollerblade couple who are now making out on a nearby park bench. He gazes with undisguised interest at their brown rippling muscles folding over each other.

Rize watches his friend's compact back and thinks of the year he did not speak to Jules, the year he spent setting up tents for the circus all across the States. Grade ten, the year he dropped out of secondary after getting suspended the second time. While Jules got caught for smoking, read Chaucer, and starred in *Oliver Twist*, Rize licked salt off daiquiris, climbed makeshift poles, and constructed tarps with two black Alabamans and a Québécois boss.

He sticks his tongue into the top nubby flesh of his newly moulded set of teeth and walks after Jules. He tries to pulls his horn off his friend's back but Jules stumbles and throws the case to the ground. He turns to face Rize.

"So much shit," Jules sputters, covering his face with his hands.

He wishes he could be brave like Jules, wishes he could cry on the spot. Could tap into that endless roving stream of sorrow flowing at the bottom of his spine.

But he can't. He's done crying and bleeding and cheating.

Instead, Rize leans over to pick up the case, realizing why Jules brought it: he'd left it in the studio before he got hurt, and now there's no studio.

Later, after three games of pool, three shots of vodka, and two pitchers of beer, Jules pulls a band flyer from his pocket. On the front is an ad for tonight's Riots' gig, with a caricature of Kellogg looking dashing and thin, his mouth full of teeth. Jules pushes it toward Rize, who turns it over to examine Jules's latest list.

– the band
– the baby
– your teeth
– kit

these are.
These are.

The things we have lost.

"And Jim," mutters Rize. "We lost her, too. So you can add her to your list."

After about ten minutes of nothing but the sound of pool shots and staticky television Jules says, "That's right buddy, you just sit there looking at me with your big whatever eyes while I tell you he took it all while we dropped like flies around him."

"So, do you want to go to this thing, or what?" Rize says, slurring his words.

Jules shakes his head.

"I don't understand," Rize says, examining the flyer.

"I sold him the name. He bought me out of the company. I couldn't think of what else to do—"

"I see." Rize crumples up the flyer and shoves it into his pocket.

Jules pulls Rize outside where it's begun to rain. He stands under the first wet drops with his mouth open and allows himself to be tugged along the mangy Main.

Jules may have the drama of tears but he does not yet know that he will die at age fifty-five of a stroke, that it will be quick and blightless. He doesn't know that he will have three sons with a woman named Jackie who lives in San Francisco, who runs her own children's theatre company.

Jules doesn't know that Rize will wake before him and go downstairs, to the basement, to play until his mouth bleeds. That, in anticipation of this day, when Kellogg and the world would have the two of them firmly by the nuts, Rize took Jules's warnings about K to heart and stole over three hundred thousand dollars' worth of musical equipment from the studio. Plus, two old mastered Riots reels Kellogg doesn't even know about. He's stashed all the stuff at his mother's apartment. Jules has no idea that it's Rize who's prescient now.

They will start again. Without K, without money, like the first time. Jules doesn't know that Rize has stood before his closet, burning holes in his socks and ashing cigarettes in his blazer pockets, trying to protect him from hexes, from Rize, and from himself. That, in spite of it all, he has tried to defend him.

That he dreamt of the baby; the image of a dried vanilla pod presented on a linen napkin. That, when he saw it, he knew it was his and not Jules's. He remembers now: Margo sitting in the corner of his room rocking on the floor asking him, over and over, "Why, if it's such a little death, does it feel so big?" In that moment he tried to crawl out of his pain, enter hers. And, twisting his head toward her, he almost blew it, told her all the things he knew. He knows about her glacial divorce. He knows Margo's been bought by Kellogg, and that she's not coming back. Instead he'd said "Let me hold your hand" while she cried about their dried-out little baby and the end of their lust.

Jules doesn't understand yet that it's Rize who's looked into the wincing hole of a toilet of the future and found out so many things! Jules has always been the namer of all things, spiller of secrets, predictor of events, destroyer of good shirts; he's the first one at the American border to have his passport slide through his sweaty palms and wail "They'll never let us across!"

He's the one who always catches you picking your nose in the van, and yet is also the first to bring you a handmade smiley-face button and pin it on your pyjama top and then call you Champ when the chips are down (Rize does remember Jules's visit). Reactionary, explosive, negative in the face of potential crisis but an utter Pollyanna in a true emergency, Jules is a prizefighter of vitriol. But now Rize sees his friend's exhaustion. Fatigued and bored by betrayal, like an almost collapsed bull, Jules is mesmerized by the glimpse of blood trickling out of Rize's mouth, which Rize wipes casually away with his wrist.

Jules reaches his hand into the night, hails a cab. A warm drop of rain slides down Rize's aching throat and Jules pushes him into a stuffy car playing reggae.

Rize wants to tell him about his year in the States—the year they didn't speak because Jules was so mad at him for quitting secondary and leaving him alone—how he spent it living with an acrobat named Susie, how he played horn with the TV on all night until he became great. Because that's all truly accomplished musicianship is: a boring kind of autism, this patience for repetition.

He'd like to explain that he's sorry for breaking his heart and busting up his marriage but he can't do anything about it now. Not even cry. And if all this, this night, that list, these drinks, this reggae cab, if these are all just Jules's way of saying goodbye, then he has to respect that.

But somehow Rize suspects that this isn't their ending. Because all the words that have been knotted and growing in his throat like blisters in these sullen weeks before summer are, finally, ready. Because Jules is right: there is so much *shit*.

He wants to tell Jules that he knows, too, about the good review in *Rolling Stone*—that he knows Margo and Kellogg have transformed the band into the kind of cheesy, stripped-down, guy-girl duo that's so popular these days. He wants to comfort his friend by telling him Margo and Kellogg deserve each other, starved as they always were for the kind of success that rots out your liver and changes your smile.

He wants to remind him that Jules promised he'd get over being terrified of Utah one day and walk into the desert with him. Needs to talk about the last night they played, the gold in his limbs that felt like coming, the tune called "Cheap Things in Honey Like Your Smile" they never finished.

And Jim. He needs to find her and ask her to come out to play sometime. He means to ask Jules if—in light of all this—if really all his hopes and dreams were pegged on being just another asshole on the marquee with cheese in his beard, stepping into the white light.

Because it's not enough. He thought it was but it isn't. It's not enough to write songs with cryptic lyrics that nobody understands. It's not enough to jump around onstage every night and have the kids think you're a genius. It's not enough to play beautiful chaotic music. To believe that amid the road, the photo calls, the interviews, love will take care of itself. Because it won't. He knows this now.

The music can wait for once, the words cannot. Yet he wants to keep Jules balanced on this wire of silence before breaking it off. Like the quick hook of a swallow's broken neck under claws, he wants to own the death of his best friend's voice, if only for an instant. But then he remembers he's broken and killed enough in Jules and, more than silence, he wants his forgiveness.

So he opens up his new grieving mouth and asks for it.

acknowledgments

I would like to thank the Canada Council for the Arts and the Conseil des arts et des lettres du Québec for their financial support while writing *The Angel Riots.*

Much gratitude goes to: Marci Denesiuk and Harold Hoefle for their friendship and feedback on early *Riots* drafts; my agents at TLS, Shaun Bradley and Don Sedgwick, for their dedication, hard work, and hustle; my editor, Helen Reeves, for the acuity of her critical eye; Mary di Michele, for her enduring support, her fine example of poetry and faith; The Banff Centre, Ledig House, and the kind people of Regina, Saskatchewan, for providing a safe place to hide and write; Montreal, Toronto, and international friends, for their constant solace and affection; Paul t. brooks, for being the quintessential life editor and rock star; and high school, for finally setting me free. Many thanks to my parents, Peter and Ibolya Kaslik, for violin lessons, a library card, and their continued indulgence of me.